Thomas the Rhymer

Ellen Kushner

William Morrow and Company, Inc.
New York

Quality Printing and Binding By:
R.R. Donnelley & Sons Company
1009 Sloan Street
Crawfordsville, IN 47933 U.S.A.

TO THE ONES
WHO HAVE GONE BEFORE:

Sir Walter Scott

Belle and Hyman Lupeson

Rose and Boris Kushner

Joy Chute

and the Jews of York, C.E. 1190

PART 1

GAVIN

Jack Orion was as good a fiddler
As ever fiddled on a string
He could make young women mad
With the tunes his fiddle could sing:

He could fiddle salt from the salt water
Or marble from a marble stone
Or the milk out of a maiden's breast
Though babies she'd got none.

—*Trad. and A. L. Lloyd*
(from Child ballad no. 67, "Glasgerion")

I'M NOT A teller of tales, not like the Rhymer. My voice isn't smooth, nor my tongue quick. I know a few tunes, everyone does, but nothing like his: from me you'll never hear songs of gentle maidens fording seven rivers for their false lover so bittersweet as to make the hardest old soldiers weep; nor yet merry ones of rich misers tricked out of their gold, with the twist of a word and a jest so neatly turned that the meanest old uncle that ever pinched a dowry still laughs without offense. Well, it's a power, surely, that music and those words, and I just haven't got it.

Not that I'm sure I'd take it, even if it were offered me. One of Tom's very tales is of Jock of the Knowe, that was coming home from Mellerstain Fair with a long face, for he'd walked all that way with his old shorthorned cow to sell at the fair, but not a man would have her. So here's Jock returning to his goodwife with no money nor goods, and winter coming on. Jock's going on down Mellerstain road with his cow, and he starts in railing at her, in a temper, like: "What wouldn't I give to be quit of you, and good money in my purse?"

Well, just then he sees a cloaked man by the side of the road. And the man says, "Good even to you, Jock of the Knowe. And how's the milk from your shorthorned cow?"

Taking the stranger for some man from the fair, Jock answers, "Why, this cow gives half cream and half honey. And if she gives one bucket at morning, she gives two at evening."

They fall to bargaining over the price of the cow. It seems to Jock that anyone wandering the roads after the fair in search of a cow must be in a hard case, so he's setting the price high. Then the tall stranger says, "Well, silver is silver, but I can offer you something worth twice that, cow and all." And he pulls out a fiddle.

Jock says he can't even play, but the stranger says never mind, this fiddle does the playing for you.

With that Jock sees that this twilight man must be one of Elvenkind. The cow's milk is wanted for some human child they've stolen. Now the fairy gold, if he takes it, could turn to grass and leaves tomorrow. But a magic fiddle's a magic fiddle; wherever you go people will give good money for music. So he says, "I'll take the fiddle."

And, sure enough, when the exchange is made, the fairy takes the cow, and walks right up to the side of the hill, and raps with his staff three times. And the hill opens up, and fairy and cow disappear into it, right into Elfland.

As for Jock with his fiddle, he never knows a day's hunger—but he never knows a day's rest, neither, with folk from one end of the country to the other calling on him for music for dances and weddings and such. His goodwife sees only his money, for he's never at home now. Oh, and every Beltane night, which is Fairies' Holiday, Jock goes to that same hillside and plays, and out come a host of gorgeous folk that are the lords and ladies of Elfland, and they dance to Jock's fiddle all night long, until his arms ache and his fingers are sore.

The way I see it, that's no way to live. He'd have done better to keep the cow.

But, then, I'm a plain man. A crofter, living high in the hills above Leader Water with one wife, many sheep, few neighbors. I don't even see a cow but twice a year at Earl's Market.

I'd never seen anything like the Rhymer before he appeared on our doorstep.

It was one of those dismal autumn nights, with the wind whistling like a mad huntsman calling up the Hounds of Hell, and you know there's rain toward. And sure enough it came, battering at the roof and shutters, and not a little down the chimney so the fire smoked up the place. But there sat my Meg, nice as you please, sewing at a shirt for her niece's eldest down Rutherford way. I was doing a bit of basket-mending, glad that the flock were well penned up already this rough night. Between the rushlight and the fire's glow we could see to work, or maybe it was our fingers remembering the way of it. Lately, light's not as bright as once it was.

Then the dog at my feet, Tray it would be, son of old Belta that was, Tray goes stiff like he's heard something, though my ears caught nothing over the racket of wind and rain. "Soft, there, lad," I say, like you do to a dog that's spooking. "Easy, lad. Silly hound, scared of a bit of weather."

My Meg looks up. "Oh, Gavin," she says, her voice strong against the noise of storm. "Gavin, it's a night for the dead to ride, and no mistake."

She sounded like she was readying to tell one of her tales. Tales go well with dark nights; like the one of that restless spirit, the Lord of Traquair, that rides on stormy nights seeking the wife he murdered in a jealous rage, looking to beg her innocent pardon . . . but her body's long, long in the mold, and her blessed soul in Heaven. It happened not a day's walk from here, across the river, some years gone by.

"The Wild Hunt rides tonight." Meg's eyes glinted with her eerie tale. "They ride on horses with nostrils like burning coals, chasing the souls of the wicked, that cannot rest for—" Then her head came up sharp. And, "Gavin," she says, "there's knocking at the door."

I thought her saying it was still part of the tale. Then I heard it too, a thud too regular for wind and rain.

Tray was growling at my side, his hackles raised. I kept one hand on his head, for there's no telling who might be abroad on such a night: or gypsy, or vagrant, or fiend from Hell. I took light in my other hand, and went and unbarred the door, good Tray by me.

Standing there was a very tall, very wet hunchback, one shoulder higher than the other under a muddy dripping black cloak. He pushed back his hood as I raised my light to his face. I saw a young man, beardless but stubbled with travel, and dark hair falling into his eyes.

"Blessings on this house," he says, not the greeting of a Godless man, or one of the Other Ones. Tray growled. "Yes," the stranger says to him, "I've had a pleasant journey, thank you—although it could have been drier. And what do you think of this new fashion in yellow garters?"

I stared at him. "You're talking to the dog," I said.

The stranger shook rain out of his eyes. "Well, he spoke to me first. I did not want to be rude. It makes such a bad impression." For all I could see of his face in the flickering light, he meant it.

"Gavin," Meg calls, "mind the wind blowing in"—which was her way of telling me to stop standing there like a gawk.

Well, we'd had the stones blessed when we built the house, and rowan over the door against those Others. And it's holy charity to shelter those wit-wandering. So, "Peace to all who enter here," I muttered quickly, and stood aside to let the mad hunchback in.

"I thank you." He had to dip his head to pass under the lintel. When he drew near the hearth he saw Meg sitting there. Still in his sodden cloak, he made a bow to my goodwife like any queen. I heard the smile in her voice as she said, "Be welcome to the house, harper."

And, sure enough, he drew the "hump" from off his shoulder: a harp wrapped tight in oilskin. While Meg busied herself wetting a handful of meal for hearthcakes, and setting milk to warm on the fire, he drew off his sodden wool cloak—more mud than wool—and if the house smelt powerful of wet sheep, there was nothing new in that.

Sometimes when you're doing or thinking on one thing, another comes of a sudden into your mind, or your mind's eye. It was like that then: the man turned to sit down, and suddenly I was seeing the flash of a bright sunny day at Earl's Market, with a woman stuffing a goose, of all things! I looked at our visitor harder. His skin was pale, fine as a maiden's, with the flush of returning heat coming to his cheeks like a sinner's blush. His cuffs were wet; he held them out to the fire, and I saw the thin wool of them, dyed with some bright foreign dye such as we don't see much hereabouts. Unfortunately, the dye had run onto the white cuffs of his shirt. Under one of them the glint of a gold band showed; he saw me looking, but made no great shift to hide it. His hands were very harpers' hands, long and supple and smooth.

Meg handed him the welcome cup, saying, "I'm Meg, and this is my goodman, Gavin, son of Coll Blacksides." We hold by the old laws in these parts, so it was right that he know the names of his hosts, and be under no weird to give his own, but only to accept our hospitality if it went not against his honor or his kin's.

The harper shuddered as though shaking the last of the bone-chill out of him, and drank deep of Meg's posset. "Never king was better feasted," he told her. Meg doesn't hold with nonsense, and she dealt him the look she keeps for troublesome bairns, or chickens that stray from the yard. He coughed, smiled sweetly at her, coughed again to clear his throat, said even sweeter, "Ah, mistress, you think I flatter! And, indeed, what call have you to take the word of a poor traveler with more mud on him than he left on the road, and a face to frighten the very bogles in the glen? Is this a man, you say, to come before the king's highness? But, I beg you, picture me washed and combed, dry-shod and clad, a song on my lips and a harp in my hand. And so have I harped before the very king at Roxburgh. He was feasting at the time, and I have gazed with pleasure at the dishes set on his table." He nodded with a grave air. "Aye; seen, but not tasted, for harpers are to kings as our friend there is to you"—nodding at Tray, who dozed fitfully at my feet, uneasy with the stranger. "Oh, I have watched our good king feast on the white bread and the marrow—and, like you, he sometimes throws his crumbs to the dogs." And making only to scratch his head, he raised his arm so that his sleeve fell back to show us the gold bracelet.

Well, it was a fool's trick, if you ask me, risking much to show off: how was he to know we'd not murder him for the gold? It made me wonder how long the minstrel had been on the road, not to think of that.

Still, I was curious to hear more: I'm not much traveled myself, but I always like news of the world, and a good tale is welcome everywhere. We don't get many passing through hereabouts, save the odd friar.

It's not that we hadn't seen harpers before. There's one usually stops at the fair, and Laverock Hugh had one resting at his place once. But none like this. I wondered if he really did know the king, and if he'd harp for us.

"Sir," I began.

But he held up one of his hands, very pretty, like he was halting a procession. "Goodman," he says, "I am not deserving of that title, nor of any. I am but a plain man, whom it has pleased God to grant some gift of music and verse, and to find favor with the princes of the earth."

Now, I'm not the sort to find fault in myself just because others do; but for all his fine words, an older man would have put that better, so I didn't feel wrong about it. Oh, he was quick and clever enough. Still, there's plenty of room for everyone in this world.

I didn't say anything, and Meg clattered loud at the hearth, turning the cakes. The minstrel looks from one to the other of us, and then his face brightens like some young dogs I've known, that think to turn your mind from the mess they've made with fetching of the ball.

"Now, surely, friends," he says, "you've heard the tale of the Cat Who Spoke Truth to Kings?"

"No," says Meg. "We have not." I could tell she wished to hear it, but my Meg is a woman of sense. "And have *you* heard," she says to him, "the tale of the lad who talked so much his tongue fell off?"

The wanderer laughed, breaking to cough. "I have not," he says hoarsely. "I pray you, tell it me, for I am always looking for strange, unlikely tales to amuse folk with on my travels."

I held my breath, waiting for Meg to give him his comeuppance. Even as a lass she'd never let folk get the better of her. The corners of her mouth quirked down, then up. She laughed a real laugh, not a tight one like his.

And, "I'm sure," she says, "you know many a fine tale. And we'll be pleased to hear them—when you've gotten out of those wet clothes and had a bit to sup. You'll take Gavin's cloak that's dry, for now, and lie next the fire this night."

He opened his hands, empty. "You understand—I have nothing to give you."

"Tch!" Meg went from sweet to sharp in a flash. "Young man, do you think this house is Michaelmas Fair? There's no trading going on here. Now, you've had a hard journey, so you'll drink up your posset now and lie down nice by the fire. And when your own clothes are dry tomorrow you'll have them back, and then if you like you can press on to wherever it is you're in such a hurry to get to."

"You're very kind." There was a sort of surprise in his voice. The minstrel coughed. Then he stood up, like in some lord's hall. My old cloak hung only to his knees, and sat his well-made shoulders better than it ever did on me.

"My name in Thomas. I'm called Harper, and sometimes Rhymer, when I busy myself to make something new, instead of robbing dead men's songs."

"Newfangledness," Meg sniffed. "There's no dishonor in holding to the old and true."

Thomas smiled. "Newfangledness indeed. But the lords who hold old lands like new songs to honor them. And who are we to dispute with them?"

"I've never had the chance," Meg says primly. I know when she's enjoying herself, however it might look to others. "Now, Tom Harper, take your cake from the hearth before it burns, and if you want some honey on it, it's in the jar."

He coughed again as he bent over to get the oatcake. Meg said, "Honey," getting him some. "And horehound tea, and good greased wool about your throat. You're sickening very prettily, as well you might, trying to cross these hills in that storm."

"I'm fine," he says, voice thick as a crow's. But soon he's drinking Meg's tea, and looking uncommon wretched hunched up by the fire. Sure enough, the cough's getting worse. Meg knows these things; she's nursed many a bairn on both sides of the river. Now the harper's so miserable he forgets even to thank her with sweet words. "This can't last," he says huskily. "I'll have no voice!"

"There," she comforts him; "you've still your harp to play."

The minstrel laughs, which only sets him coughing again. "Oh, aye, that'll give them all the dancing measure." He lifts the shrouded bundle, and unwraps oilcloth and wool with less care than I'd have thought. Then he raised the harp high, and a sorry sight to see. A smashed side, and strings dancing and jangling about the raw splinters.

"Behold Thomas Harper's harp. A gift of the spirits of the road, who saw fit to place an especially slippery bit of it under my foot, right by some fine specimens of rock."

"You'll be sore bruised, then," Meg says softly.

He shrugged, coughed and spat in the fire. "I didn't have the chance: fell atop my darling like any drunken sailor home on leave. Left her in fine shape, too, didn't I, my sweet?"

He wrapped the harp back up, coughing.

"Can it be mended?"

"At Dalkeith, it may be." This time he showed us his bracelet plainly; all covered with scrollwork like a church door, it was. "The white gold, and the yellow. I had it of the king, and thought to keep it in token—like some knight in a ballad. Vain and foolish fancy. But it'll pay my way to music now." The hand with the bauble was beginning to tremble with chill. "Circles, you see, bands around bands. Between rhyming and rhythms, songs and stories, you can see the strangest patterns."

"Gavin," Meg tells me softly, aside, "I want two fleeces from the store, for him to lie on. Thomas, rest now. There's nothing broken can't be mended."

The face he turned on her was unseely, bleak as the hills before snowfall. "Is there not? Then I have stumbled on a wondrous country, indeed." "Rest now," she repeated. "You'll feel better in the morning."

But in the morning the harper looked no better, and probably felt worse. He lay bright-eyed and pale-faced by the hearth, a spot of bright color on each cheek, and never still for coughing. If he had a mind yet to his other troubles, he could do nothing. Meg nursed him as she might, with tea and company: she sat at his side, sewing a nice bit of work that only comes out when she's forced to stay still. The way my goodwife managed the sewing, and the hearth, and the wild young harper and all the hundred other things always, our own troubles and others', it's a marvel to me. It's like the song says:

> She is all that is gracious,
> Her spirit is comely,
> The work of her hands is fair.

The rain was still falling lightly. I was busy about the sheep pens all the morning, and came in to find them talking.

"Gavin," says Meg, "Tom's been telling me all about the great All Hallow's feast they hold at Roxburgh Castle, with bonfires and brown ale and all. And stories all night, to wake the dawn, so no spirits dare come nigh."

"That's something," I said, taking some of the cakes my goodwife had set on the hearth. "I hear it's a grand place, Roxburgh."

The harper's dry lips smiled. "I've come from there. It's well enough. But even dukes and kings have their troubles. His majesty's gone from there to another of his seats, and now the duke's sore vexed with cattle-raiders. So his knights are out the nights after raiders, and up early hunting the red deer to fill his table. By evening, the hall is no merry place: it's snores and drowsing to the music of the harp, and not the fiercest battle song will keep them awake."

"No place for a harper, then." That much I understood. "Up and left, did you?"

"Just so."

"And your lord gave you leave?"

He glared at me as if I'd just accused him of stuffing the baby in the oven. "No man binds me." He started coughing again, and began laughing in the middle of it. At last he caught his breath to add, "Nor no woman, either."

Meg looks up sharp at that, and I wonder, too, is he a loose sort of man? They do say such things of minstrels. Though some are ill-made, too: blind, or lame, as though the music were a gift to make up for what they lacked. But this one would never have trouble courting.

He did see the look she gave him, and changed his tune then and there, with, "What's that you're sewing? I've never seen the like." He always spoke Meg fair as she were the lady of some great house.

She lifted up the cloth. "A Tree of Life. My minnie gave me the pattern, as she had it from hers. Folk don't do this sort of sewing hereabouts; they're more like to weave. But we always have. It's for a child's cradle. No one child's . . . any child's. I doubt I'll finish this one."

"You must." He said it so strong it set him coughing again, but he went on fiercely, "It's like a little world. You're making a little world. All those beasts and birds and leaves . . . I wish you could see the colors the great ladies use to embroider. So fine and bright. You need—here!" And he's unraveling his frayed sleeve like any starling, pulling the bright thread out for Meg to use. "Put me in your Tree of Life."

"Lie down," snaps Meg, "and cover yourself. You're shivering your life away." But the thread became a finch's breast; and later she mended the sleeve with good brown wool.

With Meg's healing, it was not many days before we had the harper on his feet. He kept to the house, with wool around his throat, helping Meg and sometimes tinkering at his harp, cutting pegs and changing strings around until he'd five notes that played true, for all the good that did him. The better he got, the more he fretted to be away; I wondered what was in Dalkeith, but didn't ask, for courtesy. Not that he fretted *at* us, mind; but when a man spends all day between the window and the hearth, and inquires hourly after the weather, you know it's time he were away.

When night came, we sat around the hearth. I was almost sorry no one'd happened by these last days, to see our guest. He looked much better now, almost fit for kings' halls, indeed. And we'd had more tales of him, too, for Meg to tell on winter nights ahead. She liked the one of the witch queen, as locked up her son's lady's womb with sevenfold spells, that she could not bring forth her babe until the young king her husband cunningly foiled the witch in her designs.

"You'll want to tell that one at the next birthing you assist," I said to Meg, and she said I'd all the sense of my sheep, as I knew she would. Our minstrel looked a bit rabbit-spooked.

"I wonder," he said quickly, as though to stop us quarreling, "if you know 'the Elfin Knight's Riddles'?"

"Some," says Meg. "But do you tell them."

He looked at the floor, and at his hands. "Well, but it's a song," he says. "It wants the harp. There's pity on it mine's broken, for I've set some new verses, and I'd like to try them out before I play them at Dalkeith." Then he grimaced, shook his head, sighed deep.

"What's the matter?" I asked.

He looked up, smiled at us. "Nothing anyone can help. Likely I'll be disgraced at this event, for want of a decent harp, but there it is."

"Won't there be other harpers there?" Meg asks. She's always quick to solve problems. "You could borrow one of theirs."

"Ha," says Thomas. "Some old pot with jangling strings and broken pegs. There's no harper will lend me a decent one."

Meg opens her blue eyes very wide. "Why not? Are you in the habit of breaking them?"

"Certainly not!" He leaned across the fire to her. "I'll tell you what it is, my honey: the others are afraid I'll show them up."

"Are they, so?"

They stared in each other's eyes, each one a brave dog staring down a wolf. I didn't know whether to laugh, or to throw water on them.

"You know," says I, "I've been thinking, Thomas. Here you are a minstrel and all. But you cannot sing without your harp. Are they all like that, minstrels?"

He flashed me a look, but a mild one. "You've been talking to Murray of Thornton:

> 'And now, my friend, you must be gone;
> Harp or carp as you choose soothely,'
> And he said, 'Harping ken I none,
> For tongue is chief of minstrelsy.'

"Wretched doggerel. Of course I can sing without the harp. What would you like to hear?"

Meg smiled behind her hand. " 'The Elfin Knight's Riddles'?"

"I'll sing it. I've made some music, and rhymes. It's not done yet, of course. And it may not sound like anything without the harp . . ."

"But do you sing it, Thomas, just the same."

He sat up straight, and coughed, and fussed with the hang of his clothes, and cleared his throat. "My voice is not right yet, you must endure it." Then he lifts his head and sings:

An Elfin knight stands on yon hill,
And he blows his horn so loud and shrill.
He blows it east, he blows it west,
He blows it where he likes the best.

Would I'd his trumpet in my chest
And was in the arms of him I love best.

When his voice rose in the house, the hair on the back of my neck prickled. It was bright and clear, like one of those glass windows, through which you see a distant scene and not the glass at all.

She has no sooner these words said
Than the Elfin knight stood by her bed.

'Tis strange, my lady, for to see
I can scarce blow my horn but you call for me.

And so the song's story shone through Tom's singing: the Elf lord coming to claim the lady's love, she that had summoned him; and how he sought to take her life after he took his pleasure, to end her power over him; but she sets him to the riddle game and so wins herself free.

Tell me what is louder than the horn,
Tell me what is sharper than the thorn?

I didn't see how the harp could make it better. His voice carried the trills and runs of notes like a river or a starling; yet nothing like water or bird.

O thunder is louder than the horn
And pain is sharper than the thorn.

Anger is greener than the grass
And you are worse than e'er woman was.

He had bits I'd never heard before; whether that's the way the story's told across the river, or if they were Tom's own, I don't know.

When he finished, his eyes were closed, his harper's hands resting on his two knees. His face was still: he, too, was caught in the song.

Meg rose, and put a hand to either side of his face, and kissed his brow. "Thomas," she said. "Harp or no harp, the music speaks true in you."

He looked her in the eyes, but his face burned with a kind of shame, as though we knew now something he'd meant us not to.

"The music," he says, "if nothing else." And he shrugs. "But that is the way of the world; a man must make his living as he can."

"Come, lad," I chided, "there's no shame in making songs. A good song's as honest as a well-made wheel, or a pot, or a—a comb, or somesuch."

"A pot," he says. "Or a comb. An honest tradesman." He shook his head like a dog shaking off fleas, and then looked up and smiled mischief at me. "Well, that's something. Perhaps I'll set up a shop: Good rhymes for sale. Wellworn tales at half price."

"A shop," says Meg, mocking his ambition; "aye, with a goodwife to mind the till, while you go wandering the hills all day after tales and rhymes."

"There's no goodwife," he says, "half so good as you, Busy Maggie—" and he leans over and kisses her seamed old cheek; nor does she rail at him for his impudence.

"I'll be off in the morning," he says, "and pray I am to Dalkeith before the wedding's over. There's to be days of feasting as Cauldshield's daughter weds the Baron of Dalkeith, with much rejoicing and plucking of harps and psalteries and loud hosannas and largesse for tumblers and minstrels and dancing bears. The Duke of Cauldshield's bade me special to the wedding"—he smiled—"although his fair daughter did not. Think you she'll like my new song?" It was a close and secret smile, that I misliked.

"Belike she will, belike she won't," I said. "But it's an unchancy song to sing to a new-made bride."

"Think you?" the minstrel asked, his face all sweet kindness and surprise—and not in the service of good, I thought.

"Ladies calling on Elfin knights? Perhaps it may please a baron's lady; I can tell you, lad, it wouldn't go down well around here!"

"Oh," says he, "but it's a very clever lady; she wins in the end, and has her own way, in that as in everything. And doesn't she just have her will of the knight, and send him riddling off with a flea in his br—in his ear?"

"Beware, Thomas," said Meg, in a voice fell and unseely as a tale's. "Look you not throw your music after pride: it's a rude servant, but a cruel master."

He rounded on her, and looked as he would speak sharp, but he swallowed the words instead. "I know it," he said tightly. "I've eaten it more than you think. You forgot to say, pride's a bitter sauce. I know the world, mistress. It's a hard place, for those of us not born to title or to lands. Easy for you to sit here, queen of pots and pans, lord of the sheepfold, generous

and kind—but out there I have seen fine men struck down, and true talent
let to waste away for want of food. No man binds the silent wound, nor
gives gold to the closed fist, whatever God bids us do. The humble minstrel
who harps nightly in the corner of his master's hall for bread and board
and a pat on the head is a cold and nameless man when his master's gone."

"Rhymer," says Meg quietly, "there's a truth for your songs."

"Oh, aye. That'll win me gold before the king."

"If it's gold you want."

"Who doesn't?" He tossed his bracelet in the air, caught it one-handed.
And with that flash of gold I saw again with my mind's eye, the Earl's
Market fair, and something else. I kept it to myself, though.

"The king's gold, the nobles' praise and a name among folk to win me a
soft bed anywhere I choose to rest—oh, and a rose from a pretty fair
maid." He cocks his head at her, and if he thinks to win Meg's praise from
such a speech, he's a greater fool than he looks. And if he doesn't, then
why'd he go on so?

Meg only sniffs, and stabs the linen with her needle. "The rose, I fancy,
you'll have no trouble getting. You're a comely lad with a high opinion of
yourself. The kings and nobles can make what they want of that, and you
serve them any way you can. Why music at all?"

First he couldn't answer her. Then he gathers himself and says, shrug-
ging, "It's a skill."

"I see." But she might as well have snorted, for the scornful look on her
face. "Like making pots, or combs?"

Clever lass, to use his very words against him! I remembered how she'd
done the same to Red Hugh, the day we both came a-courting of her.
Dullard, I'd kept silent, and carried the prize.

The young man's face was stiff with anger, but slowly a smile spread
across it. "Mistress," he says, "I fear I've met my match. I cede the field."
And bowing low, he kisses her old, worn hand!

"I tell you what, Meg, though: next time I come, I'll write you a special
song, all truth, that only you will like, and I'll sing it only to you."

Next time. We looked at each other, Meg and I, and neither read dis-
pleasure in the other's face, but a kind of hope in spite of all. I'll not deny
the Rhymer had a way about him.

"We'll see about your special song," Meg grumbled. "You'll do better to
leave out the words, and only write a harp tune. I'm not sure I trust you
with the truth."

"I am at your command," he said with a flourish.

"Good. I want you to do something for me."

"Anything."

"Then hold out your hands. I've got this wool to wind, and Gavin's are no good at all, they're so rough."

Meekly, the harper held up his smooth hands. And Meg untwisted her skein and stretched it across them, binding them still while she wound the yarn into a tidy ball.

"You'll want to leave at dawn," she says. "The day should be clear, but chill—keep your scarf on, I'll put more grease on it ere you go. If you follow the river you should reach Oxton's Ford by nightfall; my sister's girl lives there, will lodge you the night—will you take her some small things for me?"

"Of course," he says, in the stunned voice I know myself from dealing with Maggie when she's in a notion. But it's hard not to feel comfortable when a strong woman fusses over you like that. Now that he'd unbent enough to get the good of it, young Thomas smiled. "Are there any giants you'd like me to slay along the way?"

Meg tugged at the wool. "None of your impertinence, please—and keep your hands taut, if you slacken you're no good to me. From Oxton to Dalkeith's a ways; but you know that."

"I know. But I might get lucky with a ride."

"Why not go straight to the king?" I offered. "Likely he'll pay you better nor any earl."

For a moment, he didn't answer. Then he said, "The king's away. He's as like to stop at Dalkeith as anywhere else. Now, have you ever seen the Baron of Dalkeith? He'd never fit through your door. He's got arms the size of thighs, and thighs like—young sheep. They say it takes three boys to carry his armor, and his charger is half plough horse. I saw him at Cauldshield's; he munches up whole chickens the way you would a peach. Strangely, he is much taken with love songs, and weeps at the death of maidens."

Meg said, "I knew a woman once, so ugly she had to wear a veil like a heathen. Her nether lip hung down to her waist, and her ears were tied in a bow atop her head."

Well, in the way of minstrels, he had to top her tale of wonders, and did. He told us one of a heathen king, Orfeo, whose wife was stolen away to Elfland by the king of the fairies. But this Orfeo being a great harper, he followed his wife down to Elfland, and there harped tears of pity from the Queen of Elfland's eyes. So his wife was allowed to return to Middle-Earth with him—only she's eaten seven hazelnuts in Elfland, which is fairy food that mortals may not safely touch; so seven days out of each year she is bound to stay in that other land.

And somehow, with the telling of tales and the eating of supper, it was dark night and time to bank the fire. And as she laid his clean cloak over him, I heard Meg say to the harper, "Be mindful how you tread, now, Thomas."

And in the morning, pinning his cloak on him with his silver pin, "You know you are always welcome here."

And though he sweetly kissed her callused old hand, and smiled me in the eyes bright as day, it was long months before we saw Thomas again.

He waved at us as he topped the rise, and he and the corbies circling were the only black things in the grey-brown world of autumn.

My heart was heavier than it should be, and I didn't know if it was from the harper's going, or from my keeping secrets from my Meg. She was taken with the lad, anyone could see that.

Just then she gave a sigh. "That's a Valley-bred lad as ever was. He's no more seen the king than you have, Gavin. Ah, I wouldn't be young again for a thousand crowns, no matter my bones ache!"

"But—" I began, meaning to ask, *How did you know?*

"Oh, I make no doubt he's been away to Roxburgh. Once. And, if I read him right, he'll be before the king ere the year's out. He'll be back when it suits him. And then we'll know all, I suppose." She turned back to the croft, into the rising sun. "Well, talk doesn't fill empty bellies—though to hear those hens go at it you'd think it did!"

I never did learn how she guessed about Thomas and the king. I never told her of the thing that I'd remembered, of seeing the minstrel at Earl's Market.

It was last spring, when we sold off the great part of our flock, keeping only enough for wool, for weaving's easier now on my bones than wandering the hills. I'd driven the sheep in to market, and mucky work it was! I'd never'a done it without Tray. The town was busier than a stirred ants' nest, full of sheep and goats and chickens and even some cows and horses, and cloth and gingerbread and knives and ribbons and cheese: whatever a body had need of for life was there. But the people were the worst, more than I'd ever seen, for the very Earl of March and Dunbar was come to sit court for the people of his domain, there at the market where any might bring up their grievance.

So up against the wall of the earl's castle they set up a striped awning for him and his folk to sit under. First the earl's court rode circuit through the fair, which made the animals mad, with them on their horses and clothes as fine as any story, and the people shouting and cheering. There were heralds to set it all up proper, and keep order, for first the knights could bring grievance, and then gentlemen, landholders and so on, townsfolk and peasants and all. And a tedious business for the earl I'm sure it was, but we all have our work to do.

I was kept busy most of the day, with the flock and the things Meg sent me to buy, and a few more things I thought she might need. By the time I got to look at the earl, the scribes were still writing away, the learned men debating. But tables were set before them for dinner, and the fair's tumblers and mountebanks were all at it as close to the pavilion as they could get. Under the awning by March and Dunbar was one harper, and that harper was none but our Thomas. And the earl was talking to him, laughing and carping like any buttie, and the harper harped as the earl and his people ate. I tried to get close enough to hear the music, but it came to me only as a thin thread, that kept being broken by the folk jostling and yammering between us.

I'd no wish to stay and see the court of law. I'd had enough of folk by then, anyhow. But a gasp from the crowd turned me 'round again. The earl had taken a band of gold from his arm, and was holding it high to offer it to the harper. He made I don't know what speech, and the harper answered him in kind. People liked to see it. The earl's generosity was much talked on, and I meant to tell Meg about it when I got home, but what with one thing and another it left my mind.

Now, there's no sure way of knowing that Thomas the Harper's gold bracelet was the one Dunbar'd given him. But how many gold bands does one man get in a year?

Not that I hold it against him. A minstrel lives by telling tales. Rhymers live in their fancy. He'd speak of dead heroes in the same breath as porridge, you might say, as if they were his own dear companions. Madmen and dreamers, your rhymers don't live in the world like the rest of us do. I'd not say it to his face, but they don't really do any work, for one. But my Meg was much taken with him, and there's no doubt there's few can tell a tale like him, or sing such songs.

The winter was hard, with more snow than we'd seen in a long time, and water frozen even in the brooks. Autumn had been good to us, though, so there was no lack of food or fuel; all we must do was sit indoors and wait the cold out. It ended sudden 'round about March—and then, as Meg said, we were earthy mer-folk, swimming in a sea of mud. Sheep didn't like it, dogs neither. Up to their bellies in the thaw, and I forever hauling 'em out. I was up on the hill's side one day, doing just that and thinking I'd do better to pen them up again and let them miss the early grass after all, when I heard the last sound I thought to hear: a girl's laughter.

Over the dry ground of the rise behind me comes tawny-haired Elspeth,

Iain's sister from Huntsleigh Farm: neighbors of ours, and not so rare for her to pay us a visit, though this was first we'd seen of her since winter. Her brother was a man grown; their parents being gone, she lived there at Huntsleigh with him, and tried to be a help to his wife with the bairns; but everyone around knew she'd rather be here listening to Meg's stories or traversing hill and wood and dale to market at Langshaw or Ercildoun, where she'd sold butter and cheese for Iain since she was big enough to stand high-lone. Not a bad lass, though gypsyish in her ways. But my Meg swore it was spirit in her, like her own, saying Elspeth would make as good a wife when she chose.

By the look of her, she might choose at any time. Her face was rosy, her eyes bright, and her loose hair stood out 'round her like an angel's halo of red gold. She halted, just above my sea of mud, when she saw me. She was breathing hard from running, and I saw a shape to her that hadn't been before.

"Oh, Gavin!" she gasps, still bubbling laughter. "There's an uncouth outland loon roaming these hills, has taken a mind to walk out with me Sunday! And swears you'll speak for him, you and Meg, by way of his being a foster son."

"Well," says I, up to my knees in mud and pregnant sheep, "I dunno any of that. Meg's down by the beck, washing linen, for all the good it does."

So off the girl runs, slipping and sliding down the hill in the mud, clumsy with laughter.

Folk know us. We've guarded some children in our time, and Meg's brought many another woman's bairn into the world; but this was the first I'd heard of our having any son, foster or other.

I understood better when a tall cloaked figure with a hump next appeared on the rise.

"Hello, Gavin," he says politely, a bit out of breath. "I am glad to see you well!"

Thomas wasn't empty-handed this time. A bundle was slung at his side, and the covered harp across his back.

"Oh," says I, sinking deeper in the mud, "don't you try your smooth talk with me. I know we're just a convenience for you to fetch the lasses."

Under the long fringe of dark hair, his eyes brightened. "Oh? Has she been by, then?"

"Running like the Devil himself was after her. I fear you'll not get far with that one, lad," I says, to taunt him.

He reached out and clasped my two arms. It was a tricky manoeuvre, what with sheep and mud and harp and all, but he managed. "Gavin. It's good to see you. I've got so much to tell you—and Meg, is she well?"

His eyes and the corners of his mouth were tired. Close up I saw his clothes were dirty, and he'd the smell of the road on him. I thought a little more dirt couldn't make it much worse, so I got his help with that sheep, and together we heaved her out, and into a bush of gorse, which kept her dry.

Surprised, I said, "You're not so ill with the beasts."

"My hands have known other things besides harping," he said, but he didn't sound proud of it.

"Well," I told him, "you'll be wanting a meal after your travels. Come down to the house, we'll see what Meg has. She'll be glad to see you."

Meg had cheese, and barley bread, and Elspeth sitting in the corner helping her card wool.

"Blessings on this house," said Thomas, stooping under the lintel. "And how's my Busy Maggie this muddy day?"

Meg jumped up and embraced him, beaming.

Tired as he was, he cast a triumphant look at Elspeth. She sat demure, probably for the first time in her life, combing her wool as though she were a goodwife from the Year One.

The minstrel took off his cloak, and settled his harp gently in the corner. Then he sat and ate his food by the fire, that Meg gave him.

"It's good!" Thomas said. "Cheese from the sheep?"

"Goats," said Meg. "We've got two goats now."

"Just as I thought—you're building an ark. The world is turning to mud, and we will sail away. And you, sweeting, are you carding us sails of silver?"

"To steer us towards the sun?" Elspeth knew the song. "You *are* an outlander, not to know plain grey wool when you see it."

"I see," Tom says to Meg, "that you're collecting the animals first. Quite right. Why go to all the trouble of building the ark when you haven't got them all lined up? What a good thing I came along when I did. I can help the young lady aboard." Elspeth carded furiously. "You'll need a harper, you know. To drown out the braying and baying and mewing and cawing and sloshing. Of the mud."

Meg smiled at me. "Your gold bracelet's gone, Thomas, I see," says Meg. "Is that a new harp, there, in the corner?"

"Mistress," the minstrel frowned, "if you were any sharper, we could sell you at the fair for scissors. A new harp, indeed, and a sweeter lady you never laid eyes on. I had her made exactly to my needs. The sound's a bit young, yet—that's the trouble with new harps—but I'll let you judge her for yourselves when we've both had a chance to rest."

"Are harps always ladies?" asks Elspeth from the corner, busily carding away.

"Oh, no," says Thomas. "Some are right harridans."

"There's pity on it," she says, "for a man to be saddled with such a one, once he's paid golden money for her."

"Why, if a man will take one without he try her first, he's a rare fool."

"If fools were only rare," the girl sighs, "then harps might sing the sweeter."

He only smiled, unable to hide his pure delight at her rude wit. The air around him fairly crackled with desire. And she just sat there, working at the wool, the cunning innocent.

"After supper," says Meg, "will be time for harping. Now there's a bit of work you can lend a hand to. Elspeth, you're welcome at our board, if you'd care to stay and hear Tom's music."

"Oh," the girl says airily, "I doubt I can spare the time. I'm greatly wanted at home."

"Mistress," Thomas leaned forward to tell her, "the king's own fair lady of France said much the same thing to me. Just before New Year's, it was, with her and all her ladies sewing away like demons to have ready embroidered the shirts for the king and his brothers their gifts.

" 'Thomas,' she said to me, 'I pray you of your courtesy [for that is the speech of queens], take your infernal harp and voice away, for we've a deal of work to do here—and last time you sang to us we wept salt tears until we stained our silk and had to start over again.'

" 'Let me harp you something merry, then,' I offered her.

" 'Oh, no, Thomas,' she said, 'for then we would begin tapping our feet, and someone is sure to prick her finger again.'

"Her eyes flashed royally at me. And, do you know, the queen has eyes the same color as yours."

Elspeth flushed. "That's a lie."

"Well, maybe it is, and maybe it isn't." The cunning lad leaned back, satisfied to have caught her interest. "I'm the one who's seen her, not you."

"Oh?" says Elspeth craftily. "And what color are her eyes?"

"Different colors," he answers without pause. "Depending on her mood. When she's happy, almost the blue of the clear lake. When she grieves, grey as stormheads over Blackhope Scar. And when she's angry (which, of course, is seldom), they flash with green, like an Elf cloak disappearing through the woods on a May morning."

Elspeth scowled into her lap. Those were her very eyes, and the dear knows how he'd fathomed that.

"What did you do," she asked, "to see the queen angry?"

"Cruel lady. Why do you think it was I?"

"I can guess."

"Well . . . it was over this matter of the sewing of the shirts. I was determined to harp their labor lighter, and so I began to play. And into my song I wove all my care for the queen and her ladies their poor tired eyes and sore fingers . . . and do you know what happened?"

"They fell asleep."

The minstrel stared at her. "Yes. They did. All but one. Lilias was her name. And when the queen awoke, an angry queen was she."

"Oh," says Elspeth then, cool as the breeze. "And did the shirts ever get done?"

"I suppose." Poor man; he sounded for once at a loss for words. I don't guess that's the sort of answer the court ladies were used to make to him—if they weren't another of his fancies, that is. "The king looked pleased at New Year's, at any rate."

"I'm surprised," Elspeth said, "they didn't have you make up the sewing they'd lost. They do say a harper's fingers are nimble, and apt to anything."

But she did stay to supper. And after, when Thomas took his gleaming harp from out its case, and the notes from it melted like mist in the air, young Elspeth sat with her chin in her hand, and never took her eyes from him. He was wise enough not to gaze on her the whole time he played; his eyes were fixed on far invisible hills as he drew sweet music from the harp, and sang songs to us of wanderers, and of lovers parted. There was an aching beauty to the music: nothing to make a body weep, but we all found ourselves suddenly glad of the roof and the fire, and the company of mortals. Even Thomas's face smoothed to tranquility as he sang. Meg took my hand, and leaned her head against me. "Look at her," she murmured soft to me, so no one else could hear. "She thinks he's playing the secrets of her heart. And of course he is. You're so lonely, at their age."

When Thomas finished harping, he looked first to the girl. Her eyes were still cloudy with music. He smiled, as if to thank her for listening to him, as if he had indeed been telling her a long tale about himself. And she smiled back.

"It's getting late," Meg said at last. "You'd best be off, Elspeth, if you don't want to be caught in the dark."

"I'll walk with you," Thomas offered.

The girl lifted her head. "I don't need help. I know the way, harper, better than you do, I'm certain."

"Nonetheless," says he softly, "I will walk with you."

A slow smile bled across her face like a blush, she trying the same to hide it. "Have you not walked enough today, harper? And will you not be frightened, coming back on the hills in the dark, of piskies and haunts, and the White Mare of Traquair?"

"Very frightened. But the thought of your bright hair will put courage into me. Perhaps I might have a lock of it to tender. . . ."

"Oh—are you going to trade pieces of me to the Good Folk, to save your precious skin? That's a fine thing, I'm certain."

"No such thing! If I had a lock of your bonnie hair, I'd never part with it for gold or money."

She stood up sudden, and pulled her cloak on like storm clouds swirling, and the hood tight over her head. "Gavin, Meg, good night. God keep you, harper."

But he was at the door when she was. "Only to the top of the hill," he said. "And then we need fear nothing."

And he's followed her out into the damp evening.

I got up, took my staff. "I'd better see to the pens for the night."

"You can see them fine from here," Meg said.

"Nonetheless."

I was not ashamed to stand where I could see the top of the hill. I've known Elspeth since she was so high, when a big-bellied ewe came near to trodden her underfoot. I'd saved her from our sheep, and I would do my duty by this new foster son of ours, need be. But never a kiss was exchanged, though not, I'll warrant, from the Rhymer's lack of trying. I saw them stand and talk, and then she streaked off across the broad sky along the ridge like any swallow, and the man turned back to the croft.

"Can I help you?" he asked me doucely by the pens.

"All done. Let's go in."

It was late, then, but Tom must needs be telling us his news. I worked on a weeding-book of horn, and Meg took out her spinning.

"I've not forgotten," he says, "your kindness to me on the way to Dalkeith. I'm glad the welcome is still on me. I've remembered you in the world—and sometimes for the good, when the unkindness of man has been heavy on me. And I've remembered you in better times, as well." He fished in his pack. "Gavin, here's a cup, such as they make in the west—I picked the best one for you." It was a fine-looking cup of clay, baked a nice blue color such as I'd never seen. Not all show, though: it had a good strong handle for when drink was hot. I thanked him for it. Of course, we'd never take money from an invited guest, and a minstrel besides; but it was good courtesy in him to know it, and to bring gifts. "Meg, look now!" And he starts pulling something like birds' nests from his bag. "What do you think —it's silks, Meg, all colors of the rainbow!" And so they were: skeins of thread so fine you could pack them in a nutshell, and dyed bright as life. Thomas laid them across Meg's lap, but she would be fingering them, though they caught on her rough skin.

Ah, but she was pleased! Trying not to show it, with, "Oh, these are too fine for me! Oh, Thomas, they're like a church window—whatever will they do on my poor cloth!" And, "Wherever did you come by these? Rob a foreign vessel? Or ask them of the queen?"

She must have hit close the mark there, for he stopped his fussing, said, "Just so. I told her I knew a lady near her equal in grace, and skill and kindness, whose needle lacked only these to make her work perfect. She—"

"Tom," Meg stopped him gravely, "don't say such things. Perfection isn't for mankind. Something might hear you." His face was so fallen, she added, "And I don't think for one moment you spoke that way to the French queen. I wonder does she even know our tongue?"

"Of course she does! She was years learning it in her own country, before her marriage to our king. But her tongue twists it 'round: to say, 'I think,' she says, 'I *sink*!'" That made us laugh, and so he gave us her attendants, lords of France and nursemaids, and a rare show he made of them all.

"But the singers out of France," he said, "have tales I've never heard: high deeds of knights and ladies, Saracens and pilgrims. . . ."

"And we'll hear them all," says Meg firmly, gathering up her silks like any queen, "but not tonight. You'll be sorry at cockcrow else. And so to bed!"

Well, it was wonderful, the things he brought and the tales he told. I did wonder how many of them were true, these ladies and queens and French . . . It all seemed like a ballad. Truth was, I don't much care: a good tale's a good tale, wherever it comes from. But a man doesn't like to be taken for a fool. And I couldn't help thinking that a lad who sleeps at your hearth, eats your food and kisses your goodwife's hand ought to speak plain with you.

In the close dark I spoke my thoughts aloud: "There's a man never takes the straight path when he can go around."

There was none to hear me but Meg. "He's coming along," she says to me. "The queen's favor agrees with him more than bracelets." There it was, then. When my Meg says a thing, it's so. "And he came back."

"For more of your scolding?"

"Maybe."

"Well, it's a good cup," I allowed.

The days passed and Thomas spoke no word of leaving. He was no small help to Meg and me, working in house and fold like any true-born son, and glad we were of him there, and of his company by the fire.

When word went around that a harper of note lodged with us, the folk started coming by. That spring we'd more visitors than we often saw in a year, sometimes two and three in a week. Thomas was never too proud to give them a tune or a song. Nor was he loath to follow many's the wight over the hill to wedding or christening, to lend a little music to the festival, and maybe dance with the girls there! But never farther did he journey than a man could walk in a day, and still be home by dark.

Maybe he was weary of wandering. Or he needed to try new songs for the king on us folk. The girl Elspeth might have had something to do with it—or so I thought, for it was clear she'd caught his fancy, though they both took such turns acting hot and cold, it was as good as a show to see them!

The girl would come to help Meg with her brother's leave, as she said, but a day spent washing or spinning or baking would always bring a few words with the harper. Sometimes she'd let him walk her home to Huntsleigh Farm, and sometimes not.

"But it's late," he'd say, "my sweet lass, you must bide here the night."

"Oh," says she, "lie by the hearth with a singing lad? Do you think I've no bed of my own?"

"Surely, but none so warm."

"Now, how'd you know that, never having been in it?"

They'd go at it all night, if left to it. He'd sing her a rude song he'd learned of a sailor up the coast, and she'd ask him if that was what he sang to the queen's ladies, and then mimic the market women for him until they were both as useless a pair of sillies as you'd ever seen.

So March passed into April, and came time for the Melrose Fair. Thomas said he'd not go—no nobles there, I reckoned it, and the Abbey monks not good enough for him—but I thought he'd change his mind when the girl broached it.

She'd brought Meg some butter in return for eggs, for Huntsleigh hens were laying poorly. And, "I'm taking new cheese to the fair," she says, "to sell for Iain and all."

"Mind you don't put stones in them to bring up the weight," says

Thomas idly by the door, where he's carving spoons. "The monks'll be watching."

"Jack Rowan's been asking to carry my baskets, and all," she goes on. "Says he'll buy me a fairing after. Likely a green ribbon, he says, to go in my hair."

Tom keeps on carving, but I see he's near to splitting the spoon with heavy digging at the horn. "Green?" he says. "Careful, Elspeth. Isn't that a fairy color?"

"Say 'Good Folk,' " she corrects almost without thinking. "They don't like to hear themselves named."

"Well, you'll be safe enough," he considers, "with a man named Rowan. Or is rowan a charm against witches? Then *he'll* be safe."

"I haven't said I'd go with him," she retorts.

"How can you stop him?" Thomas asks, in that false-reasonable voice of his. "I can just see him following you around like old Tray, with your cheeses in his mouth."

"I am well able," she says, sounding for all the world like the Rhymer himself, "to carry my cheeses alone. *And* buy my own ribbons!"

"How nice that you don't have to."

Meg found her later, crying in the sheep-shed.

And so it went on, all the long of that spring season, the pair of them in their strange courtship. Meanwhile Tom endured with us the return of the cold, the hard birth of lambs and the icy hills; then mud again and finally the true green of May.

We learned more from him of his travels in the outside world, the sights he'd seen and the people he'd known. It was as good as being there, without the bother: the great towns whose walls rise up like cliffsides, where the folk are so many you can never know them all; and the markets with their Eastern silks and spices, French wine and Spanish leather. . . .

And Elspeth let him walk out with her, once and twice of a Sunday, where folk could see them.

"What ails the chit?" I asked my Meg. "Does she want him or doesn't she?"

To my great surprise, that made Meg laugh so hard she had to put her face in her apron. "Yes, she does, and no, she doesn't," she said at last. "And if you can't riddle it out for yourself, Gavin Know-nothing, then I've no time for your foolishness!"

"I'm no hand at riddling," I said.

"Then it's a good thing we've no daughter," chuckled my goodwife, "or you'd bestow her on the first wandering tinker she fancied, if all that matters is, does she want him!"

"But Tom's not looking to marry."

"Thank mercy!" She threw up her hands in mock-horror. "He's hard-enough pressed to win a civil word from her. Of course she wants him. But for what? It's hard for a girl. She'd sooner exchange vows with him than kisses. Oh, you think she's ripe because she has a woman's shape. But that's a girl, yet, Gavin, knows nothing of such matters, and in no hurry to find out. He's like a prince out of Faery to her." She made great fuss at straightening her skirts. "And a good thing: if I thought they were up to nonsense, I'd lay a stick to the pair of them!"

But that was just Meg talking.

It came to seem to me that most of their quarreling was a kind of love-play, after all, though not like any I've ever seen. Maybe that girl liked words better than kisses—though you could tell he liked both. And, of course, there were quiet times when he'd harp for the three of us, and sing, and sometimes she'd join in his songs, for she'd a pleasing pretty throat, and a good ear, as Tom said himself. And sometimes, when he'd softened her heart with music, he'd slip in a compliment or two, and she not turn it away.

She loved his tales of kings and queens, dead heroes of Earth and Faery. But to him they were only tales, see, while she'd been brought up in the shadow of the Eildon Hills, that were cleft in three with a blow of the giant's sword. For instance, it was her habit to leave out a dish of milk at night for the Billie Blin, to bring luck to the house, and Tom didn't much hold with that. It made her fierce, the way he never let up about it.

"It sounds to me," he'd say, "as though you're using your milk to bribe the fairies to come and do your chores for you!"

And she'd stamp her foot: *"Don't* call them that! You've got no manners, to name them so."

"All right, *Fair Folk,"* Thomas scoffed. "People of Peace. Blessed Ones. The Good Neighbors. . . . It's Elves and Fairies in the ballads, and no one minds that. Anyway," he mused once, "I'm not sure there's a rhyme for 'neighbor.' 'Labor'?"

"Don't tax your brain," she returned. "Music's different. They like verse. But you've a fine nerve to sing so about them, and then go making fun!"

"Elspeth!" he said in mock surprise. "You sound as though you're defending a friend's good name. Have you seen them, then, lapping cream with the cat, or dancing 'round the Eildon Tree of a May morning?"

"Of course I've not seen them! They don't like to be seen . . . few folk have seen them."

"Few indeed."

"Well, I've never seen your French queen, either!" she flashes. Oh, she's in a fine temper now. No one likes to be told they're a fool. To this day, I'll never know how he got his reputation with women, if Elspeth was any example—but, then, by all accounts, she wasn't. It pleased him to provoke her, but anyone could see this was no jest to her. For myself, I've heard much of Those Others, and seen precious little, but you never can tell.

"Yet I know there is a queen—though I've only your word that *your* eyes have come close to her!"

His very eyes were looking at the girl strangely: a hard look, and burning.

She doesn't see it, or ignores it, carried away in fury. And, indeed, she's something to behold, with her hair loose around her head, and her eyes flashing. "It's all just stories to you, Thomas, Elves and queens and all— just a way to get folk to listen to you. And if you don't believe your own tales, why should I?"

"But you do," he breathes. "You believe everything I can't, my bright goddess in anger."

"Oh, stop!" she cries. "Don't! I hate it when you talk like that!"

"Like what? When I say that you're beautiful?"

"It's only words."

" 'Only' words? But words are important—you said so yourself. Words are real, Elspeth, as real as anything is."

"You don't think that."

"But you do. The words of a ballad: 'And so he's kissed her ruby lips, And never asked her leave.' "

All the while he's been moving towards her, both stoat to rabbit and moth to flame. And she staring at him, flame-bright and rabbit-scared, too brave to look away.

He touched her face, and drew it close to his. And softly he's laid his lips to hers, and held her there awhile.

She started away suddenly, clamping her mouth with the back of her hand. "Wait!" he says, as she tears about the room, picking up knitting and wool and cloak. But she'll not let him near her, and she's out the door with her wool stuffed in her bag.

They've both forgotten I was there, and a good thing, too. Though I'd have been on them quick enough if I thought they were up to naught.

For a moment Thomas stands staring at the door she's slammed behind her. In the yard, the dog set up a racket. I heard a knock at the door. Thomas made towards it, then stopped, hands in midair. To help him, I said, "I'll get it." He jumped at the sound of my voice, and then darted for the door.

But he stepped back a pace when he opened it.

"God be in this house," said the man in the doorway. He was a gypsy tinker, and as likely an old rogue as ever I saw, with his dark seamy face and flashing dark eyes half-hidden in his stringy hair; and the dirty yellow kerchief twisted 'round his neck, and unseely charms and trinkets hanging there too. "May all within be safe from every evil wish and sorrow, from *uruisg* in the glens and the workings of the Blessed Ones under the Hill."

"This," said Thomas to him, "is not very funny."

"Oh, sir," the gypsy begged, "just a crust to stay my poor belly, and a seat by your fire to warm me, and I'll be on my way. And if you've any old pots to mend . . ."

The minstrel just stood there glaring at the tinker, so I rose and said, "See here. There's some cold porridge I can give you; and if you want to spend the night in the shed, you're welcome. But my dogs have sharp ears, and I have sharp eyes yet, so don't you be up to anything."

"No, good master," said the gypsy humbly. "But let me do you some small service. I've come a long way, and have news of the great folk to the east to tell; stories of the king's court, and his brave knights and fair ladies, and a new treaty with the English lords. And I have fine wares to sell . . ." He pulled out a greasy packet, and thrust it at Thomas. "Ribbons for your sweetheart, sir? Love tokens?"

Thomas pushed the packet from him as though the man held a red-hot brand.

"Something for the lady of the house, perhaps?" The rogue turned him 'round, and there was Meg, coming up to the cottage.

"Ah," she says to him, "so you found your way. I told you it was just over the rise. Sit down and I'll give you something to eat, and you can mend the handle to my cooking pot, that's been loose all this year. Don't just stand there like two posts," she says crisply to us, "or someone'll come along and tie a horse to you."

Thomas stepped aside to let the tinker enter, asking him sourly, "Why didn't you first tell us you were invited?"

"A man likes to be wanted for himself alone. . . ." the gypsy sniveled.

Well, he sat down and fell to work, and with his work he talked. All sorts of gossip I can't recall, about folk I'd never heard of, from towns as far away as Stirling and Berwick. And I'd be surprised if even half of it was true. See, he could have told us the king's daughter had borne a two-headed calf, and who among us could have disproved it? But we all three listened, nonetheless. Meg knitted, and I spun heather rope. I thought Thomas would take out his harp and cut a new string for her; but he sat by me trimming the heather stalks with a wee penknife; and if he's trimmed one right, there's three he's marred by whittling away to nothing, or breaking in two, as the tinker talked.

". . . and great woe amongst the queen's ladies—for one of them goes with child by a man of low degree, and she a girl still unwed. They've asked her the name of him that bewhored her, but she will not speak. The king is wondrous wroth, that order cannot be kept in his court and his wife be made to seem no fitting guardian to maids; and he's locked the girl up in a tower without a window, until she speak the seducer's name."

I reached down to take another stalk from Thomas, and found that he'd twisted the heather into a tricksy knot, and was holding onto it white-knuckled.

"Tch!" said my wife. "Foolish king. If she will not say, 'tis as like because she loves the lad, and doesn't want to see him harmed for helping her to do her own desires. 'Bewhored her,' indeed!"

Thomas flashed her a pleased look, as though he hadn't expected my Meg to be so wise in the ways of maidens!

"But," the gypsy went on, "there's good news as well as bad among the queen's women. For the young Lady Lilias Drummond was wed last Whitsunday to the Earl of Errol, and I hear she's with child by him already. It's a fine match for her, although they say her father paid thrice her sister's dowry for it—and if some tongues wag that she was no maiden either, well, none's heard Errol complain."

Thomas took the knotted heather, and cast it into the fire. He stood watching it catch, the twists and knots taking on the glow of heat, like some eerie jewel of gold, such as they say the old kings were buried with. Then it exploded into flame, and burnt away to ash.

There was a queer smile on his face. "Then I'm the King of the Cats," says the minstrel to himself; and spoke no more word that night.

The gypsy proved an honest rogue, for he took nothing but what he was given, and he was gone the next day before the dawn.

Thomas was restless that morning; it was no surprise to me when he set off for Huntsleigh Farm a little short of the noontide.

He didn't return till sunset, and then it was with Elspeth's arm in his. Oh, they made a fair pair to look upon, coming across the rise, he with his sleek dark head and she with her wild tawny mane, striding along together with the bright burning sky behind. I don't know what he did to put it right—more words, I'd guess, and maybe a kiss, and maybe not.

He sang for us that night, a wondrous song of Faery, of the marvels there, the feasting and the music and all. And he sang a little song Elspeth must have taught him, for it's one we know hereabouts, of the Broom on the Hill, that is lovers' meeting and lovers' parting.

And then he said, "I must be gone from here, and soon." There was no sound from Elspeth; belike he'd told her so already. "I wish with all my heart it were otherwise—" And here he caught himself, looking from Elspeth to Meg and back again, smiling sheepishly: "Well, not *all* my heart. But I'll leave a corner of it here, whether you will or no."

Elspeth said, "Then you'll be back for it." But it was a thin, pale wraith of her old boldness.

"I will," he said to all of us. "I'll come back when I can. I know—I know no one's asked me to stay. And I've taken liberties with your hospitality all the spring. But all the same—" He fiddled with his harp pegs, for once at a loss for words, as though honesty made him dumb. "All the same . . ."

"Where will you go?" asked Elspeth.

"To Roxburgh. The gypsy said the king was headed there." He looked at her, where she sat across the hearth with Meg's arm around her. "I wish—I do wish you could come with me. So much I could show you—"

It was sad to see the wild light in her face spring up, flare and die in a moment's space.

Tom saw it, too. "No, I mean it."

Her eyes looked dark and clear in the shadows of evening. "Maybe you do. But I'll not come be your whore among them all."

He flushed, hands fussing on the harp without looking at it. "Would I make such a suggestion before these honest folk? No, you shall be as chaste as dawn, and see wondrous sights. We'll tell people you're my sister, and you can mimic them for me when they've all gone to bed. I'll even harp for your dowry if you like."

She flinched. What a gawk he was, to talk of dowries to a girl who might have loved him! "You are a fool, Thomas," she said, "to think I could return here having gone off with you."

"Oh," he said, this time looking at the harp. "Yes. I suppose so. Yes."

"Never mind," she says with false brightness. "You'll tell us all about it when you come back, won't you?"

"Of course. When I come back."

And without another word he launches into harping, tunes sad and merry, filling the cottage with music in every corner.

Thomas left on a bright spring morning, taking his leave of us alone. There was no knowing when next he'd be back, so we gave him gifts to remember us by: Meg had woven a belt for him, and I'd whittled a comb of horn to pass the time.

He took them with thanks, "And nothing fairer will I find in all my travels." And, so saying, he's kissed us both.

He looked around, at the house and at the spreading hills.

"Will you be stopping by Huntsleigh," I asked, "on your way to Roxburgh?"

"No," he said, though he was looking that way. "Poor Elspeth! If she were a lad, I'd take her as my 'prentice. She'd like the road." He smiled, shrugged his harp on his back. "Now, no doubt she'll be wed by the time I come again."

Meg's face set to say something sharp; but remembering it was his journey's start, she only said, "No, no, she's far too young to wed."

"Well," he said. "Well. Maybe I'll find her some young lord. She can't spin straw into gold, by any chance?"

"You'd know that better than I." Meg added crisply, "And are we to expect any more gypsy messages while you're away?"

"Messages—?" His face looked so blank you might have drawn it on. And drawn on also was the smile, careless but for the corners of his eyes: "Did you not enjoy our dark friend's court stories?"

"Surely," says Meg, "the people of the king's high court are becoming like my own gossips to me. But I doubt we'd have heard the half of the news, had I not told him you were lodging with us."

"Oh," says Tom, "so that's what you think. No doubt he heard of a minstrel hereabouts and came for music; too bad I disappointed him."

"He'd not the look," she said, "of one disappointed. Said he was a friend of yours, when I met him."

His two eyes shifted back and forth, like an animal's caught in a trap. "Hardly a friend," he says, haughty-like. "We travel in some of the same circles. Nora's Bevis is also handy at court."

"That gypsy tinker!" I cried. "Never tell us you know the rogue!"

"As well as anyone would choose to," Thomas says stiffly. "But don't you fear; he'll not be back to trouble you."

"Oh, I dunno," says Meg, wicked-like; "he was that handy with the pot-mending, I might welcome him again."

"Well," Tom smiles, "after Gavin's fair welcome of dogs' teeth, cold porridge and all, he's sure to call next time he's in the region."

"Perhaps next time he'll bring you a lady's token, as well."

The harper looked on her in a kind of fear, as if she were a witch-wife.

"Oh, Tom," Meg sighs, "I'm not an old fool yet. When I hear tell of Lady Lilias twice in one spring, I can work the tale out."

His face broke into a laugh. "Well, there it is, then. I'll own I got into some mischief lately, and a risky business it was: her brothers would have killed me, had I stayed at court. There are not quite seven of them, but all it takes is one sword in your ribs to end the song. But clearly, cooler heads have prevailed, and she's well wed to a man of high degree, and no harm done."

But Meg looked grave, and I must have shown what I felt. "Do you think," he defended himself hotly from our silence, "a woman can't seduce? Lilias Drummond is not pining of a broken heart, I do assure you."

But I didn't give two pins for Lady Lilly. "Do you mean to tell me," I demanded, "that you might have brought Drummond and all his kin down on our heads for sheltering of you here?"

"If they'd found me—but who would think to look for me here at the back end of nowhere? Drummond doesn't burn sheep crofts for sport. Anyway, I've told you, it's all right now!"

"Oh, aye, with your gypsy friend on's way back to Selkirk maybe to spread word of your safe nest!"

At least he had the grace not to look to Meg for help now. "Gavin," he said, looking me full in the face, "you know me a little. If they had come here, I would have gone out to meet them. By my harp and hand, I swear it."

"Oh, make me no great oaths," I grumbled, for I did believe him. "Just don't look so hard for trouble everywhere."

"I never meant to," he said like a child. "I'd never bring trouble on you willingly. You've been nothing but good to me. I do know that, as I knew I'd be safe here." He was looking at the ground, more ashamed of this confession than of his whoring and lying. "I can't explain."

"No," says Meg, "you can't explain what you don't understand. But never mind," she says to us both, "be easy. The tinker was only up to mischief, amusing himself at your expense. The tinkers are strange folk, they're not like us. They're human, right enough, but they like to think of themselves as being like the Fair Folk, just stepping in now and then to help or make mischief as the fancy takes them. And in your case, Thomas, you should be grateful he brought you the news he did."

I asked my wife, "How do you come to know so much of tinkers?"

But she only repeated, "I'm not an old fool yet."

And so the Rhymer made ready to leave us.

"Setting off to seek your fortune," Meg sighed, "like the lads in the tales. . . . And if Nora's Bevis hadn't come with the news, or your Lady Lilly'd proved with child by you, what would you have done then, Thomas?"

He answered her with a line from one of his own songs: " 'Set my foot on yonder ship, and sailed beyond the sea,' I imagine. I might have left a little more quickly—and not come back."

"But now you're free to return." Meg smiled warmly at him, that smile that'd melt the snow off the hillside.

"If I stay out of trouble. . . ."

Meg embraced him, tall and cloaked and laden as he was. "God be with you, our Tom." And he didn't bridle at the name.

Well, it's no secret that our Tom found his fortune, and another name as well. As summer passed we began to hear his tunes in other people's hands, and his name on their lips. Fiddlers at the fair drew silver with his tunes, and a riddle song I'd heard Thomas make myself was said to be one of Merlin's own! A passing piper told of an enchanted harp of white ivory he'd heard played before the court at Rutherglen—which made Meg snort. Those who knew him now spoke his name with a kind of pause before it: *Thomas the Rhymer;* or else they said it too fast, to try and sound familiar. I hoped he was staying out of mischief.

We never said aught to Elspeth of the gypsy, or Lady Lilly. The girl kept on coming by, as though to prove that she'd never come just for Thomas, and I'll not say we weren't glad of her company, her saucy tongue and pretty voice.

With the minstrel gone, other lads started coming 'round after Elspeth, but I could have told them to save their shoe-leather. She'd sit with Meg at loom or hearth, or laboring in field or yard, and make mock of them, good lads all who'd been neighbors since she was small. For one spoke too slow, another too fast; one was tall and thin as a corncrake, another small and wide as a dwarf, nay, *two* dwarves . . . oh, she was a merry lass for days, and then a black humor would fall on her, and she'd sit melancholy silent, attacking her work as though it were some task set for her release. As weeks passed without Thomas, she began to soften towards the lads, but only to walk out with one one week, and then another the next.

"I cannot like them, Meg," she'd say despairingly; "I'll never be a wife! Perhaps I'd better be a nun."

"Wait and see," my goodwife answered her, uncommon gentle for my Meg; "just wait and see."

The Rhymer came again in autumn, between the harvest and All Hallow's. He came on foot, but appareled like a prince, in bright colors and broidery, his harp beribboned and his boots well soled. He was full of cheer, his bag full of gifts, which he laid before us full of pride, like a kitten that's caught a mouse and leaves it at your bed's feet.

"I'm on my way to Roxburgh," he said, "for the great night of singing I told you of." By that we knew he'd stay just a fortnight. It was good to know these things: easier on Meg, not having to wonder always when he'd be off. She'd grown uncommon fond of that boy. It's natural, us having no children of our own. And if he'd people, he never spoke of them. Later Elspeth told us Tom had been raised by a brother, same as her, only not so kind as Iain, and the brother's wife only too glad to see Tom run off with an old blind harper, to be his boy and learn from him.

Now, it was strange how the girl took on at his return. She seemed to lose all spirit. Far from mocking of her suitors, which he'd have enjoyed, she kept silent about them, and if Meg or I said anything, she'd fall in a little rage, like a wet hen. Even I could see she was taking great pains to comb and dress her hair, plaiting it fancy and binding it up with ribbons.

"Blue," says Tom, who noticed right away, "very pretty."

"Oh," says the girl, busy about the house, not looking at him, "it's nothing."

After a few days she stopped coming. Although the summer was fine, Thomas gloomed about the house—oh, he was good enough company, but a certain laughter was missing. Nor made he any shift to tryst on the hillside, as he'd been wont.

Finally, Meg, who could fathom them no more than I could, took matters in her hands and asked him to carry some eggs to Huntsleigh Farm. He rounded on her in sudden anger: "Why didn't you tell me she had a sweetheart?"

"Well," says cunning Meg, "she couldn't wait for you forever," but I spoils it by exclaiming at the same time, and louder, "Sweetheart! What on the earth put that in your mind?"

"She's changed completely," he rages. "She won't even look at me, and she minces and prinks like some—some . . . lady. And she's lost her tongue. Clearly, she's mad for some young idiot. You might have told me."

"They grow up fast at that age," says Meg happily; but I'd heard her a moment before make that snorting noise people do when they're swallowing a great laugh.

Well, there was no time for them to sort things out. Iain's wife bore another child, and Elspeth was needed at home. Thomas had to leave before the christening, which was a shame, for I've heard it said there's nothing like a good christening to bring folks together.

He told us he'd be back in spring, and so he was. He looked pale and tired, though he said that all was well, and showed us a ring the king had given him, and baubles and suchlike tokens from sundry nobles. "The queen's brother out of France, the cardinal, is coming at Easter," he told us briefly. "I'm to present a new song." Then he bade us good night, and slept the night and most of the next day through.

Well, he'd nothing but good to say of his fame, and of the honors bestowed on him for his harping and his song. But the drawn look he kept for some days, while Meg plied him with viands. It put me in mind of his own tale of the fairies' fiddler.

Tired as he was, he didn't stint us his music; indeed, he seemed to take pleasure in playing us the old tunes we'd always delighted in. At least, he said they were old, and not in the new style.

"You'd laugh, Meg, to see the new fashion in hats. The ladies wear them so high, they must stoop like swans to get under doorways"—and he did a funny hop to show us—"Some look like dizzy geese, instead!"

"You're a fine one to talk of fashion, Tom Rhymer, you with that earring you look like you got from the gypsies!"

He fingered the small gold hoop. "Yes, Busy Maggie, I knew you'd like it. All the ladies do. I'll take it off next time, before I cross Leader Water, shall I?"

"You must do as you like," she says crustily, but fond of him the while, as anyone could see. "You're as headstrong a man as ever was."

"But I beg to remain your goodwife's only minstrel."

"Oh, Tom," she sighs, "someday you'll talk yourself into something you can't get out of."

"Such gloomy predictions! And speaking of predictions, how are my bonnie Elspeth's wedding plans?"

Before Meg could get up to her mischief, I told him, "There's no wedding, Tom, and well you know it. What, must you be marrying off every girl you pay court to?"

He looked at me surprised as though a jug had prophesied. Then he collected himself. "She's a good lass," he said mildly. "I just wondered."

"She'll be by sometime this week to help me with the washing," Meg said. "You can see for yourself."

With her skirts kilted up, her long legs planted in the stream, Elspeth was not ill to see. I heard the splashing and shouting coming from there, but Meg was in charge of washing, so I kept to my own tasks. I wondered, though, what sort of care Meg could have been taking of them when I saw a half-naked Thomas streaking through the yard, followed by shrieking, dripping Elspeth. Even her hair was soaked to deep red. It hung around her in wind-whipped rats' tails. "GOLIATH!" she shouted, hurling what looked like a wet stocking after him. It fell short of its mark, in the dust. "Turn back, Philistine, stand and fight like a man!"

Ducking, darting, he retrieved it and flung it back at her. "I tell you, *I'm* David! I play the harp!"

"I don't care! I'm no giant! Anyway, I win!"

Back went the stocking, or maybe it was one of a pair of hose.

"You win!" he scoffed, still at safe throwing distance. "You look like something's just crawled out of a hole in the ground."

"*You* look like something carved on the underside of a pew!"

"I do not!"

"Yes you do!"

"Philistine!"

"Gargoyle!"

She sat down in what quickly became a pool of mud, laughing too hard to stand.

"And they say it's wine makes folk draggle in the mire." He bent over her while she half tried to fend him off. "With you, my girl, water alone will serve. Degenerate. Shocking." But he didn't plant his feet far enough apart, and in his efforts to draw her up, she pulled him down.

"Well," says I, in case they've forgotten I'm there, "that's the first I've heard pigs quote Scripture."

There was no doing aught with them the rest of the day, though the wash did get laid out on the new grass to bleach in the sun. Any remark set them laughing like two babes. The next day being Melrose Fair, he took her for a fairing. But even Meg gawked when she came back covered in green ribbons: she wore them in her hair, as laces for her gown, even tied up her shoes; and around her neck a blue glass bead on another ribbon. They laughed that evening away, and sang part-songs, and Thomas walked her home—at least, that's what I hope he did, for he was gone long enough.

Even when he left us, she was blithe enough. She sang about her work, and sometimes laughed to herself, remembering something between them. We came to miss her when she was at her brother's, which was where she belonged, after all. But she was a pretty, fair maid without a sweetheart, and folk would talk. This time, though, she made no mockery of anyone, just kept to her own ways, helping here and at home, and wandering the hills for all the world as though she were still a child. Meg said the other girls misliked it; it made it seem she didn't care for them, or for their swains. And near as I could see, she didn't, and not much they could do about it.

Tom appeared from time to time, expected or unexpected, staying the night, and maybe a day or two, then leaving again to follow the king or the knights, harping and rhyming for their favor. He was invited hither and yon, and seemed never to miss a chance to see a new sight, play for new folk. He did say most minstrels sought to keep just one patron, but that he'd keep 'em all, if he could! Well, he knew his business best, I suppose. But I fear he was the same when it came to women. He did always have a bit of a token for Elspeth with him, a ribbon or a pin or comb, and if he went away in too much haste to visit her, he'd leave it with us like fairy gold for her to find when next she came.

I allow that it was strange: a harper she never saw, to be her sweetheart. And if she didn't think he'd lady-loves aplenty in kitchen and hall, then she was fooling herself. It seemed to make her happy, though. I said to Meg when we were private, "I dunno. If it was me, I'd have his bollocks on a platter."

Meg laughed. "You would, too! But it's different for her. She's never wanted what she could have."

"Oh," says I, "she could have him right enough, if she laid her traps right."

Meg snorted, at me or at the thought. "Much good it would do her. Can you see the Rhymer yoked to a plough? Or Elspeth sleeping on the castle hall floor?" Funny, I'd never given thought to where he slept. I'd imagined feather beds, like other castle folk.

"Folks should wed," I said. "She could have a nice house, and babes, and he could bring her money to keep them with, from his travels. I'm not saying that's right, but it's no worse than she is now."

Meg took my hand. "Well, we'll just have to bide and see. She's young yet, to wed, and he's not so old, for all his worldly ways. But don't you go saying anything, to set her heart on it."

"Me give a maid love-counsel? I've no use for maids—although I didn't do badly with the one I chose."

The last time he came was in autumn. It was bright, crisp weather, and Thomas came over the hills singing.

Meg took one look at him and said, "I'm going to wash and mend that blue cloak. It's a disgrace. And you'll need it, too, with winter coming on. I shouldn't wonder there'll be wolves this year."

"And your stitches sure to keep the wolves out!" he laughed. "Winter's weeks away yet. We won't think of winter until it's time for me to go."

"You'll be staying a while, then?"

"A while," he says. "Long enough to hear myself think. I've got too many words and tunes jangling 'round in my head." His look was fever-bright, as though he'd still the court's applause jangling in his head as well. He kissed old Maggie's hand: "Dear Meg. Of all my women, you're the only one who would ever mend a cloak for me."

Meg looked at him sternly, knowing when he was coming the gallant with her, and, I'll be bound, not liking the way he spoke of "all his women." But she held onto his hand nonetheless.

He was in such good spirits, I thought he'd won some great favor, maybe to be the king's own singer. But it seemed the court was removing from Selkirk to Jedburgh for the hunting, and Thomas had cut loose for the nonce.

"I thought I'd try a change of air," he explained, or as close to explaining as he ever came. "Plenty of time before I have to go looking for a place with thick walls for winter."

Next day he went to see Elspeth on his own. And a fair day it was, the skies deep blue, the air so clear you could see the hills spreading out into beyond, all the way to the haze of the sea, and, westward, smoke rising from the chimneys of a town a day's walk away. The pair of them returned late after noon, the girl in a temper, but for once not with him.

"We *caught* the blessed cow!" I came 'round the house to hear her complaining to Meg. "It's not my fault Thomas is a dolt about gates, is it?"

"I'm not—" he began, but she cut him right off.

"And suddenly they think I can't look after myself. I never go anywhere, I never do anything, and they treat me like a child. Just because I'm not—I don't have— It's not fair!"

"Elspeth," Meg says as the girl drew breath. "Are you here without your brother's leave?"

"I *told* him where I was going."

"Well, you'd best turn 'round, then."

"Oh, Meg—"

But my goodwife pointed out over the Scar. Far and away, we could see a storm cloud black as rooks, and the grey shadow of rain below. A pretty sight to see, far off on a sunny afternoon. But Meg said, "That'll be between you and home by evening, if you don't scamper."

But Elspeth stayed rooted. A kestrel cried above us, and a mouse skreeked down below. "He'll thrash me," she muttered. "He said he would."

"I'll come," Thomas offered quickly.

Elspeth looked hard at him. He'd chosen the wrong time to be gallant, to try and come between a girl and the head of her house over a matter that, know it or not, concerned him. "No," she said with dignity, "thank you. Oh, let me stay," she says to Meg. "I'll go tomorrow. Maybe Iain'll be easier then."

If I were her brother and she'd spent the night out, I'd thrash her the harder—and likely he would, too, and she knew it. "If I don't stay here," she says, turning her fierce look first on Meg and then on me, "I'll sleep out in the hills, for I'll not go home tonight after what he said!"

Thomas looked a little helpless, not used to family quarrels. "Come," he says awkwardly, "it wasn't so bad as that. Your brother was just worried about the cow—"

The girl gazed stricken at him. "No one understands. And you! You're the worst of all!"

And she runs off around the house and toward the holly grove.

"Well?" Meg snaps at the two of us. "What are you two staring at? Haven't you brains in your heads? How do you think, Thomas, she liked having her brother scold her like a child in front of you?"

"Oh," he said. "Well . . . but she should know I wouldn't pay any mind—"

"That girl," I said pointedly to him, "needs a house of her own." And I went back about my work.

Elspeth reappeared at supper, with the first drops of rain. They glittered in her hair as she stood in the doorway, her head held high. Although she must have tried to tidy herself before she came in, she was all draggled from her hours on the hills, with autumn leaves clinging to her skirts, her hair wisped and tangled with bits of fern and heather, and a few red bilberries too.

"I'm sorry," she said formally, "if I've been a bother."

But Thomas said, as if she had not spoken, "You look as though you've come wild out of the Hill."

It was the Faerie Hill he meant, and he said it with such reverence that she could not protest. And wasn't he gazing at her as though seeing marvels! She turned her proud head to look at him, and her open lips were silent.

Even I felt the change in the room; it was as though Meg and I had ceased to exist, or were seeing a tale we weren't part of.

He rose, and she came to his side, and he seated her at the table by him. And quietly we ate our supper, each thinking their own thoughts; and what the young couple's were was plain enough to see, for though they never touched, the little space they left between them seemed filled with heat.

Elspeth helped Meg to clear away the table, while Tom harped idly for a bit, and it grew dark. Then, "Elspeth, do you sleep here by the fire," Tom says. "I'll go out to the shed."

"But it's raining."

"Never mind," he says. "It was good enough for Gavin's gypsy—and Meg's mended my blue cloak."

The girl gave him a fleece, pressing it long and soft into his arms. Meg and I retired, grateful to be alone together. The rain pelted comfortably, and neither of us felt like talking.

I woke sudden in the middle of the night, not sure what woke me. The dog was quiet, and the rain had slowed. But I'd surely heard something.

I climbed out of our bed, and found that the space by the hearth was empty. The door was unlatched. I waited a moment or two. I thought about waking Meg, I took a step toward the door, thought again, and decided after a bit that the best thing a foolish old man could do was to go back to bed until morning. So I did.

They left before we were awake, he walking her back to Huntsleigh through the new-washed dawn to face her brother's wrath. Thomas later told us she was, as he put it, "a complete lady," apologizing so meekly that Iain was hard-put to be harsh—and perhaps the brother's own goodwife had given him a scolding about chiding a girl before her suitor! I can't help owning, though, that I was glad Thomas had seen Iain angry, for Elspeth's brother is a big-armed man, slow to anger but swift to act—and it was well the harper knew it, if things were to go on as they were!

We saw less of Tom after that, for he would call on Elspeth at the farm, and help her with her tasks there, so they could walk out on the hills together. (He was, he said, a great favorite with her young nieces, because he could make a penny disappear and find it in their ears!) Not that he didn't give me and Meg what help we needed; but, true to his word, he seemed to want solitude to "hear himself think," so when he wasn't with the girl he was off wandering the hills.

One fine day Tom went off walking his lone, high on the Eildons where the world, he said, was spread before him like a jeweled map, and the only sound the wind ruffling through broom and gorse. He walked out empty-handed, without even his harp, and he never came back.

It wasn't until the next day, when we found he hadn't been to Elspeth's, that we began to fear some mischance. He might have left us without saying good bye, you see, but he'd never have gone off without his harp.

Well, we roused what help we could, but no trace of him was there. No one had seen or heard him; it was as though he'd vanished from the earth entire. We even sent to the earl's steward; Iain went, and brought back two servingmen with dogs.

But though we combed the Eildon Hills, nothing could be found. And so I doubt we shall see the Rhymer in this world again.

PART II

THOMAS

True Thomas lay on Huntlie bank,
A ferlie he spied wi' his ee,
And there he saw a lady bright,
Come riding down by the Eildon Tree.

Her skirt was o' the grass-green silk,
Her mantle o' the velvet fyne,
At ilka tett of her horse's mane
Hang fifty siller bells and nine.

—*Trad. (Child ballad no. 37)*

Scho sayd, Thomas take leue at sone and mone,
And als at lefe that grewes on tree;
This twelmoneth sall thou with me gone,
And medill-erthe sall thou none see.

—*Thornton Ms., 15th century*

Now Thomas, ye maun hold your tongue
Whatever ye may hear or see,
For, if you speak word in Elflyn land,
Ye'll neer get back to your ain countrie.

—*Trad. (Child ballad no. 37)*

WHAT SONGS DO you sing to them in Elfland?

There, where all songs are true, and all stories history . . . I have seen lovers walking in those glades, with gentle hands and shining faces, their feet light upon the grass, where little flowers shone in the shadows as though the lovers trod the starry firmament. And some I almost recognized: Niamh of the Shining Hair with Irish Oisian; Fair Aucassin with his gentle Nicolette; and two kingly men with their arms around one graceful, merry queen . . . other faces, other figures strangely arrayed, each one with their own story, no doubt, and now at peace, with all stories done.

And I do not know whether their peace was real, or if it was only the illusion of fair Elfland, a game of the Elves, a work of art.

I could not speak to them.

A story may begin anywhere, as the maker chooses. My story begins under the Eildon Tree, there on the easternmost slope of the Eildon Hills. It felt strange to be sitting still, quiet and alone. A minstrel's life is not much given to that. I rested in the moment, smelling the burnt and tangy wild air of autumn and looking, just looking, out over the great stretch of hill and sky, the river valley sparkling below. Far away, for sound carries in the clear air of the Eildons, I heard sheep, and the voice the wind makes as it tears among the grasses. It was a companionable voice, off on business of its own, with nothing particular to say to me.

If I was thinking of anything, it was of how I must be mad to keep on leaving this place. My life here was like nothing I'd ever had before. Here were people I liked, who seemed to want nothing from me; people who cared whether I were hot or cold, hungry or sated, merry or sad for my own sake, not the music's. Oh, I tried to tell myself they would have been the same for anyone, that I did not especially warrant their kindness; but I knew that was the coward's excuse, and that the truth was, they had taken me to their bosoms, and I cared for them in return. By "them," I suppose I mean only Meg and Gavin; for there was grown more between Elspeth and me than kindness.

It had happened before I'd meant it to—not that I'd ever meant anything of the sort. I had liked the girl, wanted her; but in gaining my desire, this once I had not slaked it.

I didn't want to deal dishonorably with her, and not only because it would lose me my welcome here. Elspeth was so very different from the ladies and willing girls I had known; so fiercely *herself;* so innocent. She had gone from a flouting, teasing miss to a sort of trusting thing—a bird's nest, a quick-beating heart I held in my hands—oh, still full of wit and sparks, but holding nothing back. With her it was as though some question had been asked of me, and answered well. I found I wanted to be with her all the time: to talk with her, to look at her, to let her make me laugh. I wanted to protect her from everything—yes, even from me.

I was not really able to think clearly about Elspeth. When I tried, I lost my distance—in deed as well as thought, for to think of her was to set off to see her, and an end to all musings. It made me think that I should go back to court soon, sooner than I had planned. I had songs still to make for the Christmas feasts, tunes for the dancing; and I had ordered a new suit of clothes for the festivities before I left Stirling, which must be fitted, the fashion being for such closeness. A certain countess had said she hoped to see me in blue, and I heard she was new-widowed . . . and there was the head groom's daughter, gone in one year from bouncing balls off the palace walls to lurking in the hall whenever I played. . . . I had also promised the queen a new set of verses on the difference between the love a knight owes to his wife and to his mistress. I wasn't getting anywhere with them here. (I had told Elspeth all about the royal Christmas feasts, with cakes shaped like swans, and swans made into cockatrices . . . I'm not sure she believed me, though . . . what fun it would be to show it all to her!)

A flash of movement on the hill caught my eye. I sat bolt upright, staring. It seemed as if the court itself had come to fetch me, pulled out of my dream to claim me from my dreaming. A lady on a fine white horse was riding across the hill. She was almost upon me; I'd been lost in dreaming indeed, not to hear her, for the horse's mane and bridle were strung with silver bells that drowned the burble of the river, and its hooves thudded on the dry hillside.

I jumped to my feet, pulling together my court manners. The lady on the horse's back shone bright as spring against the sere autumn grass. Her gown was green as new leaves, her unbound hair like morning sunlight. The world grew coarse around her.

In a moment I knew her. "Lilly!" I said. "What the Devil have you done, to come to me here?"

The lady's laugh was like the rippling river. "Look again, Thomas. And do not curse by the Adversary."

I looked again. One strand of her hair made cobwebs seem thick, and diamonds dull. In that halo of gold, her face shone with an indescribable beauty, full of wit and warmth and pity, all at once.

Again I knew her, and knelt down on the grass in awe. "My queen . . ."

"Oh, Thomas!"

". . . and high Heaven's. Holy Mary, rue on me—"

"Ah, no." There was sorrow in her voice. "Thomas, look again."

I looked, and beheld a beautiful woman, beyond all women beautiful. The white horse tossed its head; in the foam of its mane the silver bells rang. "Lady," I said, "I do not know you."

"But I do know you. Thomas the Rhymer, Thomas of the quick wit and clever fingers. I have come for you to harp for me, Thomas, for your fair fame has reached even unto my land. Make music for me, Rhymer, and tell me your tales."

I gazed on her, and knew she spoke truth: what were lies to such a one, wild as wind yet real as stone? And I knew that all my tales could not equal one of hers.

"What," the lady laughed, "word of your fame no longer delights you?" Her lips were berry-red. "I see it does not. Do words no longer please you, Rhymer?"

Words were brittle and unreal, next to the hot blood that sang in my ears. What use for words with her? If I could but pull her from the horse, take her silks and mouth and words and all in the grass, I should have my whole desire.

"You know me, Thomas," she said playfully, "if you will only think. You may have one guess more." My whole body felt thick and heavy. I could only shake my head, and the horse's bridle rang, silver echoing the singing in my ears. "True Thomas, riddle me this: what is it you sing of nightly and rhyme daily? True love, heroism, glory, sorrow, enchantment. . . ."

But all my rhymes were gone.

She added, "No woman of Earth, nor yet of Heaven."

Her face blurred before me: all the women I had ever had were there in it, all my moments of ecstasy and fulfillment—and they seemed dry next to her promised fulfillment, stale next to her excitement, sad next to her pleasure.

"I am the Queen of Elfland, Thomas."

"I know," I heard myself say, my voice thin and tinny in my ears.

"I am not made for your earthly lust," she said, her white teeth sharp, her eyes cruel with pity. "You were best turn now and walk away."

I took a step towards her. The horse was calm and still, cropping grass. She leaned low over the saddle bow.

"Will you have one kiss of me? It will be dearly bought." Light danced on the sweetness of her lips. "Dare to kiss my lips, and know that your body follows."

I smiled crookedly, the breath hard in my throat. "That is to be hoped for, is it not?"

"Is it? You will be mine, Thomas. Let me be sure of you."

I pulled her to my mouth, and tasted fruit and flesh undreamed of. She quenched my thirst, and at the same time filled me with hunger I knew would never leave me. For just one moment my mind cleared as I thought, *I am lost.*

Then she was sliding into my arms in a hissing shiver of silk. I was enveloped in green and gold, while the red of her lips took me into the heart of flame. We lay in the dry sedge, and where it pricked my bare skin I felt only the caresses of the earth; and when rocks and roots dug into me, they were her fingers, the heels of her feet and hands. She was wind and rain, making me safe from all elements forever by making me part of them. When passion exploded in me, I felt my body disintegrate into the numberless jewels under the hills, the stars in darkness.

I lay exhausted, pressed against the earth, soaked with sweat. The Queen of Elfland, fully dressed, stood over me. She ran a cool finger along my shoulder, and licked the sweat off delicately. "You do sing well," she said. "Now rise, Thomas, and dress yourself; for we've a long journey to make."

"What?" I mumbled. The smell of autumn earth was poignant in my nostrils, so sweet I wanted to cry.

"You must come with me. Your body is mine, as I told you it must be. You shall be mine for seven years; and you shall serve me in that time as best pleases me. Come, Thomas, rise."

I rolled over onto my back. My entire front was clothed in grass and earth. Far above us the bowl of heaven was blue enough to fall into. "I can't go," I said. "This is my home." Never had my senses so reveled in the pureness of the air, the tang of grass, the very molding of the earth my body rested on, roots stretching deep into its core. To leave it now would be to tear out the heart of me.

"It will still be your home when you are in my country. And you may find your way back. But first you must come with me. Look at me, Thomas."

She stood tall and slender as a young birch above me. I wanted her again, as I had known all along I would. I rose to one knee, one hand still clutching a tuft of grass as though its roots could anchor me to the Earth. "Lady," I begged, "have pity on me."

"A bargain made is a bargain made. You must be mine for seven years. I shall mount now," the queen said, "and you will come up behind me. Or you will stand here on the cold hillside, and watch me ride away. Either way, you will be mine. Despite your pleas, it were pity on you to take you with me. You will not find the service hard, with me."

Seven years. She was all grace and music as she swung up onto her horse's back. My eyes could not leave her, rich and strange as she was against the bright beauty of the world, more than the world, and less; a riddle to be unraveled, a clue to be followed. I felt the tug in my chest with only that little distance between her and me. I could not let her go. I knew that there were reasons to stay, but could not reason them; people to bid farewell, but could not speak to them. My fingers shook as I fastened my clothes. Then I took her hand, that cold, strong hand, and swung up onto the horse behind her.

The steed took two steps forward, and then it seemed to burst into a hurricane of speed. Wind roared in my ears. I had to blink my eyes to see. The world was swimming past us at a dizzy rate; and so I was spared any sight of familiar things, places and people I was leaving. The queen rode hard, her body taut and lean like a young huntress's. A wave of pride took me: it did not seem a bad thing to be hers.

How long we rode I cannot say. The light faded fast, as though we outpaced the sun's very path. In the utter darkness, there was a moment when all sound ceased. Then I heard the steady plash of hooves in water.

For the first time since the ride began, the queen spoke: "You're going to get your feet wet, Thomas. But never mind it."

Even as she spoke, I felt a warmth I might not even have guessed was water tickling at my boots' toes. Like a warm hand it engulfed my feet and crept up my ankles, all the way to my knees. The horse walked steadily on, seeming to need no light to find its way. And my legs were borne swimmingly through the warm stream, in a sort of dream of comfort. From the sound of it we were in a cavern, making our way through an underground stream. I wouldn't have thought it would be so beautifully warm: streams I knew in the mountains were always icy. I leaned my head against the Elf Queen's back, my arms around her, feeling the water flowing past me, and the comfort of her soft body holding me. The rhythm of the horse's hooves was like a heart beating. And our two hearts beating were like the distant roar of the ocean, the sound of a seashell gives back to you.

I don't know if I slept or waked, in that deep darkness. I seemed to hear songs, cradle songs I'd known once . . . but when I tried to listen to them, they were drowned in the roaring water's pulse.

My mouth was terribly dry, my throat rough, as though I'd been shouting. "Well sung, Thomas," said the queen. "You do well to sing the songs you heard when you lay under your mother's heart.

"Now bid farewell to sun and moon, and to the leaf on the tree. For we have passed the boundary of Middle-Earth."

The horse's body under us began to climb, and the water to ebb back from my legs. A faint light began to glow around us, the grey of early dawn, but dimmer, bleaker. My legs were dark with what I took to be the stream's water; but as the light grew, I saw its color, a deep and plangent red, dripping onto the dust of the ground.

"Blood—" I rasped.

"The earth cannot hold all the blood that's shed on it. And so the stream flows below. We have passed through it now; soon it will be gone from you."

On my legs the blood of battles from that river we had been riding through, running with the blood of births and maidenheads, the finger-pricks of children's blood-brotherhood and the deeper wounds of brothers' strife; the murder of travelers for gold and the careless scrape of a nettle in summer's fields. . . . I heard myself let out a cry, as one new-come into the world, instead of one passed from it. I was intolerably thirsty. I held the queen and felt the salt sting of my own tears on my lips.

"Now look."

And we were on a great plain, that stretched on forever all in shades of grey, from the near-black of shadows to the pearly tones of the overcast sky that hung, impenetrable, above us.

"What is this place?" I asked, barely able to speak for the thirst that was on me.

"Nowhere."

With a twitch of her legs, the Elf Queen set the horse again to the gallop. The desert flew past us, one streaming mile exactly like another. Suddenly I felt the horse gather its body into a great leap, and we flew, longer than any true horse might hold in the air, and landed soft as a kiss on green earth.

It was an orchard, carpeted in soft grass sprinkled with white and yellow flowers. It made my heart ache for the orchards of my childhood, where my brother had lifted me into the branches after fruit—then I realized that this one was nothing like them. The grass here was too green, the trees' bark shone with silver; their pink and white blossoms—no, they were fresh green leaves—were summer-rich boughs of peaches and apricots—were the ripe tang of autumn fruit. . . . Every time I looked, I saw and breathed a different season. It dizzied my senses.

"Come, Thomas." The Elf Queen slipped down from the horse's back, and held up her arms for me. I needed the help, for when my legs touched earth they gave way under me, stiff and numb as they were from the long ride. I couldn't help laughing at my weakness; and the queen laughed with me as she helped me to sit down. I took off my boots, and curled my toes in the long grass.

We were in a summer orchard now, ripe with golden peaches and apricots, and dark cherries like clusters of rubies. Just above my head hung a perfect peach, golden with fuzz like the fur of a bumblebee. It was so close I could smell it. If I had had to stand to pick it, I might have fainted, for my head was light, my belly hollow. But I reached up one hand and pulled the sun-warmed fruit from the tree.

"Ah, no," the queen said. "Will you take what is not yours?"

"And do you mean to let me die of hunger, here in Elfland?" I snapped, the smell of the fruit tempting in my hand.

"This is not Elfland," she said sternly, like one reprimanding a wayward child. "In a moment, I will show you. But first, you had better learn to control your appetites. Your forefather Adam also thought it would be a fine thing to eat of the fruit of the Tree—I see he merely set the mode for mortals, and taught you nothing to profit by his example."

The queen of godless Elfland was a fine one to be lecturing me on morals! But I was no thief. Angrily I threw the peach away.

"Don't be angry," she said more gently. "You must trust me in the ways of enchantment. Had you tasted of the fruit, you were lost to me—and your soul lost to you. Here—" From a fold in her mantle, she took out a loaf of bread and a jug of wine. "Eat and drink this. They will not harm you: the bread was baked in Boulogne of the world's fair France, and the grapes pressed in Sicily."

If I fell on the food with a little less decorum than was seemly, I think I can hardly be blamed. The queen seemed at ease in the garden, and made herself a crown of cherries, and sat with the wreath cocked rakishly on her golden head, like a little girl at a party; but I noticed that even she ate none of the fruit.

When I had eaten I felt stronger. My lady had a maiden's beauty now, fresh as the orchard itself; and I couldn't resist straightening the wreath upon her head, and twining my fingers in her rich cloud of silky hair. But she caught her fingers up in mine, laughing. "Ah, no, Thomas; can you think of nothing else?"

"Madam," I said gallantly, "how can I, when your beauty shines like—" I stopped in confusion, for I'd been about to say "like cherries." Not a very pretty phrase; I knew I could do better any day of the week. But in that orchard it was hard to think of other things—as though the place itself were more real than anything else.

"I see," said the queen. "It is not you who are unable to resist, but I who

am irresistible?" There's not a woman born who doesn't adore that notion.
But the Queen of Elfland said, "Then I shall make it easier for you."

There was a shivering in the air around her. And there, in the place of
my May Queen, sat a withered hag. Her hair was lank, her face dry and
loose-skinned, and her hands crooked and misshapen. Even her gown was
old and threadbare. The crown of cherries was the only bright thing about
her; an abomination on that unseemly head. From her puckered ugly
mouth came the Elf Queen's golden laughter.

"You may touch me now, Thomas, as much as you will. Come: rest your
fair head on my lap."

I found my back was to a tree.

"Do not deny me," she commanded, steel in her voice; "come."

I knelt in the grass at her side, and laid my head on the old stuff of her
gown. It smelt of lavender and tansy, the herbs countrywomen use to store
their clothes in. My old nurse smelt like that. I remembered following her
around, my fist tight in the folds of her herb-scented gown.

I felt a clawlike hand in my hair, pressing my head down onto the Elf
Queen's bony thigh, holding it there immobile. "Ah," she chuckled, "now
is it easy to resist? But don't you want to see wonders, Harper? Look
where I show you . . . look. . . ."

Her sharp fingers twisted my head, so that I was looking out past the
trees to where a path led down into a valley—the sort of rough path a
woodman makes to mark his trail, through a dense thicket of brambles,
with barely room on either side for a body's two arms. It twisted down,
dark and treacherous, and the briars looked fierce.

"Shall we walk that road together, you and I?" the Elf Queen asked me,
and waited for my answer.

"Lady," I said, "I doubt even one of us could manage down it."

"Clever boy! You speak truer than you know. But what of this one?" She
turned my head again.

This time it was a proper road, broad and well kept, with room for a
good pair of carts, or even a company of horses. It wound pleasantly
through the grass of a glade.

"Where does it go?" I asked.

"Where do you think it goes?"

"Nowhere to interest us," I said. It had that over-tended look, like one
of the king's deer-hunting parks, where there may be no stones left for a
horse to stumble on, and people ride mostly to show off their new clothes.

"Good," she said. "And this?"

The breath almost left my body then. There was no road at all, only a
great sweep of valley and hillside, all misty silver-blue and green. As I

gazed, the mist parted to show me a tiny road of ivory winding through forest, field and stream, all the way up to a distant castle etched fine against the hilltop.

"Silent, Rhymer?"

"That," I said quietly. "That is the road for me."

"Yes, I thought so." She stood; and as she shook out her garments they turned again to her robes of green. "That is the road to fair Elfland, Thomas, even where it pleases you to go."

A strange joy filled me then. I felt that I was coming home. It was the place I had always sung of, the vision that filled my eyes when I closed them to sing. I never dared to think it could be real for me.

Beautiful again, and sweet and merry, she took my two hands and smiled at me: "I see you do not mind. Now are you glad you kissed me 'neath the Eildon Tree?"

Her eyes were blue as bright heaven. "Lady," I said, "those seven years will pass as seven days."

"Think you?" she asked gravely. "I can make it so. The ballads should have taught you that—or have you learned nothing from your own songs? We arrive: seven days of pleasure pass, seven nights of feasting and delight —and then it's, 'Up and away, Thomas! It's time to return to your own country!' 'Oh, but, lady, I've been here but one short week. . . .' 'Oh, no, Thomas. It's full seven years since your feet have trod the Earth. While you have reveled here, your friends have aged, and missed you—but now you shall be reunited with them—so!' " She looked at me with a winning mixture of mischief and eagerness, her eyes a trusty brown. "What say you?"

The mist was gathering again on the far hillside, curling over the blue-shadowed trees and weaving amongst the ridges.

"Lady," I said, "I have longed for Elfland all my days. When I was a child—"

I stopped suddenly. I'd never told anyone this.

"I remember when you were a child," she said quietly. "Go on."

"I thought—I didn't think I was really human. Nobody seemed to like me—I mean, other boys—my brother and his—his wife—and I thought I was—somehow—that I didn't belong there." It was desperately hard getting the words out, like working my way through brambles. I was ashamed admitting these things; and ashamed not to be able to say them without feeling the pain all over again. "I thought I came from somewhere else. That I belonged to different people," I blurted out finally.

"You didn't, of course." She walked moodily away, kicking dead leaves in front of her. The orchard had turned to autumn, and the crown on her head become red leaves and berries. "You are a man of Earth. Elfland is not your home."

"I know that," I snapped—because I hadn't really expected her to say otherwise; not really. "But still, give me my full seven years there."

"As you wish." Her eyes were tawny gold. "But understand this: you are not of Elfland. You think you know Faery—but all the songs and tales you know are the palest shadows of the truth. Someday it may prove too strong for your taste, Rhymer—and then you will long for the years to be over, and for your feet to tread the bournes of Middle-Earth once more. Elfland, though, Elfame, my Faery . . . Elfland holds what it has. Make no mistake: it desires you as you have desired it. Serve me well, and I will release you after your seven years. But I lay this weird on you: that you speak no word in Elvin land, or you'll never win back to your own country. You may speak to me, Thomas, and to me alone—and you may sing to the hosts in my hall, for that is why I have brought you from your land. But whatever the others may say to you, in forest, field or in hall, look that you answer none but me."

To go into Elfland speechless? That was an ill condition for a man of words to bide! If it was a joke, it did not amuse me.

"Lady," I protested, "I know the songs. In all the tales I've never heard of such a fate."

She smiled warmly. "But this is *your* tale, Thomas, whose end you do not know. And since you are so well versed in Faery lore, I need not add that all mortals are under weird to eat no food of Elfland. But never fear— you will be well provided for."

I felt again the pull of mastery; my fate was in her hands now, and if she made conditions, I must abide them, as I had—almost—always done the bidding of great ones. There was nothing for me to do with dignity but to bow deeply to her. "As you wish."

The mist was shifting on the far hill. Despite her words, I longed to be on that road.

The lady whistled to her horse, and the beautiful creature trotted up, seeming as eager as I to be off. Only the Elf Queen stood for a moment in the orchard, turning her wreath of leaves in her hand. Then, with a shrug, she lifted and hurled it high over the tops of the trees, and sprang into the saddle, and helped me up behind her.

The ivory road began almost at our very feet, in the grass of the orchard. The horse walked on it for once like a normal horse on a normal road. Around us grew all that blue-green landscape, field and trees and distant hills. My heart was light, and I sang as merrily as I doubt I have since I was a boy:

A wager I'll lay with you, my pretty maid,
Five hundred marks to your one
That maiden as you go to the Broomfield Hill,
Maiden you'll never more return. . . .

The Elf Queen laughed, and came in with me on the chorus of "Oh, the broom, the bonny, bonny broom."

We crossed a stream on a pretty humpbacked stone bridge. "Lady," I asked, "are there no inhabitants to this land?"

She turned in the saddle and looked at me quizzically. "But, Thomas—they are all around you! Haven't you see them?"

I felt my face go hot with embarrassment. "No, madam."

"You must learn how to look. It will come to you in time."

I looked, but still saw nothing. We were in a beech wood, now, the sun slanting yellow through white pillars of trees and green leaves.

"Look at that tree," she said softly, pointing with her chin. "Look sideways."

I turned my head away, and out of the corner of my eye I caught the glimmer of a woman's figure standing by the tree, tall and white and silver-haired.

"Did you see?"

"A woman . . ."

"Yes. One of mine."

I could not tell whether she meant one of her subjects, or her attendants, or even her child. I looked again, slantwise, and caught the nymph making what, among humankind, anyway, is a rude gesture.

The Elf Queen laughed. "Word of your coming will precede us. Remember: speak not a word to any of them."

I didn't, but I turned around and flipped a sign of my own back in the nymph's direction.

"You are a boy, still," the queen said, sounding not at all displeased.

"I feel like one," I answered frankly. "Like a boy on holiday." I was remembering some of my more spectacular holidays; I started telling the queen about old scrapes I'd gotten into, and gotten out of . . . it didn't seem to bore her. Moments I'd long forgotten came tumbling out of me. As I spoke, I started seeing out of the corners of my eyes some of the land's people: some tall and graceful as the queen herself; others so tiny I'd have taken them for birds if I didn't know better. I learned to keep from turning my head for a better look: when I did that, they were never there.

There were no birds, and no birdsong in that wood. All I heard was the ring of silver bells on the bridle, the clump of hooves on the path, the wind in the leaves and the distant rustle of a brook—and over it all my own voice, talking, talking, telling the queen everything about my old life in a childhood world I had left behind long ago, word, thought and memory.

"Your cat," the queen was saying encouragingly, "Fluff: was she a good hunter, too?"

I started to answer; heard my own voice and stopped. "Lady—" I stammered. "I—" What was I doing here, prattling about my past to the Queen of Elfland? What was I doing here at all? How had I come so easily to kiss her under the tree, to mount her horse out of my world and into this?

"Please—" I stammered again; then managed to stop myself enough to say with some little dignity, "I would rather not speak."

"I think that is not true," she said, the voice of sweet reason. Then she laughed. "Do you think yourself under enchantment? Is that it, Thomas?"

I hate being laughed at. And I had every reason to think myself enchanted.

"You don't understand," the queen said indulgently. "There is no spell on you. But you are mine now; and what pleases me should rightly please you too. It pleases me to hear you speak."

"And if I do not wish to?"

"Then, of course you will be silent. But why, dear man? Have you not all your life given people the pleasure of your voice, your wit and your words? You have always known how to make yourself useful. You will be useful to me, and give me pleasure. You will always know when I need to be sung to, or kissed, or brought a drink or be left alone."

"It sounds a great deal like magic to me."

"Of course it is magic! *I* am magic! And I never choose the dull or the stupid for my own. From the moment you saw me, it would have been hard for you to refuse me anything. The desire you felt for me, that made your head swim and the blood burn in your veins . . . do not confuse that with your lust for a mortal woman. I am Queen over all Elfland, Thomas—over you I have no need of enchantments."

I found even her words roused longing in me. I tried to mask my longing with stiff banter: "Nonetheless, I think I can divert you with better than tales of a little boy's pets."

"If you like," she said with cold carelessness. "But I will have it all of you before your time is out."

In answer I put my arms tight around her and nuzzled her neck. Not the cleverest thing to do to a woman holding the reins to a horse you're both riding: I nearly lost my seat when the horse skittered suddenly, flinging its head back almost into our faces. A white dove had darted across the path in front of the horse. There was a sick whistling sound, and a silver arrow buried itself in a tree trunk above our heads.

The queen quieted the horse and held up her hand, and the dove alighted onto her finger just as another beast came crashing through the forest.

It was a black horse, the hugest I have ever seen, bigger than a cart horse, but with a racer's build. Astride it was a man all in black, with long coal-black hair—but his eyebrows and his lips were the red of sunset. He held a long bow in his hand. When he saw us he pulled up suddenly, setting his horse to frothing and tossing of its head.

The queen sat still on her horse, the dove like alabaster on her finger. "Now, brother," she said coldly to the rider, "what is this?"

The elf man's face was as hard and chill as hers. "Sister, I do but sport."

"Oh? And will it be sport when I take your two eyes and give them to the Nameless to munch on? For clearly those eyes do not serve you well anymore, or you could see that this bird is one of mine."

"For a little while only," said the hunter. "His time is almost done. And he has not yet succeeded."

"Then, when he fails, he is yours to hunt. For now—" She lifted her hand, and the dove fluttered off it—but still flew 'round and 'round our heads, as though fearing to leave sanctuary.

The hunter laughed. "Ah, sister! Such mercy as you show! You are not the only one has been in the World. I have followed him there, and watched his poor attempts. You'd laugh yourself sick to see them: poor voiceless dove, a common enough bird there, and this one trying so hard to achieve the notice that is his due."

The queen looked at the hunter with amusement twin to his on her face. "Maybe. Maybe I will lend him Thomas's voice—he won't be needing it for a while." Speaking, she stroked my leg with her fingertip, so that I bristled equally with horror and with lust. It's not a sensation I can honestly recommend.

"You there!" the dark hunter barked imperiously at me. "What man's get are you?"

I, of course, remembered her weird and did not answer—trying hard the while not to wonder whether I still could now if I would, with her fingers and her words working on me.

"Come," he cajoled, but still imperious. "Thomas . . . who are you?"

"Don't be a fool," the queen said—not to me, but to him.

"You gave me his name; may I not use it?"

"Fool," she repeated with scorn. "You know less of the World even than you think. There are a thousand Thomases on Middle-Earth: the name has all the power of a walnut."

The hunter looked not the least abashed. "Well," he said, "then there will be another way."

"Huh!" the Elf Queen snorted. "You're saying so to vex me, only. You wouldn't know what to do with him if you had him."

"Maybe." Without a word of farewell, the hunter wheeled his horse and vanished amongst the trees.

The dove lit again on the queen's finger. "Go," she said to it. "Your time is short, but not yet gone." She shook her hand, and the dove flew off. "Silent, Thomas?"

Silent, yes, my mouth dry and throat tight with fear that she might have *done* something to me, and the tension of the strange battle I had just seen engaged. . . . "No," I said, and let out a lot of breath in relief. "No, just cautious."

"That is well. You need not fear my lord of the silver arrows—he does not care for mortals."

And that was meant to reassure me! But I didn't fret for long. The golden-haired woman in rich green rode with me through the woods, her bright demesne. I was in the Queen of Elfland's keeping, and all around me the Land of Dreams unfolded.

Forest turned to meadow. We had lost the ivory road seen from the orchard, although the path we took uphill through the waving grasses seemed purposeful, as though the horse's hooves knew the road invisible. Above us loomed the castle on the hill, no longer toy-sized; still bright and fine as carven ivory, but strong as steel too. It was encircled by a wall without a crack of gate or door.

The queen took a horn hanging by her side, that I had thought was for hunting. She raised it as if to blow it to announce her coming; but then shook her head and let it go unsounded, and turned to me with a green-eyed grin: "Ready, Thomas?"

I hung on for dear life as the white horse gathered itself to leap. There was a rushing of wind, and then we were clattering into a stable yard, and folk were running to greet us from everywhere.

"Everywhere" in this case meant not just door and passageway. Winged creatures glided like sea gulls down from roof and tower, their iridescent wings banking and catching the light. Several gargoyles detached themselves from the drainpipes to take a lively interest in the proceedings. Something green even crawled up out of the well, and sat on the brim with its toes dangling in the water.

There was not a plain creature amongst them. The beautiful ones were beautiful beyond belief: hearty or ethereal, they all might have stepped from the pages of some arcane illuminated missal. And the ugly ones rivaled the whimsy of a stonemason in any cathedral. The castle folk surged around us, and from her horse the queen beamed delight, warming them like the sun with her presence.

"Mistress." A great brute of a man, half-naked, with the horns of a stag growing out of his shaggy head, held out his arms to the queen. She slid into them, and he set her on the ground. Fearful lest he offer the same service to me, I slipped to the paving stones on the other side, and stood flexing and rubbing my legs.

But the Elvinkind soon discovered me.

"The queen's new mortal," announced a bluff-looking fellow with oak leaves in his hair.

"Is this a wise one, or a fool?" asked a languid lady with ivy dripping from her fingers. (Shrubbery seemed to be the fashion of the day.) "He surely wasn't chosen for his looks, this time."

I felt coarse, grimy, clumsy among these Elvin folk. I also hoped that I could hold onto my temper as well as my tongue.

A radiant creature with vast folded wings fingered a lock of my hair. "Bright," it said. "Rich."

"Aye," said a short, squat man with a voice like falling rocks. "Give him leave to speak."

I looked anxiously for the queen; but she was all the way across the courtyard from me, standing on a flight of stairs, surrounded by courtiers.

"He's shy," a tall Elf said kindly. He had the largest, darkest eyes I have ever seen. But for his height, and the not-quite-possible cast of his features, he might have been a youth of seventeen summers. "Come, child," he said, "tell us your name."

The ivy lady sniggered, and he cast her a venomous look. "I think he is a learned man," she said. "A monk, perhaps. Ah, mortal, you laugh at that? Pity. I have always wanted to see a monk. Is it true they have no—"

"The Riddle Game!" A tiny girl with a voice like an unoiled hinge drowned the others out. "That will test his learning."

"Right. Start with an easy one:

> *What is whiter than the milk,*
> *And what is softer than the silk?*"

They looked at me hopefully, and it nearly made me sick not to be able to answer. That's a nursery song—every child knows the answer is "snow and down."

"That's too easy," said the dark-eyed Elf; "you've offended him. Here."
He knelt in front of me, putting his eyes on a level with mine. His eyes had
the melting beauty of an animal's, with human intelligence deep in them.
He held my gaze as though he knew the power his eyes had, but when he
spoke it was again kindly:

> "In the forest lies a well.
> In that well lies a cup.
> What king's hand dropped it there
> And whose will fill it up?"

I shook my head: that one I didn't know, nor do I think any mortal
does.

"You see!" the unoiled hinge creaked. "He knows nothing!"

The tall Elf rose gracefully to his feet. "Well, he's the queen's business,
not ours." He put his arm around the burly fellow, and they wandered
away.

"Pretty fool," said the winged creature. It unfurled its wings; they were
a living rainbow. I gasped in admiration, while the others stepped back to
give it room. A breeze caught it, and it pivoted until it rose towards the
wall.

"My dear," the ivy girl said vaguely, walking past me, "you may come
to me. I shall be as a father to you. . . ."

"No, no—UNCLE!!" Hinge shrieked.

I would have laughed, but I was shaking with the strangeness of it all,
and the weariness on me. One by one the Elvin folk drifted away.

I felt a gentle touch at my elbow. A woman in a grey cloak put her arm
in mine. "Come, Thomas," she said; "we must rest."

I knew her for the Elf Queen, although she seemed shrunk and weary,
like any mortal woman who has wandered far from home. No one attended us as we crossed the fair courtyard and climbed the staircase into
the castle. We passed through corridors rich with tapestries. I saw jeweled
windows, and walls of living flowers. Finally we came to a door we closed
behind us. In the center of the room lay a great bed of pearl, curled like a
seashell. I took the Elf Queen's cloak from her, and unlaced her gown. Her
body was supple and fair. She weighed almost nothing in my arms, and she
smiled, when I laid her on the bed, like a sleepy kitten.

When I woke I was somewhere else.

I heard the splashing of a fountain, and was brushed by a warm breeze
smelling of flowers. My bed was soft and narrow, and I lay in it naked,

lightly covered by a sheet. The floor was set with white painted tiles. The walls were pale blue, the ceiling white.

I did not know who I was.

I held the memory of a room of grey stone, and being cold all the time. There was a little house made of earth, the constant smell of wet wool, and an old couple, my parents—not my parents—I turned onto my side, facing the wall, to think. The sheet slid silkily over me . . . it was silk! I was a prince—the favorite of princes—Oh, God, that was it, I had to play my new song at supper for the Italian envoy and I'd only half finished it—

"Sir?" said a voice. I rolled over, but saw no one.

"Sir, I have for you the juice of West Country apples." A silver cup on a silver tray hung in the air perilously near my head. The voice came from somewhere near there too. I yawned hard, and rubbed my hands over my face.

"My lady bids me remind you not to speak to me. If this food displeases you—"

I seized the cup, hoping to silence the strange, sexless voice. It could have been a grown woman's, or a boy's before it changes. I needed silence to think. My situation was coming back to me. I had been lost because I was nowhere on Earth. I was become the Elf Queen's lover, now, living in the land beyond the blood river, the land of mist and ivory.

I hoped all my wakings would not be this hard.

The questions that rose in me must for the time remain unasked. I swallowed the juice and went to the window the breeze came from. It was like the arches of a cloister, the window an entire half a wall, floor to ceiling, supported by slender, twisted columns. I stood among them and looked out onto a green garden, set with paths around a pool of lilies. At the center of it splashed the fountain.

A blue silk robe drifted onto my shoulders. My invisible servant said diffidently, "You have been lodged in the Summer Rooms, sir. Mortals find them the most comfortable at first. There are clothes laid out in the next room for you to try."

Voiceless as I was, I couldn't oppose the suggestion without being rude. So I passed through a curtained archway to the next room.

It was another airy chamber. All its furnishings were cushions big enough to sit on, and a collection of musical instruments the like of which I'd never seen. Along one wall ran a bench, on which clothing was laid out.

It was a prince's wardrobe. From soft wool jackets to silken hose and velvet caps, all was fine and beautifully cut. I have known lords dressed meaner. My hands went out to finger the brocades—at home I sat at the feet of those that wore them. These were rich with shifting colors, patterned like mazes; supple they hung from my arms, and flowed when I turned.

My servant's feet, if he had any, made little sound. Unless he spoke, I could not know whether he were there, watching me peacock it like a bridesmaid. It was a pleasure I intended to indulge in private. I laid the ostentatious robes aside. By the light in the courtyard I judged it to be mid-morning at the Elvin court. And so I chose a plain white shirt with luxuriously full sleeves, and a grey linen tunic cunningly pleated at the shoulders. The cloth was deceptive, though: grey in the shadows, it shone grass-green when it caught the light. There were grey hose with it. I didn't think my lady would object to my showing a fair bit of leg. If her folk were to think me a fool, fit only for her pleasure, at least I should be a well-made fool. I found high leather boots meant for riding, but all of the house shoes seemed to be of velvet, so I chose simple green ones free of embroidery.

"Now, please, you follow me, sir."

I opened my mouth to say, "I can't follow you if I can't see you—" and closed it again, the words unspoken. There was a rattle of cup on tray: what I followed was my empty cup, winding its way through the halls.

We did not seem to go far; but as we walked, the shadows lengthened. We passed into a dark stone corridor, like that of any keep I knew at home. My servant took a torch from the wall to light us. It burned blue and cold, and despite the wind of our passing the flame held steady. The light was bluer even than moonlight; when I looked at my hands, they were the color of a corpse, and the silver cup I followed shone like some holy grail.

The torch stopped before a door, which opened at my servant's hand. Inside I beheld a night-scene: a great hall full of Elvin feasting, with music of all kinds, and tumblers performing in the center—like many halls I've been in on Earth, save that some of the courtiers were winged or horned, some of the tumblers goat-footed; and all brightly lit by the cold blue torches. It gave the whole scene a sea cast, as though they were feasting underwater. Only at the high table were there real wax candles burning—but their golden light met the blue torches' at the edges in a dapple-green, as if the feasters at that table dined at pic-nic in the greenwood. I watched, fascinated, trying not to be repelled at the changes the light made on face and clothes, telling myself that, after all, it was only light, no more. I had never before realized how sun- and fire-light warm our eyes with their glow, granting even a sick man the ruddiness of health, and gilding lovers' skins like gods'.

A lady most fantastical stood up at the high table, her hair bound up in braids strung with jewels and tongueless bells, her gown a bright brocade whose true color I could not begin to read in the shifting light, all puffed and slashed in curious ways. I saw it was my queen. She beckoned to me, and I came, making my way not behind the diners' benches, as would a modest servant, but down the middle of the hall, past minstrels and jugglers, to kneel before her on the high dais.

Of course, all eyes were on me, the newcomer. I was not dressed for the feast; but my elegant simplicity was well chosen nonetheless: it spoke of proper humility in the queen's minstrel, arrogant grace in her consort. It remained to be seen which I would be greeted as.

"Rise," the queen bade me kindly. I did, but I stayed where I was. On her right the seat was taken by another lovely lady, and seated at her left was the dark-haired hunter from the woods.

"Good evening, Thomas," he said, civilly enough; but I saw from the look of the Elf on his left that the use of my name was a discourtesy. I pretended not to note it, and bowed my head to him graciously.

The hunter raised one crimson eyebrow at the queen. "Is it a silent pet, then, sister?"

She answered, "Truly, his words are for me alone—and yet he is not silent."

"Riddle me once," said Hunter. "An instrument?"

"The wind cannot what ten men can."

"Riddle me twice: a piper?"

"A voiceless tree, a bladeless sword."

"Riddle me thrice: a harper!"

"Done in three!" cried the queen, and those around them clapped their hands. "But you have divined only the half."

"Nonetheless," said Hunter, "surely a harper of note: your judgment in music none can excel."

His hands were clasped together over the table. Slowly he opened them; and as they grew apart, the space between them filled with a small harp until he held the instrument in his two hands.

She was white wood, curved like a swan's breast, with a white dove carved at her head. The silver strings seemed to beat of their own accord in the flickering light. My fingers tickled to try her. The hunter lord held her up for me.

"Dear brother," the queen said with the exaggerated politeness I have heard at many another court, "giving my harper gifts already? How generous, when he has done nothing yet to earn them." Her tone was a warning, and it snapped me out of the present of court gifts and compliments, and into the story-time I have so often sung of, where people who accept faery gifts often are bound by them to their sorrow.

The queen spared me further need for thought by taking the harp in her own hands. "Lovely," she said, examining it; and as she did so, its color turned to ebony black, the dove headpiece to an intricate carved knot trimmed with silver. "By all means, you shall hear the harper play."

I took the harp gladly from her hands. Her dark kinsman was smiling at her without any malice. I ignored him, and ran my fingers softly over the strings. They were perfectly pitched, and the tiny sound cut the air like Damask steel. I had been afraid that it would take me time to learn the ways of any new harp here, that I would need to practice until I'd got the feel of it, the subtleties of tuning and of tone that shift along the strings as you play; but I knew that this one was made for my hands and would ring true under them from the moment I took it up. With it I would not shame my mistress or myself before them all.

"Give us a tune," said the queen, like all the others I have ever known.

Only the table where she sat was paying any attention to me; the rest of the hall had gone back to its own revelries. To draw their attention, I might have struck up with a dance or a battle tune; but the deep-sea color of the light put me in mind of something other. I have found over the years a strand of truth in a harper's impulses; it's as though the music comes forward to tell you when its time is come to be heard. So I heeded it now, and sounded forth the opening notes of "Drowned Ys."

In Lesser Britain, then, the princess betrays her people for her lover; she opens the seaward gates to him, and the water rises up over her father's kingdom in retribution. It's a long piece; I played only the lament of the drowned land, now lost to the sea forever. That's always been a showpiece, tender and sad; to play it well, the notes should be held a moment longer than the rhythm suggests, just as a person telling his grief pauses in pain before revealing it . . . until at last the sorrow overwhelms him, and it comes rushing out, like waves onto the land. The song concludes in a passionate, shrill wail, as the last deep notes of the earth are lost to the cry of the gulls, one bass string only droning the slow roar of the waves, until it is all that is left.

When I played the first notes, the queen's table all listened politely; but soon they were caught up in the music's own flow. I played softly to them, feeling the attention of the hall gathering behind me, like a great warm beast preparing to spring, and welcome. I began to harp louder, playing to the whole hall . . . and the whole hall was mine.

I know that giant hush as I know the air that I breathe and the water that I drink. In village inn or castle hall, it is the same. Its power worked its way into my hands, into the strings of the harp and the very echoes of the walls around us. It built like the sea of Ys, until I brought it all down with me on the same final wave.

And the hush continued, past the last echo of that note.

I stayed still, my hands quiet on the harp. Whatever broke that stillness, it would not be I: it is the minstrel's highest accolade.

What broke it was the unexpected: a man's voice roaring, *"Drink! Drink! I've the red thirst on me!"*

I looked up, startled, at the queen. She gave me a sign with her lips pressed together, meaning, *Be still. You will understand later.* Behind me the whole hall was crying hard for drink, as though the music had taken them into the desert, not the ocean. For the first time since I had arrived, I was truly frightened: there was no merriment in their cries, but the desperation of the parched. Even the queen took a deep draught from her chalice before she said to me, "That was well done! Now, feast with us, minstrel!"

She motioned me to an empty place down the table from her. So, before her court I was to be her minstrel—but her favored minstrel, seated at her table if not at her right hand. I sat between two courtiers who made as if I wasn't there; but it was a respectful ignoring, as though they knew better than to touch a coal while it still glowed, as I did from the music. I took care to touch nothing of the food or drink set out for the Elves, but ate the human food that was brought me: grapes from Smyrna, as I recall, and Dutch cheese; Welsh cakes and Spanish figs.

The hall quieted again when everyone had been served. I wondered if I would be asked to play again. I wondered if I would get to take the harp back with me to my rooms, or whether it would turn to dead leaves or chicken bones when it left the hall. Being bound to silence, I heard the conversations around me:

He said she was tired of him, but her *kind don't get tired. . . .—I'm having it made for the Dancing. . . . Of course when I was there last that wizard was there too. . . . Her time is come, and he doesn't know it. . . . True moonlight gives more power than candles. . . .*

I looked out over that sea of wonder, and I was alone. I could speak to no one, and no one could say anything familiar to me: there was no link of blood or breeding between me and these folk. Even the simple kinship of bread and wine was denied us. The beauties, the antlered, the winged ones, all awash in their sea of blue light. . . . I thought, God help me, seven years of this, and this the first night. . . . I tried to think of Meg and Gavin, but the blue light came between me and my image of their hearth fire, and blurred the sun on the hillside. For the first time since I'd mounted the faery horse, I thought of Elspeth. I seemed to see her as I had when we first met; like a drowning man, my memories of our time together flowed vivid through my mind, clear with the distance of fair legend, of song. Strange, how vivid she was to my mind's eye, against the eerie lights of Elfland. How she would love to be here now! She, who wanted to travel far and see strange sights, who set out milk for the faery folk. . . . And wouldn't she have words to say about the green-haired hussy clothed in cobwebs on my left! I smiled to myself, wishing Elspeth were here with me —and then froze the wish and the smile, afraid. At the heart of enchantment, anything was possible. I had chosen this fate for myself; all that I had ever been and done had brought me to that trysting on the hillside with that unearthly, immortal queen. What did Elspeth know of such things? I was bound to seven years apart from humankind, and in some way I'd deserved it. Whatever the queen said, I knew that I was both too good for the mortal world, and not nearly good enough. Elspeth was . . . along with Meg and Gavin, was what was *good* and true in humankind. She had no place here. To think on them might be to put them in danger; and so I resolved to put them out of my mind. Let her mourn me as lost, and find another lover. The Elf Queen was my lover now.

As if she heard my thoughts, the lady on my left spoke to the queen: "Sister, your harper grows weary."

"Indeed," said the queen, "he is not used to our hours." The high table laughed hard at that, although I couldn't see why. "You have done well," she said to me, "and now you shall rest. Go with Ermine, here."

Ermine was an elf girl wearing a small cape of ermine-skin and little else! Despite her furs, she played the part of servant. She led me out of the hall, and I took the harp with me. Ermine was small and round, with clear white skin and a saucy eye—just the kind of servant girl a minstrel can always tease a kiss out of. Nevertheless, I looked at her dispassionately. Why drink beer when you can have wine?

But that's a false excuse. The truth was, that I felt no desires towards the pretty servingmaid at all. And if I had, what could I have done— *gestured* my admiration for her, like some poor wordless bumpkin at a fair? The poets say, "Tongue is chief of minstrelsy"—and in amorousness, too, it cannot be bettered.

There was, of course, nothing to stop Ermine from talking, corridor after unrecognizable corridor: "Well! You certainly did them a treat! The red thirst on them, and no mistake. You mortals do have a way about you. Is it something they teach you, or are you born with it? Born with it, I expect; it's in the blood, so to speak, ha, ha. You gave a lot with your harping; no wonder you're tired, poor thing. I'm tired, too: this feast has gone on for days. Oh, yes, I know about mortal time, not like some I could mention, who dress in peacock feathers, and only see the sun when they stay out too late on Dancing Nights. . . . It does me a world of good, too, I can tell you: you don't see *me* getting the thirst, and bawling like a changeling for drink. . . . Well, we all pay a price: I'm getting old, I may have to spend some time as a stone, soon; or maybe a nice tree, in a forest where I can get a little sun. . . ."

I was indeed terribly weary, as though I had spent days at the feast instead of a few hours. After my feat of minstrelsy, I was not expecting to be spoken to like a pet dog; but I was too tired to make any sense of her words anyway. She said nothing of where she was taking me. When it proved to be the queen's bedchamber, I was surprised Ermine let pass the occasion to pronounce on human prowess there as well. But she made no comment as she showed me to the queen's bed and left. Perhaps the queen's mortal lovers were an aberration not to be spoken of; or perhaps they were as common as finches.

I put my harp down next to the bed, and managed to get shoes and hose off before I sank into the heavy down and slept a dreamless sleep.

Dawn light woke me. The queen was pulling back her curtains to let it in, clothed only in a white shift, her gold hair unbound spilling down her back. As I propped myself on one elbow, she turned and smiled at me, as radiant as if she had not been up feasting all night.

"Well!" she said cheerily, "you've slept long." I smiled sleepily back. "Thomas . . ." she chided at my silence; "Thomas . . ." And then she let out a peal of laughter. "Thomas! Where are your manners? Answer me!"

I had forgotten that I still could speak to anyone. My speech was unlocked to her, alone, of all the land. "Yes," I said huskily, and coughed to get my voice back. "What?"

She pirouetted, as lively as a girl after her first ball. "How did you like our feast?"

"It was . . . splendid. Do stop, you're making me dizzy. Come to bed, you must be exhausted."

Again she laughed. I would never have spoken to her thus if I hadn't somehow known that she would like it; her girl's delight told me what tone to take. "Sweet child. Feasts are for pleasure—they don't tire me out." She came and sat on the edge of the bed, stretching her bare arms like a cat. "But we must feed you—it's been days since you've eaten, you'll waste away to nothing. . . ."

"Days? What about my meal last night?"

"Last night . . . ? Oh—you mean when you feasted. That was some time ago. I'm not sure how long. I really can't keep track here. You'd be surprised to know how much of your own time you spent in the hall, though." Then days had passed in a single night? I thought of her promise to give me a full seven years of Elfland—although now I was not so eager to hold her to it. But she said, "I've done what I can to let you live in our time here. But you can't expect to grow accustomed all at once. I've made your room always be morning when you wake up, though—that should be nice for you."

I was very hungry. She brought me a tray of food, its earthly origins carefully named as always. But I could hardly eat it, for her bright chatter, and the attention she couldn't seem to help paying me. She fluttered around me like a hummingbird; and now her fingers were in my hair, and now they were unfastening my shirt, picking up grapes to feed me and stroking my back. I must have made a pretty sight at last, sprawled out on the bed with my clothes coming off me, surrounded by bits of fruit and cake, that she pressed into my mouth with her hands, her mouth. . . . When I took her at last she moaned and cried out like a mortal woman, clinging to me as if to squeeze the life out of me. We squeezed a few peaches instead, and I had great to-do licking them off her after. Then I finished the wine, and picked up the bread from the floor where we had tossed it, and ate that too. She lay on her back, her hair becomingly curled in damp tendrils around her face, watching me with a very satisfied smile.

As yet, she'd said nothing about my bravura performance of harping. Maybe it had happened so long ago she had forgotten it, I thought sourly. But she hadn't.

"Now, play to me, Thomas," she said lazily.

The black harp was still there, at the bed's head where I had set it last night—before I fell asleep. It was still in perfect tune. Between the queen and the harp, my feelings for Elfame once again took a turn for the better.

I sat on the edge of the bed, and played a few simple airs. The queen stretched, and smiled. "You will want to know," she said, "why your harping took them as it did last night."

Now that I remembered it, I wanted to know what had been poured in their drinking cups. Not all the old tales of Elfame concern lovers; some are very grim. But I judged it best to say nothing.

"As you will have gathered from songs and from your own experience," she lectured, still lying naked on her back, "mortals and the mortal world are very attractive to us, although we also despise them. In truth, no Elf can live without sometime coming to Middle-Earth, whether it be twice yearly on our great Dancing Nights, when the Solstice moon draws us to it like the waves of the sea; or if it be those hobs and brownies who so delight in the life of farm and human hearth that they are seen but rarely here in their own land. Humans themselves are . . ." She stretched again. "There is a heat in you—a warm glow like the sun, like flame . . . it warms us. When you harp, Thomas, the heat comes off you with a great radiance— no, that's wrong: it isn't heat, it's . . . it's . . . it's like gold. Like sweet air. It's the sun, Thomas. The sun of life that burns gold at zenith, and the molten red sun that sinks into the earth, red as the blood flowing out of you when you die. . . . Tell me: do you fear death?"

Her voice was ragged with passion, her breath coming in small gasps. Irresistible. I seized her in my arms and kissed her deeply. "No," I answered her, the life pounding in me. "Not now."

"Tell me about death," the queen said. "The heart stopping in you, the breath stopping in you, the cold and the dark."

"Lady," I said, "I do not know. No man is given to know his own death." Our bodies were pulsing together now. I was talking wildly, as always in such a case. "When mine comes, you may attend it and see for yourself."

"You could be old and ugly then," she said. "Does *that* frighten you?"

"Yes—" I said, "no—"

I was spent; but she played her passion out on me, and I could not but enjoy it.

As soon as she was done, she nearly leapt from the bed, pacing like a green-eyed tigress. "Go to your room," she said, looking over her shoulder at me, neither pleased nor angry. "I've work to do."

I pulled half my clothes on, and took the harp, and went out into the hall. So I never did learn what the Elves drank when the red thirst was on them. I thought of the deep dark river we had ridden through, that was the border between the two lands, and of the injunction laid on mortals to eat and drink nothing in this world. And I thought of the bright clear fountains and streams of Elfland, forever denied me.

I stood alone in the hallway outside her chamber. Nothing looked familiar to me; I didn't know which way to go. Walls that had been grey were now white, and there were doors where there had been walls. It was as though the whole castle had changed its shape while I slept.

A few Elves went by. They glanced at me, but said nothing; and I couldn't speak to them. I held the harp firmly to me like a talisman.

"Sir."

I looked around, saw no one. There was a gentle tugging at the harp. "Shall I carry that for you, sir?"

I recognized the voice of my invisible servant. I held the harp tighter, shook my head mutely.

"Follow me, then." As if coming out of some folds of clothing, a large brass key appeared at about my knee-level (held at a shorter person's side?). I followed it through unrecognizable corridors until we came back to my blue and white rooms off the garden.

It was still mid-morning.

I drank from a pitcher of juice, this time pressed from *oranges*—a fortune squeezed to pulp for me!—and then I sat on a bench against the wall of the garden, and watched the light grow stronger, felt it glow golden warm on my skin, until it was as hot and bright as high noon. The water of the fountain pool sparkled, dazzling. But there was no sun reflected in it.

When I had had enough of the basking, I went back into the cool of the inner rooms. All of the fine robes were still laid out, but I had stripped to my shirt in the heat, and saw no need to add more to it. Instead, I picked up one of the strange instruments. It was a sort of lute, with a long thin neck and only three strings, and huge ebony tuning-pegs. I slid my fingers up the neck experimentally; the strings twanged, and when I plucked them they made a sound brittle but sweet, because of the flatness of the sounding box, which was stretched skin, and could double as a drum. I played with it for a while, but was not satisfied; it was as if it had been made for another music than the one I knew. But it did not seem Elvin; I had seen nothing like it in the hall last night. Though nothing like, it reminded me more of the little rebec the lord of Coucy's minstrel had brought back from the Holy Land. I'd had a good time quarreling with him about whether he could possibly have remembered the tuning right.

Hours must have passed, though the courtyard was still bathed in noon light. I was getting some nice sounds out of a sort of mechanical psaltery worked by ivory tablets connected to hammers, one for each triple-string —but working it was slow going, and I was forming an idea for a tune.

So I went back to my new harp, which was by far the most beautiful instrument of the lot, and I sat in the courtyard and plucked out the start of a new melody.

I was dismayed to realize that it was nothing but the tune to the old song, "Unquiet Grave," set to a different beat, for *dancing,* if you will! I worked at the variations a little, but there really was no point—you're never going to get people to dance to "Unquiet Grave," however you ornament it. So I gave in and just sang the song:

> *I'll do as much for my true love*
> *As any young girl may.*
> *I'll sit and mourn all by his grave*
> *For a twelvemonth and a day.*

> *When that six months were gone and past*
> *The dead began to speak:*
> *Who sits and mourns at my graveside*
> *And will not let me sleep?*

I had not played a verse or two, when I felt a chill shadow fall on me. But it was still bright noon, and no shadows were in that land. I sang on:

> *'Tis I, my love, sits by your side*
> *And will not let you sleep.*
> *I crave but one kiss of your clay cold lips*
> *And that is all I seek.*

Over my head, a whirring sound: wings parting the air. Facing me, sitting on the marble edge of the lily pool, was the white dove of the woods.

It looked very becoming, decorating a garden clearly made for pretty birds. The dove fixed me with a clear amber eye, but I saw no reason to quit my singing:

> *Green grass grows over my head, sweetheart,*
> *Cold clay is over my feet*
> *And every tear you shed, my love,*
> *It wets my winding sheet.*

> *Down in yonder grove, sweetheart,*
> *Where you and I did walk*
> *The fairest flower that blossomed there*
> *Is withered to the stalk.*

As the dove looked at me, a terrible thing happened. Its eye seemed to film over with darkness; but the darkness overflowed, and from the dove's eye fell crimson drops, splashing like rain on the fountain's edge, and staining the soft feathers of its breast.

> *When shall we meet again, sweetheart?*
> *When shall we meet again?*
> *When oaken leaves fallen from trees*
> *Turn green and spring again.*

The dove was weeping tears of blood.

My hands fell still on the harp. *Why?* I asked silently. *Poor spirit, what has befallen you?*

For the dove had a tale of his own; of that I was sure.

What had the queen and the huntsman said in the wood? *Poor voiceless dove. He is one of mine. His time is almost done.*

In that heat that was not the sun's, a chill shook me. Had he been a mortal man, been to the queen what I was, perhaps, and broken the weird she laid on him?

"Sir."

Behind me stood my invisible servant, evinced by a platter of food hanging in midair. Perhaps because of the bird, I suddenly pictured myself as a goose being fattened for market. But it wasn't my servant's fault. With a sigh, I took the platter, uncovering fruits and meat and surprisingly fresh rolls. At home, maybe it was suppertime. People might be sitting down to table at the end of a long day's work, laughing and joking; talking about what had been done that day under the sun, and what was yet to do when it rose again.

The dove still perched on the fountain's edge. Tears no longer fell from its eyes; they had dried on the feathers of its breast like the crusts of tiny wounds. I broke one of the rolls; it was soft and white as clouds inside. On impulse, I scattered a few crumbs from the crust on the ground between me and the fountain.

The dove fluttered down. It ruffled its handsome fan of tail feathers, and began to peck at the crumbs.

It did not, however, seem to be swallowing any; rather like a polite dinner guest who has dined somewhere going through the motions.

I got curious, in the fussy way of invalids and boys held too long in the schoolroom. What *would* the dove eat? In turn I cast down a little fruit, a little meat, even a few drops of wine. It seemed interested in the wine. Maybe it even drank a little; it was hard for me to tell.

I felt a sharp tug at my tray. "Sir," said my servant, "if you are going to play with your food, I shall be certain you don't want it anymore."

In that moment the alto timbre definitely resolved itself into a woman's voice: the familiar tones of a child's nurse. I held doggedly onto my tray, and the voice resumed its neutral tones: "Very well. Just leave it on the ground when you're done."

The white dove had flown up onto the eaves of the roofs overhanging the courtyard garden. I nodded amiably to it, and it ruffled its feathers.

It remained there while I finished my meal. I might have tried to coax it down again after, but there was a knocking at the door to what I suppose I may call my apartments. Since I couldn't really answer it, I waited to see what my servant would do.

I heard the door open, some low conversation, and then a voice saying contemptuously, "Ah! So this is where you've been hiding. And a fit place, too, vile creature."

"Yes, sir," my servant said humbly, like a schoolboy chastised.

I didn't like the sound of it. There was too much cruelty in the stranger's voice, and too much humility in my servant's.

I jumped up when I heard the snap of leather. Biting my cheek not to shout, *Stop that!* I rushed into the other room.

The doe-eyed boy stood there, looking innocent as a fresh dawn. Behind him was the ivy lady, and the tiny girl with the squeaky-hinge voice. All three were dressed in green velvet, and booted to the thigh.

The tall boy smiled disarmingly at me. "Harper! We're riding out hunting this fine morning. Would you like to join us?"

A leather crop dangled from his hand. There was, of course, no sign of my servant, and I could not ask what had just happened, nor come the mighty over the dignity of my "staff."

"Yes, come ride," said the lady draped with living ivy. She had ivy leaves worked in green-gold thread along the hem of her cloak.

"If you know how," the hinge squeaked.

"Harper rode with our lady," the boy admonished her gently; "of course we'll find a steed to bear him."

The Elves seemed friendly enough, to me; and would they bring me to harm, knowing whose I was? I was curious to see more of the Elvin court and lands. So I nodded and went to change my clothes. To my relief, the Elves stayed in the other room to wait.

I'd already noticed the hunting boots laid out; now I found a suit of the green velvet that must be hunting gear. It fitted me wonderfully well.

"Ah!" they cried when I reappeared in it. "Splendid! Come!"

The great courtyard was full of clattering hooves. The Elvin mounts ranged from the fine blood-horses to funny little mules and goats for the shorter set, things with horns and triple-tails I'd never dreamed of. My trio stuck close to me, and from the milling throng produced a brown mare for me. I'm not much of a horseman, being seldom able to afford a mount, but the mare seemed positively eager to show off her competence at being ridden. She might really have been anything from a lineal descendant of Pegasus to an enchanted dishmop; but for all that, she felt warm and alive under my body, making me feel a certain kinship with her amongst these outland beings. In a moment of sentiment I found that I had named her Mollie.

Doe-Eyes was up on a rangy dapple-grey, Ivy on a white palfrey and Hinge on something endearing like a large, ambling goat with twisted horns. All heads lifted when the notes of a glorious hunting horn rang out on the air. The music bounced off the castle walls and out into the hills, calling us to follow.

Follow we did. "Now, Harper!" Doe called gaily, and I held on with hands and knees while my horse streamed with the others out the gate and over a bridge that seemed to be made of nothing but air.

All around me were figures of Elfland, large and small, horned and leafy and wild, clad in green, bobbing across the wide hillside like a mad tapestry. An arrow of front runners formed, with the rest of us fanning out behind.

I wondered what we were hunting. Possibly nothing: I noticed that hardly anyone was actually armed. A few Elves carried long silver spears. But everyone was whooping and galloping onward. I made no cry, but reveled in the glory of rushing air around me. We wheeled on the hillside and cantered across the slope, effortless as birds. The horns rang out. It was like a child's dream of freedom. I was laughing to feel Mollie surge underneath me, and myself a part of the wild Elvin ride.

We started downhill, moderating our pace only a little. The shadows of the hills closed over us, and we soon found ourselves in the forest.

The horses spread out in all directions among the trees. The riders were streaks of green against the dappled light. I could hear their calls as they pressed on, but Mollie fell gradually back from the hunt, until she and I were alone in the forest.

I gave her her head, since she seemed to know what she wanted. Her pace was easy under the trees.

At last we came to a clearing. I heard water: a spring bubbled up out of the earth into a little pool. Someone had built a small stone wall around the pool. Moss grew in the clearing, studded with the tiniest of flowers. In this pleasant spot I dismounted, and let Mollie take a drink.

I noticed then a gleam of something on the rim of the wall. It was an old earthenware mug, highly glazed so that it shone where it wasn't caked with dirt. Just for something to do, I dipped it in the spring to clean it, and brought it up brimming with cold, clear water. I wished I might drink, but did not do it.

A strange sound took me then; for if a sound can fill a man's senses, surely this one did. I've tried many times to get the feel of it into harp music, and failed. It was high but sweet, cold and clear as crystal, or the water itself; it shivered right through me with deliciousness.

A man stood across the glen from me, on the other side of the spring. I knew he was a man, and not an Elf, although he was uncommon tall and splendid of face, with broad shoulders and a great beard falling over his chest.

"Who calls?" he asked, his voice as deeply penetrating as the crystal sound had been.

I shook my head to show I could not answer him.

Mollie whickered, and went and nuzzled him. He rubbed her nose.

"These woods are full of enchantment," he said to me, rather unnecessarily—but it was kindly meant, by way of excusing my dumbness. "Have you need of me, man?"

I shook my head again.

"I believe you," he said, and there was that in his voice made me want to weep—as though no one had ever believed me before, and meant it, as this one meant it. "You are a bard, I think, and so are bound to truth. Sometimes there is gained truth only in silence." He stretched and shook out his warrior's arms, smiled a little. "I am not a bard. Sometimes the silence wears on me, man; but so must it be."

Somehow, his patient smile was more poignant than tears. I would have eased him if I could. Helpless, I held out the brimming cup to him. "Not yet," he said, with a true smile for me this time. "Not until the need is great. Then will I drink, and gladly."

I returned the cup to the wall's edge.

"And yet you did call. You are not wholly theirs yet, though you wear her raiment." I looked down at my green velvet, the supple leather boots. I wanted to explain: that he could not help me, nor I him.

"Now tell me only this," he said gravely: "When the last ride comes, where will you stand? Will you be among the host of Faery, or will you ride, singing, at my side?"

I crossed the glen to him, and knelt before him. And I took his hand and pressed it to my lips in fealty, needing no words for that. His hand was strong and warm.

He touched my bent head. "It is well. Go now, brother; and tell your lady that the King waits still. And fortune attend you on your road."

Mollie gave a little whuffle of disappointment. He was gone. And the cup bobbed, empty, in the well.

I leaned against Mollie for a bit, embracing the scratchy warmth of her, breathing in the comforting horsey smell. On Earth I have known lords, kings, men who were counted great; but next to him they were children, or toys that children play with. And yet he seemed more human, not less; there was no taint of Elvinkind about him. In him all things that are best in us—love, faith, courage, patience, generosity—were strong; but he had burned out all lesser passions in fires I dared not imagine. I fixed the memory of him as a bright coal of true fire in my heart, among the flickering spells and colors of Elfland.

Then I mounted up on brown Mollie, and the two of us rode slowly out
of the glen, until it was swallowed back among the trees.

I was, of course, completely lost; but for once it was someone else's
problem: Mollie's, or the queen's, or the ones' who'd invited me hunting.

It was the latter I came upon, Doe-Eyes and Ivy and Hinge, along with
a few of their companions, sitting on a ring of tree stumps drinking out of
silver flasks, while their mounts cropped the grass around them.

"Ah!" they sighed happily as I rode into the clearing, not at all surprised
to see me. "Harper! The Hunt is past. Come sit with us."

I obligingly dismounted. Next to the image I still held of the King, the
Elves all seemed fragile, insubstantial. They must have felt it themselves:
they leaned into my presence as though I were a winter's fire. I remembered what the queen had said about our mortal golden heat, and came
close to pitying them.

"Thirsty?" Doe offered me his flask. I could feel the others watching
with great interest to see if I would take the bait. He must have known I
would refuse; I think he just couldn't resist playing with my humanness, as
when he'd asked me my name the day I arrived.

"Now—" Ivy waved the flask away languidly. "Harper doesn't want
your silly drink. He's the son of a monk and a famous princess, and he's
much too clever for you."

"How do you know whose he is?"

"The queen told me."

"Oh, liar."

"Stop it," a green-haired woman with fingers like tree roots interrupted
them. "It's too nice a day for challenges. Let's have a dance instead."

"The horses are in the way."

"Send them home. We can walk home; the Hunt's over anyway."

"Did they catch anything?"

"Yes, but they had to let it go."

"Let's not go home; let's go to the mountains."

With a wicked glance at me: "Let's make a changeling."

"Oh, no," insisted the tree-root woman, "let's dance. I bet the Harper
can make you dance."

"Without a harp?" Doe asked maliciously.

Indeed without a harp, I thought, and stood myself up on a tree stump,
and opened my mouth and sang:

> *Drunk since ever I saw your face*
> *Drunk since ever I met you*

Drunk since ever I saw your face
And the devil if I can forget you!

It was an old dance tune from my youth, that I have often heard played
on fiddle or harp. But when I was a child, there wasn't always a fiddler or
harper around, and so the folk would *sing* the tunes, to whatever rude
rhymes should please their fancy. Mouth music isn't the easiest singing in
the world; it goes fast and steady, and you have to time your breathing not
to break the rhythm of the tune.

Oh, who's *that by me pulling the blankets off*
Who's that by me pulling the blankets off
Who's that by me pulling the blankets off
Nobody, only Conla . . .

The Elves were nodding; they all caught on to the rhythm fast enough.
Then, like slender trees themselves, like little bushes and rocks and flowers
in their earthiness and strangeness, they began to dance around me. They
danced no steps I knew, but danced the *rhythm* of the music, the dips and
weavings of my voice, the pulse that beat through the singer and the song.

Leezie Wright, oh she's a sight:
Her petticoat wants a border;
Old Gil Brenton in the dark
He's kissed her in the corner!

While the Elves danced around me, I saw back to a Yuletide of my
childhood; people dancing in my parents' house, impromptu, while a
sturdy old woman stood on a table, reeling off verses about them all.

Harry's neat and Harry's sweet,
O, isn't he the dandy
And doesn't Harry kiss the girls
And do it right and handy?

When I closed my eyes I could see them all, Harry and Gil and Leezie
and pretty Susan, see the very sweat beaded on their faces and the colors of
the ribbons in their hair. I had been so small then; when I tired of capering
around the dancers, I had crouched under the table and listened to the old
woman singing. All of her words came back to me now: the double enten-
dres I'd been too young to understand, as well as the nonsense words she'd
filled in the music with when her rhymes dried up. I had grown up to

become a different singer making music for different dancers in an un-earthly land; but, in a way, I was become her, too, now. The music brought it back so strongly, I could almost smell the sap of cut pine branches, the honey-and-rosemary steam of the wassail bowl, the tansy and lavender crushed under the dancers' feet. . . .

Then I opened my eyes to the green world of Elfland, the fantastical creatures stamping and swaying to mortal music. And there among them, where he had not been before, was the dark head of the hunter lord.

Like a soap-bubble burst, my vision of the Yule dance was gone. The hunter lord looked at me, and the rest of them faded.

They faded like ghosts, like a weak memory: the others became *less,* and Hunter became *more.* He seemed cut out of the air, his red eyebrows and lips very vivid. He said to me, "Well, Thomas."

For the first time, I felt the pull of my name. Maybe I had been too long in Elfland, and their ways were seeping into my skin. Maybe I had grown so unused to hearing my true name from anyone that it was like the call of a friend. Whatever it was, I listened. And when, like the queen before him, he said, "Come, Thomas," I followed him out of the clearing, down a path in the woods to a little stream.

Hunter sat on a rock and pitched stones into the stream. "Once," he said, "there was a knight. He married a fair and clever lady, and as time went by they had one child, and they were very happy. All would have gone well for them, but the lady's mother was a jealous woman, who grudged her daughter the happiness she found with anyone but her. The jealous mother hired a gang of ruffians to set upon the knight in his house, and they killed him and the child. The mother thought that now her daughter would come home to her. But the daughter buried her dead that dark night, and then she did something very strange. She cut off all her long brown hair, and dressed in a suit of her husband's clothes, and she walked for days until she reached the king's court. There she did not seek justice, but service: the knight's widow became a servingman to the king. And, over the years, her service so excelled that the disguised woman rose to the rank of chamberlain. Now, riddle me this, Thomas: what became of the knight?"

So saying, he threw a final stone into the stream; it sank with a decisive *plunk.*

He's dead and buried, I thought; knowing it could not be the riddle's true answer. Nonetheless, I picked up a stone myself, and pitched it in. To my pleasure (and relief) it made as loud a sound as his. What did I care for Hunter's riddle? I was not an Elf; the games he pleased to play with the queen and the court were none of mine.

But the question had been asked; the hole had been opened in the fabric of things, and there is something about a hole, a tear, a rent in anything that is irksome to people of character. One wants to fill it, to mend it, to close it. I have heard Elves say that humans' greatest strength and weakness both is their curiosity, which leads them to invention. Elves are not very good liars; they're not even very good storytellers, as we account storytelling: most of it is not invention, for with the rich stuff of Elfland in their hands, they've no need to invent.

Hunter stood, brushing the leaves from his green velvet, and whistled low through his fingers. My Mollie came trotting up to me through the trees, and I mounted her and rode away.

Of course I could walk away from Hunter's challenge; I fully intended to. Even if I came up with the answer, I couldn't say it; I'd have to sing it to him—ridiculous! But if, by some chance, in my adventures I did come across the answer to his riddle . . . well, it would be interesting to know. It was a curious story he'd told me.

Mollie took me back to the castle. Fortunately, the gate stood open; I did not have to try if the brown mare could leap the wall like the Elf Queen's steed.

As soon as I dismounted, an Elf came to tell me that the queen waited for me in the tower. I found her in a high round room, bright with Elvish sunlight. She was sitting at an embroidery frame, looking terribly domestic —until I saw that what she was doing was unpicking threads in a sort of tapestry so densely woven it was impossible to tell what would happen when a thread was severed: a whole patch might unravel, or one color only; or the lone thread might just hang there. There was no telling what the original picture had been—if it had been a picture at all—the threads were so tangled and raveled now. But the queen was enjoying herself; it seemed to be a game, or some sort of craft.

A dwarfish Elf was playing the lute to her. The music wasn't very good, I thought; more of that tuneless Elvin stuff.

The queen tilted her face up to be kissed, domestic still. "Hunting, Thomas?"

As always, I needed a moment to remember that it was all right to speak now. "I suppose. Never did find out what, though. But I met the King Who Waits; and Hunter is making very free of my name."

"Ah." She seemed to consider for a moment. She touched my wrist, listening, and then she made a face. "Be careful of him. He cannot harm you, but he can trap you through your own folly."

"Hunter? But why should he want to? You said he does not care for humans."

She turned, and waved the lute-player out of the room. "You're mine, and so you interest him. I'm afraid I can't help that. It's possible"—she sighed and picked another thread—"that he is bored. It happens sometimes."

I kissed her again. "You're never bored."

"No; you see to that," she said complacently, answering my kisses.

"You, I will amuse gladly; but never Hunter. Queen over all Elfland . . . why not give me Hunter's name? That would amuse *me.*"

"Oh, no, Thomas, that never can be, for one of humankind to name a lord of Elfland."

I pulled away from the intoxication of her skin, leaned my back defiantly against the warm stone wall.

"Then it cannot be, for one of humankind to pleasure the Queen of Elfland."

My lady plucked one more thread. "That's quite enough," she said frostily. A strand of blue unraveled on the frame.

"You don't want Hunter's name. Come here, Thomas."

"I'm helpless," I said, the wall rough behind me. "I'm alone here."

"You have me. Come to me."

"I'm lonely," I said to her, staying where I was. "I'm lonely and confused. I have a servant I cannot see, and an enemy I cannot speak to."

"I am here," she said. "What more need you?"

"No more . . . if I could have you always." I said it once, surly; and then, filled with wonder at it, *If I could have you always.* It was so simple, I should have realized it before.

"Come here," she said again, this time full of such warmth and grace as drew me to her. The Elf Queen folded me in her arms, and kissed me, cheek and hair and brow. "Always come to me. Here is my ring." She placed a green stone on my finger. "When you want me, you've but to breathe on it, and I will send for you at once."

I thanked her with silent lips, kissed her hands a thousand times, breathed my gratitude into her scented skin.

"I know you're lonely. I know it's hard for you here. Thomas, my Thomas. . . ."

Held in her arms, enshrouded in her hair, I believed her. I kissed her until I couldn't stop; and in the final moment of release I felt, for just that instant, perfectly understood, body and soul. I wept, as men do, to feel that moment pass away.

That night I played the harp again at a smaller feast. The hunter sat down the table from the queen; and though he looked often at me, he said nothing. His riddle was scarcely in my mind; I could feel the queen's gold ring burning on my finger, a little tug of allurement all the time, a promise pulling to be kept. I looked at her, shining among her shining company, knowing soon she would be mine again. When I'd made my bows to them all, and carried my harp back to my rooms and put it by, then I breathed on the grass-green stone of the ring. No sooner had I done so than a solemn Elf was at my door. I followed him through the ever-changing corridors of the castle to the queen's bedchamber, where my lady already waited, her gown unclasped.

"See?" she said. "Thomas, I am here."

I woke to morning in my own rooms, feeling so well rested that many hours must have passed. Perhaps I'd slept a mortal day, or even two. I rose, and ate, and bathed in the lily pond. My servant handed me a thick towel. I dried myself, and went into the music room that was also my wardrobe. Except for the formal velvet of the hunt, it seemed anyone could wear anything anytime here—time being so fungible and elusive a thing. I surveyed my extensive wardrobe with satisfaction. It was strange to see that no matter what color the clothing first appeared—and they were all hues, from earthy copper and garnet to the blue of sky and shadow—in different light all turned to some shade of green, as if there were a third plane to the cloth's weaving beyond the warp and weft.

This time I caught up everything of fine brocade, shimmering silk and softest linen. Carefully I put them on: shirt and tunic and houppelande and cap and sash; even down to the embroidered shoes, I lacked no vain splendor. Then I breathed on the ring, and went to the queen again to let her take them from me.

She was always there when I wanted her. Alone in my apartments, I taught myself to swim in the lily pool; I learned new instruments and made new songs to sing to the queen and her court at their feasts, their unpredictable mornings on the lawns and evenings in the myriad gardens of the castle. But when I grew tired of my solitude, tired of the attentions of my invisible servant and the one-sided conversations of Elves, I misted the green-stone ring with my breath and found my way to her. She was in her bed; she was in the tower; she was sitting in the garden; she was walking under the trees in the orchard. Her arms were always open to me, her body always ripe as fruit, rich as spices.

And soon there was never a day passed without I spent some part of it in her company; and not garden nor music nor the strange sights of Elfland pleased me more than her voice, her skin, her touch. My harp lay still, I made no new rhymes, for why make songs when you can take the very mistress of all song in your living arms?

Once, we were in the long grass under the trees, below the glade where the ancient lovers walked in their glad contentment. We had stood in the shadows of the tall trees, holding hands together, silently watching their graceful forms and shining faces, until we could look no more, and had come away to the long grass to seek our own contentment.

"Do the dead come here," I asked the queen, full of my own quick life, "to be happy when they die?"

"No," she said, pushing hair back from my face—my hair was growing long—"you're speaking of Paradise, Thomas. I showed you that road already."

"Don't be irreverent," I said, suspecting a jest over what was not a jesting matter. "When did you so?"

"In that Other Orchard: remember the thorny road you thought no one could pass down?"

"Oh, come now—do you mean to say that if I had taken that road, I would have fetched up at the end of it in Heaven among the blessed saints?"

"Not you," she chuckled; "not you." I poked at her until she giggled, inducing her to add, "Few men are given so clear a choice while yet they live, though."

"But those people," I insisted, "here in the glade—did they not all die the death in Middle-Earth?"

"Aye. Long ago." She pulled my hair, this time, twining it about her hand. "Now, enough of questions, Thomas. The dead do not come here to be happy—if they do come, it is for quite another reason."

"What reason?" I asked breathlessly, trying to resist her just long enough to learn something.

"Not to live—would you want to spend your Eternity here?"

"I wouldn't object," I murmured in her ear.

"No," she said sternly. "You are wrong. It would be different for you then. This is an ill land for a human soul that would be at rest. Unless you were like the King in the Wood, whose last breath was never taken on Earth . . . but even he paid a price. Oh, the dead sometimes find their way to us, but what they seek is never happiness such as you mean. And what they pay, you would not want to pay." She laughed, rolling me over on top of her. "But they are a pretty sight, those sweet lovers in the glade. They are creatures out of song, sweet songs of love and fate that even warriors weep at. Perhaps, some day, you and I shall join their number. . . . Should you like that, Thomas, to be a song yourself? To hear one night in the hall of how you loved the Queen of fair Elfland for seven long years, and how at last you returned, changed, to Middle-Earth?"

"Shall I return?" I breathed. "And shall I be changed?"

"Oh, you are changed already," she answered carelessly. "And shall be more so or ere your time be out."

"I'll tell you the song that will be sung," I teased her, putting thoughts of home out of my mind: "Of how Thomas the Rhymer returned to Earth, and how the Elf Queen sighed and pined for him, until at last she must—"

She silenced my lips with her finger. Her eyes had gone deep blue. "Vain Thomas. All my other mortal lovers are wind on the hill, dust in the glen. You would like to be the one exception, to out-charm the charmers."

"Of course," I said. "And why should I not be?"

"Presumptuous mortal." She caressed me, her eyes soft with laughter. "For that, I shall turn you into a hazelnut tree, and let you serve out your time to me in some useful fashion."

"If my lady thinks that is the best way I can serve her. If she is quite, quite sure . . . shall I be the world's only musical hazelnut tree, then?"

"No," she murmured, "you shall not. . . ." and we spoke nothing more of any moment.

Perhaps it was the queen's ring protecting me, or maybe something had come up to alleviate his boredom; at any rate, the hunter lord was gone from the court for now. The queen said nothing, but I was unwise enough to make a jest of it.

"Someone has found out Hunter's name," I said, "to draw him from your side. Maybe a pretty nymph has him locked up somewhere."

The queen slapped my face, light but stinging. We were naked in bed, where we'd been for hours, showing no inclination to depart. "Leave off," she said, "this talk of names."

In that moment I had a sudden sharp vision of Elspeth, as she had been the day we had our quarrel over the naming of the Fair Folk. The memory flowed through my body sharp as pain: her voice, her hair, the curve of her cheek and the flash of her hands. . . . How long since I had seen her thus, or even thought of her?

There was no counting the days. Enough time had passed that my hair was grown so long it swept below my shoulders. But the queen, and all around me, never changed. They were young, and beautiful each after his kind . . . only I was doomed to mortality, and to change. Before them I would wither, fade, and die. For the first time, the thought terrified me.

"Lady." I clasped her cool, dry hands in mine. "Look at me."

Her eyes, green as forest leaves, were pleased with what they saw. "I'm looking, Thomas."

"Lady, am I the man you kissed under Eildon Tree? Or are the seven years burning away my beauty, and will you be casting me out in the end for that?"

"Never." She kissed me on the eyes. "You are fair, and ever fair, and will be so for years to come. It is my will that Elfland not age you."

I shivered under her hands. Even in this, my body bended to her will. I was learning to love the feel of enchantment that she carried about her always; knowing that, she did less to mask it from me now.

"Do not fear the loss of your beauty, Thomas, while you serve me here."

I kissed her hands. "I want it only for your pleasure, lady."

"Yess," she hissed contentedly. "That is as it should be."

"And if I misplease you," I murmured, letting her taste the curling edges of my lips, "will you be turning me to a loathsome shape, or yet cast quick age upon me?"

"I could. You know the songs. But you please me, Thomas; very much you please me. . . ."

We came together then, and I rolled away exhausted. But the queen would not let me sleep yet. She stroked my hair, and brushed my face with butterfly fingers. "Tell me; when did you first discover that your beauty brought you women?"

I couldn't help but smile at the memory. "Oh . . . very young. When we all got interested in girls—my friends were always complaining, but I never had any trouble."

"Mmm . . . and you pursued the advantage?"

"Mmm."

"You look like a cat with cream. Who was she?"

Lying on my back, my eyes closed, I told her about Brown Meg, the kitchen maid; and Lizzie in the dairy, and the tinker's daughter of Inveralloch. All when I was too young to do more than buck and sigh. . . . I'd not thought of those girls in years, but now their faces came back to me sharp and clear; and their words, and their tricks, and mine.

The room was in dusk, and my throat was dry. Candles were lit around the bed; the queen's skin glowed creamily. "Go on," she said.

"What, more?"

"Oh—you're tired, aren't you? Poor Thomas, you must eat."

Bordeaux grapes, and Cornish pastry; and then more kisses, and the queen pulling away from me: "No, no," so playful, but steely; "one more old love, and then back to me."

I felt angry, my passions used and toyed with; but I knew my anger was useless against her. "Who, then?"

"The last one. The one you were thinking of when you thought of growing old."

"That was you."

"It was not. You know which I mean."

"Oh. A girl—a farm girl. No one, really; the last, as you say. The next to last, now, there was a treasure. . . ."

In place of Elspeth I gave her Lilias Drummond entire: the curve of her lips, the mole on her neck; all the secret things we had done, and what I'd thought of it all, things even Lilly didn't know.

"But you lost the lady. What a shame. Because you were of too humble a station—what would her people think of you now, do you suppose, of where you are now?"

"Envy," I said. "Pure greensick envy. Lilly married with an earl; but I am mated to a queen."

There are women who like to hear themselves compared (favorably, of course) to your others, and even some who thrill to hear of long-ago exploits. But the Elf Queen was plumbing my humankind, following it like a vein of silver buried in a hill.

I did not try to refuse her; I doubt I could have, and as her pleasure was mine, it was no bad thing.

She asked, "And have you lain with a man?"

"Once." She pressed me for more. "When I was young, and curious, and easily impressed. I didn't like it: it made me feel used."

"What was it like?"

I told her. To my surprise, even the telling roused me; maybe it was the feeling of her drinking in my experience like water: my stories seemed to feed the same dry spring in her that the use of my body did.

I stopped listening to myself. I fell asleep talking, and maybe I kept talking in my sleep.

When I awoke it was black night. The queen was gone. The sheets were cold, except for the tangled patch I'd rolled myself in. My mouth was dry, my throat raw from talking. I reached out my hand for the beaker that always stood at the bedside. As I raised it, I felt a strange lightness on my finger.

The queen's ring was gone from me.

I caught my breath, desperate for light. Like the blind harper, my old master, I felt my own hands, but they were bare as any pauper's. I felt the length of my body—perhaps it had slipped off—and then I groped among the silken sheets, listening in the heavy darkness for the clink of metal falling on the floor. The slippery sheets were cold and empty. My heart was pounding, and I was alone.

It had fallen from my finger when I slept, surely, fallen to the floor unheeded. I slid down off the bed and to my knees on the stone, feeling every inch of the cold marble with my hands. Around the bed nothing, nothing, nothing.

I got to my feet, standing naked in the darkness. Surely it was only a joke, a test. Perhaps I no longer needed the ring; perhaps I had only to call her now for her to come to me. "Lady," I said aloud. My voice sounded fragile in the dark and silent room. "Lady?"

I held my breath. There was no sound, not even the wind.

"Lady!"

She did not come; she was not there. I closed my hand hard around a polished curl of the bed frame. I should not have shouted in that raw, helpless voice. It was the voice of a child, lost and alone.

I was not a child. I tore the sheets from the bed, flung them to the floor, shaking them, my ears straining for the sound I knew I would not hear now. The chilly room, the fathomless dark cast the wrong noises back to me; the hiss of the silk and my own harsh breathing were too loud there to endure. In the blackness I stumbled toward the door, barking my shins on something that had never been there before. I groped my way along the wall, finally found the door handle—a bronze satyr's head cast by dwarves in the mountains—pulled the weight of the heavy door inward, and stood in the hall.

Elvin starlight shimmered through a tall window, casting shadows of columns down the hall. The hall was grey stone, the floor streaked with silver. There was no one there. I heard a painful, tearing sound; no one had made it but I. I held my breath a moment, another moment, to show that I could.

My body was trembling. I put my hands down, pressed them to the wall behind me. Surely she would come to me now.

"They are gone," said a voice at my side. "All of them. It is Dancing Night."

Where the voice came from, there was no one. I knew well enough who it was.

Foolishly, I groomed my hair back with my hands. I was quite naked, and now I was shivering with the cold of the stone wall and floor.

"We were left behind," my servant said. "They wouldn't take me either. Come, sir, you should lie down."

You should lie down. But I had lain down, and risen bereft. I had been nothing but lying down since I got to Elfland, and where had it gotten me? Cast away like a used tumbler, a cup drunk dry. Only the habit of silence kept me from cursing her aloud. To be taken and used by a woman thus— not a woman, though, a demon. A witch, a queen with the rich blood of enchantment, who provoked as she fulfilled, who satisfied with endless change. . . .

Oh, I should lie down, I thought, laughing, and then the laughter gathered itself into a sort of hammer in my chest that struck out through my throat and beat me to the ground. I heard my own cries, felt the jerking of my lungs. I clenched myself into a coil, holding all I had, myself, waiting for it to be over.

"Oh, sir," said my servant worriedly, "please don't. Please don't cry." I would have liked to stop, but the sobs were like those endless tales about magic coins that everything sticks to. Being a singer, I had the lungs for it. It hurt. "Please don't cry. Sir—"

I felt a little hand on my shoulder, warm and clammy. The touch jolted me from my weeping—I sprang to my feet, hands outthrust to fend him off.

"I'm sorry!" my servant shrilled breathlessly, as desperate as I. "All right—I won't—I'm sorry. Please, I'm sorry—"

That reached me where nothing else could. Those were the same terrified tones I'd heard the day the Elves came to my rooms. I, who had served in my own turn—here I was, striking terror into my own servant, the poor creature even the Elves had abandoned, I who had served and knew what it was to fear. . . .

I raised my two hands in a placating gesture, and nodded to show it was all right. My breath was still coming in spasms. My stomach ached, and I was shivering from the cold.

"Come on, sir," my servant said resignedly. But in his distress, my invisible guide went off without showing me an object to follow. I waited, dumb and patient as cattle, and at last he came back with a candle.

"We're not supposed to waste real fire," he confided, "but tonight they won't notice."

The gold light cast grotesque shadows all through the halls. I tried to keep my eyes fixed steady on the candle flame, not to look at the shadows and the patterns they made.

My rooms were also in darkness. The candle was comforting. I went first to my wardrobe, and took a long woolen robe to cover myself. I was thirsty, but the jug was empty.

"There's nothing, sir," my servant said. I hadn't been sure he was still there. "Tomorrow it will be all right again."

The stars in the sky above the garden were as big as toys, but pale, without the sharp, crisp clarity of our own. I took the only thing that felt truly mine, my harp, and played there in the garden, under the fuzzy stars, in the warm and scented Elvin night air.

And because I could not speak, I sang my challenge.

> *O, what is whiter than the milk*
> *And what is softer than the silk?*
> *What is louder than the horn*
> *And what is sharper than the thorn?*

As if I were working a spell with them, I sang all the riddle songs, one by one, without their answers: a challenge to the Elvin stars, giving nothing where I got nothing in return.

> *Can you plow me an acre of land*
> *Between the salt water and the sea strand?*

> *O, where are you going? says Miller to Moser*

> *Who's there, who's there at my bedroom window*
> *Disturbing me at my long night's rest?*

I sang the dawn up: a surely grey dawn without color, without sun.

The queen did not send for me that day.

I was used by now to having her when I wanted her; and I had wanted her more and more since I had the ring. The time spent out of her company had been time to eat, to sleep, to rest. Now I tried to bide alone, but there was no savor in it. The courtyard's fabulous flowers were only plants, the instruments wordless voices. I wearied of my own singing, of my own company. With her there was speech; and when there was no speech, something better for soul and body's comfort.

There was nothing I could do, no one I could ask. The need for her was burning in my blood, and I could not sit still. My hand strayed ever to the finger where the ring had been; she, who had been a touch away, was now as distant as the moon. I went out into the halls, but their shifting order was baffling, and I feared I should be lost. She might send for me at any moment; if someone came to fetch me, I must be where I could be found.

I paced my apartments as though they were a cage, waiting, waiting for her. The Elves were back; I heard them in the halls. No one came to me. I ate when food was given me, with no idea of how time passed. I stayed awake all that day, that night and the next—such days as they might be, with the light growing and waning around me, however the hours might count. When I felt sleepy, I swam in the pool. If I were asleep when she wanted me, I might miss the call.

Helplessly restless, I started searching my rooms for the ring. If I had the ring, I could have what I needed. Maybe her game had been to hide it there for me to hunt and find. I prowled my rooms, looking in inlaid drawers, turning all my clothes inside-out, emptying pockets, sweeping high shelves, searching amongst my instruments. But the queen's ring was not there.

I could not sit, could not stand. My harp felt too heavy; the sound of the notes was harsh, shrill, intolerable. The robe I wore hurt my skin. It chafed, tugged, weighed me down. I pulled new clothes from the mess of them I had made on the floor: a silk shirt, loose-collared and full-sleeved, cream-colored except when the light turned its sheen to pale green. I'd never seen it before, nor its companion, a pair of loose trousers; it felt like wearing wind and water, the light silk brushing my body with its feather touch.

I was leaning against the wall, my face resting on the cool plaster, when the knock came. My heart started pounding; I could feel the blood flushing through me already. In my loose silks I felt strangely vulnerable; it was as if I walked the halls the Elf Queen's naked lover, as I followed her servant to my mistress.

She was sitting in her chamber, reading a book. I hadn't known she could read. I stood in the doorway, waiting. She held out her hand to me; I came to her and knelt and kissed it.

She laid her hand on my hair. "Thomas. Have you been missing me?"

Her voice pierced me like arrows. I had forgotten its penetrating sweetness. I gasped as though stricken indeed. "Yes. I have. You know I have."

"I have been busy," she said.

I felt as if I were drowning, and only her hand could save me. "I love you," I said, cradling it against my cheek. "Please don't do this to me, I need you."

"There." She stroked my head, pressing it to her. "There, it's all right."

"I'm lost without you."

"Yes," she said, "I know. But I don't think you did. You know now, don't you?"

"I know now," I said, reaching for her shoulders, her neck, her face. "Shall I have my ring back, now, sweet lady?"

"Oh, no, Thomas. That ring is mine, it stays with me; it was for your brief use only."

I sprang to my feet, looming over her precise, delicate beauty. "Damn you! False as glass—" raising a fist to strike her.

The Elf Queen laughed up at me. "Oh, would you, Thomas? Would you indeed?"

My hand fell to my side. "I would," I said coldly, numbly. "If it could, if it would keep me from—"

"Well, you cannot, and well you know it. So come to me, Thomas, and lose yourself in me." And when I hung back, "You cannot do otherwise; you know now you cannot. There is no blame, and much ease."

She opened her arms to me, and I went to her. It was comfort even beyond a child's comfort, for what does a child know of a man's grief, or a man's hunger? "I love you," I said to her.

"Yes," she said, "yes, it's all right now."

And now the world was become simple: her presence was my joy; her absence, my pain. But it was not all right. I had no control over our meetings; she might promise to send for me, and forget, or she might keep me by her for days at a time.

I loved just being near her, watching the way she moved, hearing her voice. Sometimes she let me stay while she worked, talked to her people; sometimes I was silent, and sometimes I harped for them. Sometimes we made love in the places where we used to do, and sometimes she told me more of Elfland then, and sometimes her pleasure was to hear me speak of me and mine. There was a laugh she laughed only for me, when we were alone together.

But other days the summons did not come. I paced my rooms, feverish —even the silks were too heavy for me then. I swam in the lily pool, I practiced my music—but my ears were ever turned to hear the knock at the door.

The green-stone ring was again on her finger. I tried to make a joke of wanting it, to wrestle it away from her; but she grew angry when the wrestling got too rough, and I was afraid to lose her goodwill. I knew her moods by now. It was become so clear to me, when I was pleasing her and when I was not. When I pleased her, we were both happy, and she would see me more often.

When she was melancholy, or on edge, I must choose my words with care. When she was feeling easy, I could say almost anything. I scolded her, teased her, made demands; once I even asked her for her own name.

"Call me Maggie." She smiled and stretched in that familiar, catlike manner. "Call me Lillie—any of your girls that pleased you."

It gave me a particular shiver to hear the intimacies of my past from her lips, one not altogether displeasing. "No," I insisted boldly, "it just won't do. It's not right. Where I come from, we all have names. Nobody has a proper name in this place: everyone seems to be called by their most distinguishing characteristic. You'd think my mother'd christened me 'Mortal.' Or 'Harper.' "

"Oh, yes," she laughed, "and you call my people things like Hinge and Tree-Toes. It's perfectly polite, Thomas, here. You understand, we are not given to christenings. What do you call me, without a name?"

" 'Lady,' " I answered. " 'The queen.' Not very romantic."

"Well," she said, "it would not be very romantic if you knew my true name, either. It would be very ugly—for me, my dear: *you'd* love it. You may well be the hero of this story of yours, but you are not the kind of hero who tricks people's secrets out of them in bed." She laughed my particular laugh. "And think how it would sound in the songs! 'The Elf Queen's False Lover.' "

"It would be a new twist, anyway. In stories it's always the woman who tricks her lover's secrets out of him, not the man his lady's."

"That," she said, "is because people never think mortal women have any secrets worth having. Is it true, Thomas; have they?"

"None so fine as yours."

When I cried out for her, it was always a wild and wordless cry.

Hunter came back.

His eyes were always on me in the feasting hall when I harped, when I sang, when I sat eating and listening to others. I felt naked before him, as if my very silence proclaimed what the queen was to me. Although I never was the man to ask directly when I could find out by indirection, after a time I would gladly have walked up to him and demanded what in this world or any other he wanted of me. Meg was right: the Elves are not like us. A gypsy tinker is your own dear brother next to an Elf.

He looked at me, but he never spoke.

And because it made me uneasy, because I did not know what it was he really wanted, my thoughts turned to his story, of the knight and the widow-chamberlain. *What became of the knight?*

I didn't give a horse's hey for his riddle. I was not in Elfland to solve riddles for him, or anyone.

Or so I believed.

They had one child, and were very happy. But the lady's mother was a jealous woman. The daughter buried her dead that dark night, and then did something very strange.

On those grim days when I sat in my rooms waiting for the summons that never came, or restlessly wandered the hills around the castle, walking off desire, seeking sometimes the ghostly company of dead lovers who were happier than I was, then his words came back to me.

She did not seek justice, but service. Rose to the rank of chamberlain. Once there was a knight. He married a fair and clever lady. . . .

I could not get the story out of my mind. It had beauty, and tragedy; and it had no ending. Maybe it was only that.

Or maybe it was something worse, the magic of Elvin compelling. I had been weirded once before, when I kissed the queen's lips under the Eildon Tree though she warned me my body must follow. I should have known better, that time, but that I was so dazzled by her; for I knew the tales, like "The Blue Falcon." I'd told it myself: the story of the unlucky prince out hunting, who brings home the feather of the blue falcon, whereat his father's wife lays her weird on him, saying, "I set it as crosses and as spells on you, that you shall not be without a pool in your shoe and the wet chill on your head until you get for me the bird which that feather came from." And he must endure hardship and mystery until the deed is accomplished. Strange that, even then, I didn't think of myself as being in a tale. Was I under a like compelling of Hunter's, or was I only bored and restless?

I should have asked the queen. But when I was with her, it all seemed so unimportant.

All would have gone well for them, but the mother hired a gang of ruffians. . . .

Alone, I thought of it perpetually.

What became of the knight?

How on Earth—or under it—should I know?

Since the story wouldn't leave me, I decided to play with it. It might make at least the first half of a ballad, with its sorry tale of jealousy and murder. And there were images that touched me: the young wife burying her dead husband and child alone at night; her weary walk to the king's door. . . . Harp in hand, I began to pluck at the words and the tune.

The tune came quickly, mournful but urgent. And I minded me of another story I'd once heard, a true one, about soldiers using their own swords to bury their comrades.

> They left her naught to dig his grave
> But the bloody sword that slew her babe
> They left her naught to wrap him in
> But the bloody sheet that he lay in.

It was grim, but it served. Now, follow the body's wretchedness with the heart's pity:

She buried him, herself alone,
She buried him, making her moan . . .

And think you not her heart was sore
As she laid the mold on his yellow hair?
And think you not her heart was woe
When she turned about, away to go?

For the first time in days, I felt at peace in my own garden. I'll finish the song, I thought with grim satisfaction, and then I'll play it for my lord Hunter in the great feast hall before all the Elvin court—that will show him what a true minstrel does with his riddles!

I wondered how it should begin. There were the usual openings: *Once there was a lady fair . . . a knight so bold . . . Come gather 'round, good people—* No, no good. This called for the unusual. My beginning must be as strong as the verses I'd already written, but sweet as the death was grim.

Her love built her a bonny bower
All covered over with lily flowers
Where they might rest them all the day
In loving sport, and sporting play.

It was well enough. A bower, true lovers to be parted . . . But something was lacking. There was too much distance, the whole thing was like a picture viewed from another room. That's not the way of true minstrelsy. *Hunter's* story had felt more true to me than this. I was damned if I would let him tell a better tale than I! Was it beyond me? I wondered uneasily. Had I made all the good songs I would ever make? Maybe this was the best I could do—

Of course, a ballad is harder than a tale to tell. Not that I've ever had trouble finding rhymes; if anything, they're too easy, and can quickly mar a tale with doggerel. Rhyming was no problem. What I sought was some twist of the story's path that would draw the hearer closer in . . .

I laughed when I thought of it.

My love built me a bonny bower
So sweetly set with the lily flower
A finer bower you ne'er did see
Than my true love he built for me.

It was so simple: I should have known, when I began despairingly to compare myself to Hunter, that the solution was in sight. I always hate myself just before I think of something good. I would follow the lady, be in her heart, feel what she felt.

> *It was my mother's deadly spite*
> *For she sent thieves in the dark of the night*
> *Put my servants all to flight*
> *They broke my bower, they slew my knight.*

It was, after all, her story: her love spent most of it dead.

> *They swore to do to me no harm*
> *But they slew my baby in my arms*
> *Left me naught to wrap him in*
> *But the bloody sheet that he lay in.*

I sang the verses until I was sure I'd remember what I had rhymed so far. Again and again I harped the tune to it, changed a few notes. I grew venturesome with my harping, tried adding an ornament or two.

"Sir." My servant came up behind me. "I have food for you."

But I shook my head; I couldn't stop now.

I cut my hair, I changed my clothes . . . rose . . . nose . . . toes . . .

No, *I changed my dress*— no, sounds like a ball gown—

> *I changed my clothes, I changed my name*
> *I cut my hair just like a man . . . to seek*
> *for fame*

No, no, no. I began the song over again; sometimes if you just sing what you've got already, the next line comes naturally.

> *. . . And think you not my heart was woe*
> *As I turned about, away to go?*

> *I cut my hair, I changed my name*
> *Changed* something *to something . . .*

I hadn't even heard the white dove arrive. But I looked up in annoyance when I struck a false note, and saw it sitting on the fountain. There was no question but that it was watching me.

"My love built me a bonny bower," I started over, "so sweetly set with the lily flower . . ."

And as the song went on, the dove wept its terrible tears.

If you don't like music, I thought crossly, go sit on someone else's fountain. But I played on. *"Changed my name, Played my game, Sought for fame. . . ."*

"Sir," came the insistent, irritatingly calm neuter voice of my servant, "you *must* eat."

I turned in a temper to the tray held in midair, lifted my free hand to push it away—and gashed my thumb with the tip of a fruit knife.

I hissed between my teeth—only sorry I could not properly curse my servant for holding the knife so carelessly—and shook my hand hard in pain. Drops of blood flew across the courtyard.

I pressed on my thumb to stop it from bleeding. I was surprised that my servant hadn't yet become all apologies and bandages. The dove had ceased its weeping. It hopped clumsily down from the fountain rim, balancing itself with its wings, and waddled over to one of the spots of blood—my blood—and bobbed its head.

So that's what the dove ate.

I rose, disgusted and a little frightened, to shoo it away. And to think that I'd played good music to it, twice.

"No, sir! Don't!"

My servant's cry didn't even startle the dove. But I froze in my tracks. My servant had never sought to hinder me, nor commanded me in anything.

Then the dove spoke.

"Alas the day . . . Eleanor . . ."

It was a man's voice, and a man of my own country. "Eleanor . . . alas the day."

It took all my strength to keep from speaking to him. My hand fell, forgotten, to my side. The white dove walked on its ugly feet, coming closer and closer to me as I stood still, watching it come. It stood beside me and ducked its head again, and wet its beak in my dripping blood.

"Eleanor, Eleanor, my love."

At last I apprehended. As with the ghosts of the ancients, my blood gave the dove voice. I pushed at the gash in my thumb to open it further, forcing drops of blood to the ground. The dove drank.

But still it did nothing but mourn.

I turned to the tray, the knife again. I needed my fingers to be whole for harping, so I nicked a vein of my arm as surgeons do to let blood. It trickled onto the tiles of the courtyard, and the dove took its fill.

"My time," he cried sorrowfully. "My time is almost gone. I cannot make them see—I cannot make them hear—Eleanor, my love, my heart's joy—it is for you I left the road to Paradise, for you I crossed the bloody river, for you I wear this shape and soon will lose my soul; for you, for you, you, youu, youuu. . . ."

Its voice had become a dove's cry.

I cut another passage for my blood; but I thought I knew the tale already.

"Her tears on my grave, I could not bear them; my new-slain spirit burned with pity and revenge . . . Revenge . . . Revenge . . . her mother must die, must die; my Eleanor must live, must live, must have back her youth and womanhood. . . ."

Once there was a knight. He married a fair and clever lady . . . and they were very happy.

> *I cut my hair, I changed my name*
> *From Fair Eleanor to . . .*

Thus, Hunter and his riddles! What become of the knight, indeed? You hunted him through Elvinwood on a big black horse, you canting bastard!

I opened my arm again. I was not a surgeon, and I feared to lose too much at once.

"They will not see, they will not hear . . . I can weep on Earth, but cannot speak . . . I am dead, Eleanor, dead and lost and cannot help, dead and lost forever, no more time. . . ."

"There is time!" It was my servant's voice, thin with tension, fierce with care. "You don't understand. You must return to Middle-Earth, where the years pass slowly. You will have more time, then."

But what good would all the time in the world do for him if he could not speak? *Poor voiceless dove . . . you'd laugh yourself sick to see him. . . . Lend him Thomas's voice . . .*

I would gladly lend him mine; but song was all the voice I had now.

I could make him the song. That was all. But if somehow Eleanor's king could hear it, and know the truth—her mother exposed, and justice done —then the knight could rest easy, his weird accomplished.

Helpless to tell them this, I took up my harp again, plucked out the new tune to express my will.

"Yes," said my servant breathlessly. "Go back now—and Thomas will finish your song. There will be a way. You must not despair."

Thomas? My servant was a new creature now, compassionate and sure. And of course he knew my name; the queen, or even Hunter, must have told him. It didn't matter; in this matter we were one, whomever his orders came from.

* * *

I knew the answer to Hunter's riddle now. But the answer raised even more questions. Hunter's desire towards the dove had been clear enough, when the queen and I met him in the forest. He wanted the knight to fail in his quest, so that the knight's soul would be trapped in the dove's body forever, fair game to Hunter's bow. Everyone knows the Elves take their sport in hunting the restless spirits of humankind: just as some ghosts on Earth torment the living, so do Elves torment our ghosts. Perhaps it was even better sport on home ground.

So: the dead knight's spirit had found its way to Elfland, struck some kind of bargain with a power here, some means to help it to revenge. Likely the knight had not chosen—or had been tricked into choosing—the mute dove's shape. He had been given a set amount of time in which to right the wrong done him and his lady. If the time ended in failure, he would not rest, but become Elvin prey. What would happen to his soul if Hunter shot the dove, I did not like to think.

Why, then, had the elf lord set me on the path of the riddling? Hunter must have known that I would want to help. All that I did would be to work against his aim. Perhaps it would merely amuse him to watch me fail? Unless . . . unless he didn't know the dove had found his way to me. For without the dove I would never have unraveled the tale so easily and quickly.

If he meant to vex me, or only to take my mind a little from the queen, he had succeeded. But did he know I divined all? My servant might tell him—but my servant was leagued with us, with the mortal souls.

Leagued with us . . . but what, really, was I to do but listen and rhyme? I was no wizard, no Elvin power. I must have time—time to think, time to finish Eleanor's song. I wondered if she was pretty.

"The king loves her," the dove said suddenly. "The king loves his flower among servingmen. I roost outside her window. She weeps at night. Eleanor, no time. . . ."

Then it cocked its head, looking for all the world like any garden dove, and flew off.

I got slowly to my feet, feeling a little the worse for the blood-letting. My hand shook as I took a cup of cider from my servant, and I drained it in one draught. My arm was a gory mess, streaked with dried blood from little nicks and places where I'd missed the vein. I rinsed it in the fountain, where the cold water staunched any last bleeding.

I meant to get back to the song; but suddenly I was tired, so tired I could hardly move. I put my harp in a safe place, and stripped myself for bed.

Then the queen sent for me.

I wrapped a long robe around myself, and followed her servant through the hall. We came to the queen's bower, half chamber, half garden, with roses and morning-glory, honeysuckle and jasmine growing up the wall to form a canopy of living perfume. The queen reclined under it, dressed— but barely—in a robe of sheerest silk, the shape of her body, the very texture of her skin contoured against it. She opened her arms to me, and I fell onto her in that fierce burst of passion that can come just before a man yields to exhaustion.

Her touch and my feelings drove all thought of the dove from what there was of my mind. I fell asleep still clinging to her.

I woke because the queen was stroking my arm, the sensitive inner skin of it. Her fingers brushed the crusts of scabs.

"Thomas," she said, stern but gentle, "I don't like this. Have you been ill, Thomas, or has one of my people been taking advantage of you; or have you been feeding ghosts, Thomas?"

I did not know what to answer her. But her hands kept on with their stroking of me, and it seemed she did not require an answer just at present.

The knight's poor ghost seemed so far away then. It was hard to think of him when I was rapt in the smell and smooth clutch and grip of her shining body.

Yet here I was, taken into the very arms of Elfland. If any could help us, it was she. In the woods, the queen had looked kindly on the dove—or had that been only to annoy Hunter? If it was, and Hunter knew it, then my speaking for the dove might anger her. That was reason alone to be silent. To lose her kind, delicious hands, only for an instant, seemed unbearable now. If Hunter sought to drive a wedge between us—

I took those hands, ran them over my body, sighed to hear the Elf Queen sigh. The contest was between me and Hunter; she should not be brought in unless she must. Instead I brought myself in where I would be, shuddering at the familiar strangeness.

"I love you," I said over and over to her, until it was one more piece of sensuality that meant nothing to my mind, everything to my body. And she was saying words to me, but never that she loved me, never that. I pleaded with her, my sobs a thorny rose of pleasure. There was no pride left in me; I have never loved a woman more. She was not a woman, of course.

She was shaking me out of my satisfied lethargy, saying sharply, "Thomas! You must tell me who you've been giving your blood to!"

"I don't . . ." I tried; "I can't."

"So." She was tight-lipped, furious. "Is that how you love me?"

I met her eyes. They were blue and cold. "You know that has nothing to do with it," I answered softly.

She started to cry. I'd never seen her do that. "How *can* you? How can you say all that you did, and now—"

Gently I pulled her hands away from her face. Her eyes were dry.

"Do not try to deceive me," she said. "Do not deal double with me. Your whole allegiance here is to me. It is I you are bound to serve, and no other—do you forget that, Rhymer?"

"No, madam."

"I take you to my bed; I give you everything of comfort and ease—do you think I mean you harm?" Her voice had changed to pleading. "It is in my hands that all your fate lies; through my agency that you will win home again—if you cannot trust me, who is there for you here?"

It was true. It was all true. But the King Who Waits—I thought of him now, not because he could help me, but because he had called me *brother.* We two, and the dove, a poor murdered man of our own kind. I did depend on her, and none other. But that did not make her one of us.

Hunter's name was on the tip of my tongue. To blame it all on him; to let her deal with it, let them fight it out on their own eldritch terms. But it was my challenge, not hers.

I remembered her saying in the woods, "This bird is one of mine." Had the knight's bargain been with the queen, then? Was it my sweet lady had bound the murdered man to dove's shape? Perhaps she had not meant to be cruel; I knew, none better, how she did not always see matters as mortals do. The rules of magic were strict. If she had laid the weird on him herself, even she might not break it.

"Well, Thomas?"

My escape came easily: the human tricks the queen had learned, I knew from birth. Curling up miserably, I burrowed my way into her arms. "I do," I gulped, "I need you. Please don't be angry with me, I can't bear it."

"Well . . ." the queen said, softening; "well . . . but you mustn't lie to me, sweetheart. It's only for your sake. I'm not angry, really. . . ."

"How can you say"—I was nearly really crying now—"how can you ask if I love you, if I trust you? Do you want to see my heart cut out on a platter? I'm wretched every minute I spend out of your company! I've never been like this before—not with anyone, ever. I say things to you I've never said to anyone—what more do you want of me?"

All that I said was true. But if I had been sincere in that moment, I would never have admitted to any of it.

Whether she knew that, or whether human melodrama just tickled her Elvish humor, the queen did a terrible thing: she started giggling over my misery. I quivered; when she pulled my hands away from my face, I was laughing too. We rolled about the huge bed in a welter of silliness.

She was the first to pull away. "Well," she said, grinning down through the tangle of her hair; "let it be, then. Whatever you're doing, don't do it again. I'll know, of course."

Of course. But what could I do but sing? "Madam," I said, "sweet lady —how can you think I would do anything to drive me from your side?"

I did not, then, leave her side that day or that night—as Elfland measured time. For when I got back to my rooms again at their eternal midmorning, the nicks on my arm had healed; only a few white specks of scar marked the passage of the knife.

I set to work on the song again. The tune still pleased me, always a good sign.

> *I cut my hair, I changed my name*
> *From Fair Eleanor to Sweet William*
> *Went to court to serve my king*
> *As the famous flower of servingmen.*

Then Hunter came to see me.

He came on the arm of the doe-eyed elf boy, who had found his way to me once before; and they were carrying on disgracefully. When I came in from the garden, Hunter mock-swatted him. "Finch, wait outside. You never can keep your mouth shut."

The boy moved away, light as air. "Oh, Flame; how can I leave you here with that *creature?*"

"Why, Thomas will protect me." As always, Hunter took delight in the use of my name. But if *I* was not "that creature," who was? My poor servant? "Off you go, then—but wait for me nearby. The way is getting close for one."

As Doe-Eyes drifted away, an invisible hand slammed the door shut behind him. I smiled: there was no love lost between my servant and him.

"Now, Thomas." Hunter seated himself without invitation on one of my chairs, and put his elegantly booted feet on another for good measure. "How do you fare with my riddle?"

Angry, but trying not to show it lest temper betray me into speaking, I shook my head.

"Have you put it out of your mind?" he asked lazily. "Distracted by other matters?" I knew he could not hurt me. The queen would not let him hurt me. "Eh, Thomas?" It reminded me forcefully of an obnoxious master talking to a schoolboy. No one had invited him here: I was not a schoolboy, and I would not stay to be baited in my own rooms.

But the door handle burned when I touched it. "Not yet," said Hunter comfortably. "Don't you want to know where I've been?"

Between his hands, a glass globe appeared. It was the most perfect glass I'd ever seen. Despite myself, I drew nearer to look at it.

There was a picture in it: just an illuminated Elvish toy. But as I watched, the tiny picture in the glass globe *moved*. It was like being high on a mountain, looking down at the affairs of men with an eagle's eyes. The scene showed a young man, with a boy's soft features, still, standing in a rose garden, holding a golden chalice. His ash-brown hair fell almost to his shoulders, and his clothes were good, displaying a nice expanse of leg. He looked up, suddenly, as though he'd heard something—looking up directly into the globe, so that for a moment his wide grey eyes seemed to meet mine. Then a man dressed for hunting came into view. He was very richly dressed, and well attended, but the disarray of his party showed that the hunt was over. The youth offered him the cup, and the rich man drank. But he was agitated; he kept talking to the boy, describing something with his hands—the quarry, perhaps, that had escaped; a bird by the look of it, although if they'd been hawking their hawks were already mewed—and sometimes the man touched the boy's shoulder for emphasis—a little too often, to my jaundiced eye. All the while, though, the youth looked up at him steadily, with his clear grey gaze.

At last the rich man and his train moved off, leaving the youth again alone in the garden. He stood for a moment looking after them; then he went inside what looked like a castle, and gave the cup to a servant, and went up some stairs and into a small bedroom where he began to undress himself.

Under the boy's clothes was a woman's body; and what she sought solitude for was not right for anyone to look upon. Yes, the knight's Eleanor was beautiful; and, yes, she loved the king.

Moved to my heart, and disgusted with Hunter's invasion of her privacy, I turned away. But the elf lord's long arm shot out; his hand closed around my wrist, and he tried to thrust the globe in my face. "A pretty piece of flesh, is it not? Or does your own kind no longer please you?"

Enraged, I seized the globe from him, my fingers closing around the obscene picture, and hurled it across the room.

The noise of its shattering was louder than glass.

"Sso, Thomas," Hunter's fingers were still tight on my wrist. He began to draw me closer to him.

I shoved him, hard, so that the chair fell over with him in it. He scrambled to his feet angrily, his red brows bristling like a cat's.

"No!"

Hunter seemed frozen in the midst of his attack, arms uplifted, balancing on his toes. Then I realized he was struggling against an invisible force: my servant. The elf lord gathered his strength and flung my servant across the room—I followed his trajectory by the slam of chairs and tables, the final crash and thump against the wall near the pieces of the globe.

"How dare you!" Hunter raged at the wall. "How dare you lay one vile finger on me, you hideous, ill-faced monster!" He turned to me. "Oh, yes, my fine singer, that is the way of it: beauty and the beast. You may serve the queen, but did you know that you are served by a creature no one in Elfland can bear to look upon?"

I didn't much care. I wove my way amongst the fallen furniture to the empty spot against the wall, and groped for my invisible servant, to help or comfort him.

"Touching," said Hunter frostily, bilked of his scene. I was close enough to hear my servant's harsh, blubbery breathing, someone trying hard not to cry. I felt the rough cloth of a sleeve, remembered how I, naked, had fled my servant's touch in the hall that night I'd lost the queen's ring, and shivered but persevered. "Do you know what you seek to hold, Thomas? Shall I show you?"

"No!" he shrieked, shrill as a girl. "My lord, *you promised!*"

"I promised." Cool and in control again, Hunter gloated. "Alone among all the folk of Elfland, you are the one no one can stand the sight of." The poor creature *felt* normal enough; my hands closed on small, sloping shoulders. I tried to help him up. "You, who were once so beautiful. . . ."

The thin shoulders were shaking now with sobs. His body was rigid, neither coming with me nor casting me off.

"I promised," Hunter went on, "and I will hold to it—just as long as you do not betray me. Or lovely Thomas will see you as you really are—"

Weeping with a child's raw sobs, my servant broke away from me and fled.

"Well, Thomas," Hunter said to me; "and what became of the knight?"

The things I would have said to him if I could. . . . As it was, I turned my back on him, and walked slowly and deliberately into my garden.

When I heard the door close behind him I returned to the room. I straightened the furniture and swept up the shards of the broken globe. They were cloudy, like dirty water. Then I went back to the garden, and picked irises and some tall yellow flower, and put them in a pitcher on the table for my servant to find.

I dreamed that night, the first dream I remembered in Elfland. Fair Eleanor was walking across the slate-river roofs of the castle in the moonlight, carrying a boy's slingshot. She was shooting shards of cloudy glass at the white dove. In the dream, *I* was the dove—as an arrow-shaped piece of glass flew towards me I gave a cry, and started up in bed.

My room, for once, was bathed in starlight. The flowers on the table were moving, being rearranged in the pitcher.

"Oh!" My servant gave a little gasp when he saw me awake. I rolled over onto my side, my heart still pounding from the dream. When I looked at it now, it seemed a pretty picture: the moonlight of Middle-Earth picking out the edges of the glass, silvering the sharp slate and Eleanor's white shirt. . . . But it had been a terrible dream. It took me a long while to get back to sleep. And so I was aware of the secretive hand, gently and cautiously brushing the hair out of my eyes; the feathering touch of fingertips stroking my hair until, at last, I slept.

Since Hunter did not tell the queen about his visit, I had the pleasure of doing so. When next she sent for me, I knelt formally at her feet.

"How now, Rhymer?" the Elf Queen asked, amused. "What's this?"

"Madam," I said with my best court manners, "one of your people has struck my servant without just cause."

"It is Hunter," she said certainly. "I shall bar his way to your rooms, Thomas; you need not fear."

"But my servant—"

"That is between Hunter and your servant. Do not interfere."

I bit my lip in frustration. It was not safe to tell more without giving the game away. "Your servants are mine, too, you know," the queen said kindly. "It is not you who are responsible for their welfare in the end." Then she laughed. "Oh, my dear Thomas! You look so concerned. Being responsible for someone else becomes you. You are quite the young lord—I suppose you have seen the part well played before." She didn't mean it unkindly; and I had.

Still I persevered, hoping, maybe, to win a little of the truth behind Hunter's mysterious statements. "Hunter was cruel, lady. He said my servant had once been beautiful, but is now so ugly none would look upon him."

"I will bar his way to your rooms," she repeated firmly. "It will be all right."

I knew from her tone that the subject was closed. So I took her strong, slender white hand and kissed it.

"What did Hunter want?" she asked as an afterthought.

"To plague me. Is he jealous?" There. I'd finally said it.

"Not the way you would think." The Elf Queen pulled me to her. "He is not a mortal man. He hasn't got a soul—or, rather, he has; but it's bound up in his name. It dies with him." It sounded brutal, even coming from her. It made me feel brutal, too.

"What does he do," I said, kissing her hard on the mouth, "when the red thirst is on him?"

"It isn't what he does; it's what he *has* done that concerns you, Thomas, if you knew it."

"I'll kill him for you," I said, "if you ask me to." My mouth was hot against her neck.

"And you'd die in the trying. I'm not ready to lose you yet, sweet Thomas. . . . Don't go seeking to be a hero, my Rhymer, my beauty. My heroes are all dead: bright Oisian and tender Manannan. . . ."

"I'll join them in Hell," I murmured in her ear, intoxicated by the very thought of my peril.

"No you won't—or if you do, there's no justice in high Heaven. Your way lies a different road."

She said it with such certainty that I stopped, my body still pressed, clothed, against hers, where I sought to batter the gates of her rich array. "What do you mean," I asked hollowly, " 'my way'?"

"I know, you see." Breathless, she pulled my head down to kiss her. "The more you tell me, the more I know—your past becomes your future to me—"

"I don't understand—"

"You don't have to—"

I threw her back against the cushions. "Enough! Enough of your riddles!"

Her eyes were wide, a strange, unseely yellow. "Would you know the hour of your death, Rhymer?"

"I—"

"Soon I shall know it. Quite soon. It is important that I know it, for to be there when it comes to you."

"Stop—" It was so frightening it was almost funny, like children telling each other ghost stories.

"I will be there for you, Thomas—"

I felt terribly cold. The wild queen descended on me, and kissed my cold lips, drinking in my fear of death like nectar. It was her right, payment for my challenging her.

It was horrible. I thought, Perhaps this is how Elves make love together, drawing feelings out of each other that are not desire: fear, cold, anger, hopelessness. . . . I did not want her, but I did not want her to stop.

The things she said to me then come back to me sometimes in dreams. She did not stop until I lay there, still fully clothed, drained and exhausted. Her face was flushed with exhilaration, her eyes bright. "Thomas," she said, "I'm so thirsty."

She touched me till she roused me, and I made love to her as a man does to a maid. Then the queen lay there in perfect innocence, all golden hair and rosy cheeks. I loved her so much *I* felt thirsty. "Sweetheart," I said, touching her hair. "My own dear love. . . ."

"Oh, Thomas." She hugged me fiercely. "What shall I do when you are gone?"

"There's time," I comforted her. "Years, yet."

But her silence told me there were not.

"Come back with me," I said deliriously. "Live with me—marry me—be my wife—"

She flung her arms out wide. A rainbow shimmered between them. She wrapped it around us both; the colors spun and dazzled me. " 'Marry me,' " I heard her acid voice from the middle of the rainbow. " 'Be mine—' "

Lost in the colors, I couldn't tell up from down; couldn't see my own hands, feel my own limbs.

"I don't think," her voice said pleasantly, "that this is how your mortal girls feel when a man proposes marriage to them. I had better stop it." The rainbow coalesced again between her arms. "No one ever has asked to marry me," she said. "You're an odd man, Harper."

"I've never proposed before," I said drily. "I suppose it would take the Queen of Elfland to bring me to it. What a shame you've refused me: I bet you come with a magnificent dowry."

To my utter amazement, "What's a dowry?" asked the Queen of Elfland.

I told her.

I dreamed again of Eleanor, of the dove and the king. The Elf Queen might have barred Hunter's way to my room, but his riddle had already entered. I dreamed that I had finished my ballad. Somehow Eleanor had learned it, and was sitting all alone at night with a harp on her lap, singing it. The harp was in my hands: I was Eleanor, my fingers dainty and small, my body her body—I could feel her tears coursing down my face. I woke to wipe them.

Sad Eleanor, who haunted my dreams . . . *could* she learn my song?

Would she then sing it to her king? I did not think so: if she had wanted to be discovered, there were a hundred ways; she did not need mine. It was the dove who sought revenge for himself, freedom for her. The dove, who moved so easily between the worlds, he should carry my words—if I could give him speech.

My servant had retreated into deference again. I wished there were some way to tell him that I spoke to the queen on his behalf, that his care of me did not go unnoticed . . . I had tried with the flowers, but what real good were they? I was beginning to know without words when my servant was nearby: his presence rearranged the air somehow. I made the effort now to be especially gentle in his presence. Whenever I sat in the garden harping or singing, I could feel him hovering in the background, especially when I worked on Eleanor's song. The air took on an anxious, expectant quality. That quality's fuel to a performer, but hell when you're trying to work things out alone; nonetheless, I did not chase him away.

> So well I served my lord the king
> That he made me his chamberlain
> He loved me as his own son
> The famous flower of servingmen.
>
> But all at night, to myself alone
> It's there I sit and grieve my song:
> Alas the day that I become
> The famous flower of servingmen.

There it was at last; I had taken the song as far as it could go. All the tale was there: the jealous mother and her cruel deed; the burying of the knight and Eleanor's transformation; the king's high favor and her midnight tears. It was time to bring back the dove.

I played "The Unquiet Grave," and he came in a flurry of wings. I fed the poor knight's ghost some of my blood, and it spoke: "They hunt me. Through the woods. I am here, I am there, I am gone. Soon the king will hear of me, and follow. Soon, soon, sooon. . . ."

As its voice deteriorated to cooing, I did not feed it more, but sat and played for it the entire song I had made, adding impromptu the final verses:

> Our king is to the hunting gone
> Taking no lords nor gentlemen
> To follow after yon white dove
> He's hunted over hill and grove.

He's hunted up, he's hunted down
As though the wood it made its moan:
Alas the day my love became
The famous flower of servingmen!

Well, they'd bear improving; but at last I had the riddle's answer set in rhyme. Now I must only put into effect the story as I had told it. For we were of one mind, the dove and I; he to be hunted through the woods until the king caught up with him; I to give him there a song to sing, and voice to sing it.

Of course I'd rather have sung for the king myself; but easier far to win the dove a voice than to bring myself back, untimely, to the world of men. (And the king in Hunter's glass had been no king I knew. Either more time had passed on Earth than a few years, or the world of men held other gates to Elfland.) My part lay all in defeating Hunter: to answer him his riddle, and to free the knight's soul from him.

If I guessed right, the answer to both conditions lay in the feasting hall. For the queen's harper to sing there would not be amiss, and so would Hunter be answered before them all . . . but *double* my triumph when I took the dove from under his very eyes, by getting there the blood to set him free!

I mean, of course, the drink that quenched their great red thirst. If it was not human blood, it was something else that fed their mortal desire; might it not serve a ghost, as well? I thought it must. I would beg it if I could, steal it if I had to; give him enough to drink to send him back to Middle-Earth with my song in his throat.

My love built me a bonny bower . . .

The dove sat still as marble while I sang. His eyes were dry this time. I sang again, and again. I wished I could tell him what was important: don't leave out the repeats, don't take a breath just before the last line. I did it by example.

My servant brought me wine to drink. I sang the song through once more. The dove fluttered its wings, cocked its head, hopped down from the fountain and back again. I cut my arm and watched the dove take voice, and listened to the dove sing.

Chills ran up me. It was not a man's voice, nor yet a bird's. It was as though a flute had come to life, and learned language as well as music. Only when it had sung the song through did the dove begin to weep: perhaps it, too, could scarcely believe the sound it made.

Some say a man knows when his fate is on him. It might be that; or it might be that I was just too excited to bide. I did not wait to be summoned to the hall. I went to my wardrobe, and picked out the grandest silks and brocades there were in it. Thus arrayed like a Prince of Singers, I cradled my harp in my arms and stood at my door. The courtyard glowed lavender twilight behind me. My servant knew the way to the hall, that I was sure of, and knew my purpose there.

I followed a blue torch through dark halls. Quite out of character, my servant was chattering nervously, the torch bobbing with the words: "I don't know if it's now or not, sir; we haven't been called for. Of course, feasts happen all the time; if we wait, we wait. They'll get there eventually. I must say you look very nice—that style becomes you. I hope you won't be too warm, though. Oh, dear, there's no one about—is it Dancing Night again, so soon?"

No, it wasn't Dancing Night. There were Elves in the feasting hall: the winged ones were disporting themselves among the rafters. They looked like ornaments up there between the painted beams. Two of them glided down to us. Their frail wings gleamed like hard silver in the torchlight.

"Rhymer. The queen's Rhymer."

"Come to sing. Music."

"Make us music, Harper." Another one drifted down beside me. He was tall, with twisting lilac hair.

I shook my head. I had one song to sing tonight.

There was murmuring in the rafters. The shadows shifted over the floor, across our bodies and our upturned faces. The winged Elves had hold of the torches, and were flying around the ceiling with them. Their lazily beating wings did not even cause the light to waver; it burned in its eerie blue globes. The Elves' murmur turned to humming. It swooped and rose with their flight, with the approach and distance of the lights held in their hands. Their faces were grave and full of peace as they wove their dance of humming, wings and light.

Presently, servitors began to set up the tables. I recognized Ermine among them, but did not acknowledge her or any of them. They were looking at me, though, there where I should not be.

They covered the tables with linen, and garlanded them, and decked them with gold and silver dishes and branched candelabra. Theirs was as fine a dance, in its way, as the flyers' above them.

I stood at the center of the room as the Elvin court began trickling in. I stood, harp in my arms, and did not move as they walked around me, looking, curious but not surprised. Word had gone out that I was there.

Tall and dwarfish, jolly and wraithlike, grave and merry, they all found their places at the tables lining the hall. Last to come in were the folk of the high table, the stately and elegant Elves nearest the queen, who called her "sister," although they were not kin. Hunter wore red tonight, that perfectly matched his lips and brows, his hair dark as night against his clothes. On his arm, the queen shown like the sun of Earth in gold brocade, gold even in the blue torches' glow.

I did not look away. I watched steadily as they proceeded to the dais. It pleased the queen to call me a beauty; but before her Elvin companions I felt coarse and earthy, even my Elvin brocades so much cheap gaudery.

No other entertainment appeared. I was all of it. I waited, silent, as everyone sat, drank, began to pick at whatever was set before them. I could feel their eyes on me from all sides. And for a hall full of feasters, they were strangely hushed.

Hunter was looking very happy. I met his eyes once, twice, again, and read there pure delight—that, and the riddle. It was all I could do to keep from shouting out the answer then and there.

The queen was ignoring me. It didn't matter. She might do as she liked in public.

My body grew weary, waiting there standing in the hall. I hate to think of the mortal time that must have passed while the Elves ate and drank their fill. But a good minstrel knows how to judge his moment.

It came when the first course of the meal was over. Platters were being cleared away. The Elves were sufficiently sated now to heed me. I took a stool, rested my leg on it to hold the harp and began.

At the first note of harping the hall fell silent: no need to woo the audience tonight. I called on the power of my voice, and sent the first words of my song soaring rich and plaintive into every corner of the hall.

> *My love built me a bonny bower*
> *So sweetly set with the lily flower*
> *A finer bower you ne'er did see*
> *Than that my true love built for me.*

Wrapping myself entirely in the song, I resisted the urge to see how Hunter was taking it. Instead I turned Eleanor's story outward, giving it to the Elvin court as rich and full and clear as I could make it. Usually when I present a new song I'm nervous. In the hearing of others, it can sound stupid to me, all of its faults exposed to their imagined criticism. I've learned to ignore the feeling, but tonight I didn't have to. My song had a purpose beyond entertainment, beyond admiration, and I was not afraid.

> *The king stood fast, all in amaze*
> *So loud unto the dove he says:*
> *"Come, pretty bird, what means this rain*
> *This mourning for my servingman?"*

> *O, it was her mother's deadly spite*
> *For she sent thieves in the dark of the night*
> *Put her servants all to flight*
> *They broke her bower, they slew her knight.*

The dove told all of Eleanor's story again to the king, up to:

> *She cut her hair, she changed her name*
> *From Fair Eleanor to Sweet William*
> *Went to court to serve her king*
> *As the famous flower of servingmen.*

The song ended in a circle, its ending also its beginning. It is a device much favored by magical folk, as I know. I stopped there; I had taken Eleanor's story as far as I might. Its ending now depended on what happened next.

As I played the final notes, lightness took my spirits. The weight that was my love for the queen was still on me; but Hunter's weird was lifted. Almost merrily, I raised my eyes to the Elvin court.

Silently, they heard the song end, and just as silently now they drank, one and all, drank deep from the pitchers forbidden me.

Hunter was the first to speak. He toasted me with his golden goblet, and "Well riddled, Thomas," he said. He turned the goblet over. Red drink fell splashing to the floor below the dais.

At that the Queen of Elfland stood, and an angry queen was she. "Brother," she said, "that was ill done."

Hunter looked at her, one corner of his red mouth quirked in a smile. "Nevertheless, sister, it is done." And to me: "Thomas, you have guessed my riddle and may beg a boon. For the sweetness of your song alone you might have one gift of me, richly deserved and without any binding on you."

But I looked only at the queen, my mistress. Her beauty tonight was cold and pure as marble. I looked at her, and for the first time let my voice be heard speaking in that hall. "Lady," I said. I spoke to her alone: that was my weird, and not to be broken. "I will take no boon of the lord of the silver arrows. But for my service to you, let me ask one."

"Mortal man," she answered regally, "do not ask it."

"Please," I said to the queen my lover. "I must. You may refuse it if I have in any way displeased you; but I pray you do not deny me the pitcher at your right hand, and the drink that is in it."

The queen smiled. Her whole face was springtime to me. "Gladly you may have it," she said, and lifted the golden vessel. I came forward to take it.

But it was Hunter who took the pitcher from the queen's hands. "Rhymer," he said, "you have chosen ill. This is not the answer you seek."

And he turned the pitcher and poured more red drink out onto the floor.

All around me the Elves in the hall gasped. The liquid was trickling across the floor to my feet. Only the queen remained as she was, cool and stately; but her face was deadly white, her eyes dark.

"Brother," she said again, "and that was ill done."

"Nevertheless," he answered her, "it is done. The first cup was for your promise to me in the woods, that I may hunt the dove when it has failed in its quest. And the pitcher was for that harp you took from me, that you changed to give your Rhymer."

"Thomas." The queen leaned forward, looking down at me. My name, that she loved to use, she had never spoken before them all. "Thomas, you have had your boon of me. It is time you were away."

"Lady," I said, "that time is not yet."

"Thomas, the time is almost come that cannot be turned from."

"Lady, I will bide."

"Thomas," she said, "for the love I bear you, turn and go."

Even in the cold of danger, a great warmth welled in me. She did not order, but beseeched me, by words I would have paid dearly any time to hear from her lips. But for the sake of the dove, and my kinship with the King in the Wood, I must deny her.

"Lady," I said, "for the love I bear you, I cannot."

Slowly she straightened, and slowly turned. And she lifted her own cup. Her wrist glimmered white as she turned it over, and spilled it on the floor.

"Now, brother," she said to Hunter, "your challenge is met and answered, the players determined. Begin. But if you fail, know that my wrath shall be terrible on you."

"Then I have succeeded already," Hunter smiled—and in his place there rose a tongue of flame. It spoke in Hunter's own voice: "You chose the players yourself, sister; and by your own words you doomed them. Your latest reign has been marked by an . . . unnatural interest in things mortal. A fascination, perhaps, that is a weakness. They do not play by our rules; they don't even recognize the game when it is played. You know that; but do you know that they have rules of their own? I challenge only humbly to show you that, in the end, those mortal must betray you."

I stared, fascinated, at the man-sized flame burning nothing but air, flickering orange and red and blue with Hunter's words.

"We are not children to be lectured," the queen said. Her hair had come unbound; golden, it fell around her like a mantle, and waved in a wind none other felt. "Speak your words."

"I challenge only this, then: grant Thomas his true boon."

Do you remember the dares you took in childhood—the window you had to jump from, the old log over the ravine to walk across? And how your heart pounded, and you *knew* you were going to die, really going to die this time, but you had to do it because you couldn't give back the dare? Oh, the Elves were children—but no more so, I suppose, than our own knights who hurl down their gauntlets one to another, or our kings who wage war for their proud honor.

"Thomas," the queen said to me. She was calm now, composed and clearheaded as many people are in crisis, or at chess. "Can you name your true desire?"

The question caught me off guard. My true desire . . . It was love, her love, and it was music better and truer than anyone's, and to go home and be a whole man again, and more besides. To be the greatest in the land, wealthy and sought after . . . and to be ever great in minstrelsy, my name a legend, my songs remembered. Her voice spoke everything possible: I stood in the high court of Elfland, and she was sworn to grant me what I asked.

And a fine fool I should sound, asking for it. My errand here was for the murdered knight; those other things I would get of my own deserving, or not at all.

"I desire," I said, "to give a voice to the white dove, even as you gave his shape to the knight's spirit."

"Why, then, did you not first ask that of me, instead of the pitcher?"

"For fear you would refuse," I said. "The pitcher seemed a small thing to ask." It was half a lie. I had known better than to ask her for the dove's voice, because the thing might be impossible for her, by reason of the weird binding the knight. I do not know the ways of Elfland, but for a mortal king to promise a boon and then not grant it, even through no fault of his own, it is a grievous thing. I had hoped to avoid exactly this, what Hunter had forced me into.

"The ghost will speak only at great sacrifice to another of humankind," the Queen of Elfland said. "You know it must be fed on mortal blood, and much of it, more than one man can give and still live. Only then can your tale be told as you have rhymed it, your song sung."

I swallowed. My fingers were cold, clutching the harp. I was not prepared to die for the knight, his lady and my song. But the dare was on me, as well as on her; I had brought it on myself, thrice denying her warning. Still, I did not quite believe that I would die; that was no way for the story to end. No doom was yet pronounced.

I closed my eyes to think, blotting out the court, the gold, the flame, the beautiful and grotesque, the lights. She was giving me the choice. Was that honor in her, or was it punishing me for inciting the challenge? I thought, with a twinge of pain, No; the queen is moody, but always fair. It had begun as Hunter's challenge; it was Hunter's fault. She must know that. She is Queen over all Elfland. She must be good at the game.

And I was chosen as a player. Hunter chose me for my weakness; my lady for my strength. I must not fail her; my death would fail her, for then she would lose. And she must not lose the dove.

Better the dove than me, though. But better no one's blood at all. To sing the song as I have rhymed it. . . . Oh, I could think of other endings; but all too fanciful, and not, I felt, to the purpose. The dove had already begun to attract Eleanor's king to follow it; soon, soon it must have a voice to sing its tale. The dove must have a voice—

"Sister," the flame spoke, "your singer is silent."

"He remembers," said my queen, "the conditions laid on him, and the price of his silence in Elfland. He is not silent; he is cautious."

Like a body blow, the memory hit me hard. Behind my closed eyes, the woodland scene unfurled, and I wished I, too, had a cup to spill, for the queen's other promise in the woods.

She had just told me what to do. But it was mine to speak. Speak it I would, and try not to count the cost. For my own honor, and for the queen's; because fate and folly and Hunter had brought us from that point to this, and I must not fail her now. I felt sick with relief at escaping death, and cold at the thought of what I must yield up. But if this were to be my last feat of minstrelsy, it would be a grand one.

"Lady." I prepared to speak in the high noble style of my own land. And in my lush brocades, standing before the glittering Elvin court, for once I felt like a true prince: Earth's emissary, and no servant. "It were great pity that so fair a lady should lose any part of her desire, and that so mighty a sovereign compromise her will. Let us therefore choose another way, that the dove might speak and achieve his quest, and I yet may live. Have I your gracious permission to recall your own words, as expressed in that same wood where my lord took such offense?"

Somebody laughed. Mine was not the language of the Elvin court; it was of ours, and I did it well enough to entertain. A slow smile broke on the queen's face. "You have."

"Then let the dove take no unwelcome gifts from his living kindred to bring his own dead voice again; but freely let him have the gift of mine from me."

The Elf Queen flung out her arms, and laughed triumphantly. *"So speaks the tongue that cannot lie!"*

Hunter again stood glowering in Elvin form, looking sulky and perplexed. "Sister, why do you laugh? A compromise is hardly victory."

Still she chuckled. "Brother, true, you have not lost. I yield the Rhymer's voice to the challenge, and humble myself before your art and craft." But my mistress looked anything but humble, standing tall and proud and definitely amused. "I laugh for the gift the Rhymer has won for himself by this deed; and you have helped him to it."

"'The tongue that cannot lie'?" Hunter sneered. "I wonder if he will thank you for it."

I had no chance to ask, with the voice remaining to me, what they meant. My lady summoned the dove, and in he flew through the high hall. He came to rest on the head of my harp, where Hunter had once, many feasts ago, set the dove ornament.

"Friend," I said to it, "do not forget my words, or the voice is wasted."

"Friend," he answered, and my heart sank to hear his voice now, "you may be sure of it."

I had to bite the inside of my lip to preserve my dignity. It had happened faster than I was ready for.

The queen did not bid me stay and harp. I bowed to her, though not to Hunter, and turned and walked blindly out of the hall—but slowly, and with my head held very high.

One corridor was like another; all different, all the same to me. Finally I sat against a wall. No one was by. I lifted my harp, and played. The harp was sweet. I opened my mouth and made a sound like iron being dragged on gravel.

After my fit of tears I felt much calmer. I was horribly tired, and hunger had begun to gnaw me. How long had I been in the hall? How long had the challenge lasted?

I got to my feet, picked up my harp and began walking. Some places looked familiar—I thought I recognized a tapestry, an oriel window . . . once I even thought I'd found the queen's bedchamber, but when I pulled on the nymph doorhandle, the door opened on quite a different room. I kept going. The light was that of mid-morning now. When I heard the pleasant gurgle of water, I knew I had found my way home.

In my rooms, with the door shut behind me, for the first time since the feast I felt safe, bone-weary, but in safe harbor at last.

I set the ebony harp in the music room, and sat on a pile of cushions, too tired even to strip off a layer of brocade. When my servant brought me cheese and apples to eat, I accepted them gratefully. My servant said nothing, and I was glad.

I must have dozed for a while. When I awoke there were long afternoon shadows across the yard, and Hunter was standing at my feet.

"I am leaving," he said without preamble, "going on a journey for some little while." He wore a great sweeping cloak of black, the exact color of his hair. "I have come to pay my debts." I scrambled to my feet, poised to defend whatever might stand in need of it.

But Hunter made a dismissive gesture with his hands. "A debt of art, Rhymer. I cannot leave the world with an unfinished song; it would be shame upon me. Listen, then:

"When he heard the dove's tale, the king was filled with pity, but also with elation. He raced his horse back to the castle, and pulled up in the courtyard, all in a lathering foam. And when his chamberlain came out to give him a stirrup cup, the king picked Sweet William up onto his horse, and kissed his famous flower of servingmen full on the mouth. The court stood all amazed. But soon the case was made clear, and Eleanor was readily persuaded to stand revealed as a woman whose devotion to the king had more in it than loyalty. She and the king plighted their troth on the same day that her mother was burned for her sad cruelty."

Hunter shook back his hair, and turned from me. "And now," he said in a soft, unpleasant voice, "for my other debt. Come forward, my child."

There was no reason for my servant to comply. But the rattle of a key on the table showed that he had.

"You have no right," my servant said in a tiny breathy voice. "What I did didn't harm you."

"How do you know that?" Hunter snarled—really snarled, like an animal. I began edging closer to him. "No, Thomas," he said without turning around. "You will hurt yourself." I stopped, but still prepared to spring.

"Thomas," my servant said with desperate courage, "please go away."

"Thomas is going to stay and protect you," Hunter said. The ugly growl in his voice frightened me more than anything. "It's his new business, looking after people. He'll look after you—"

"My lord, *please*—"

"You knew about the dove, and how to make it speak. I don't mind that, it served my turn. But you made a mistake to let me see where your love lies now. . . ."

"*Get out!*" It was a frightened, cornered hiss at both of us. I took a step forward.

"If only you had stayed small." I wanted to hit Hunter, just to stop his awful voice—but, magic aside, he was too big for me to hope to bring him down. "You were charming when you were little. I tried to keep you so, but I haven't the knack. It was a mistake to take you to my bed for those few years of beauty you grew into then—I should have known you'd turn on me. Ugly like all the rest—"

"You might have asked the queen to help—" My servant was gasping with repressed sobs. "I begged you to—"

"The queen wanted none of your foulness by then. We thought it a mercy to hide you away here. . . . And see now how you repay us. Well, here's my debt to you."

Hunter lifted both his arms, his cloak flowing like night behind him. His hands moved as though he were weaving knots in the air. I waited another moment to see if he would offer any violence—and then I didn't have to.

There stood, visible, the hideous creature no elf could bear to look at: a woman, a mortal woman of some fifty years, who had betrayed Hunter by growing old. She was not fair to see: her hair was lank, her breasts fallen under their ragged covering, her skin no longer supple. None of the ravages of illness seemed to have touched her—but the sickness of defeat was in her rounded shoulders and woeful eyes.

I stared in perfect horror—to think they had done this to a mortal woman! And I hadn't known, had taken all that service with no idea. . . . I saw her raise her eyes to me—and saw, a moment too late, how she read the horror I showed.

With an awful cry of anguish, she ran from the room. I followed as far as the doorway and stopped. If I still had my voice, I would have used it despite all weirds, to call her back, and try to explain— Useless, my anger turned on Hunter. Voiceless, I could not charge him with the vile names he deserved, but I needed to hurt then as never in my life.

I slammed my fist into his belly—and found it circled with living flame. "Ha, ha," he laughed, a parody of laughter. "Harper, how will you harp? What voice will then be left to you?"

But the flame held no heat—like all of the artifice of Elfland. I hated him the more for having the magic to change his shape, but not to keep the girl her youth. Stubbornly, I thrust my other hand in, hoping to find some core that was Hunter, there in the center of the flame.

The fire was all around me—somehow I had stepped into it, although I felt nothing. "Looking for my name, Rhymer? If I tell it to you now, how will you speak it?"

I flailed in the flame like a scarecrow flapping in the wind, knowing I was ridiculous, hoping my rage alone would somehow harm him. I smelt burning, but my limbs were cool and intact.

"Bargain with me. What will you give me for my name, for the chance to do me ill? Seven more years in Elfland as my own? Seven years a fish in the flood, and I a kingfisher? Seven years a bird in the wood, and I a falcon? What's the word worth to you, Rhymer?"

He must be mad, to think I'd make any bargain with him. Human rage such as mine is so passing a thing, next to seven years of a man's life.

"Why are you not grateful, Rhymer? It was I who gave you back your rhymes, not your queen. She would eat you alive if she could, and leave nothing for even the Nameless to hunt. . . ."

Somehow, I found my way out of the flame that was Hunter. It burned still for a moment; then it went out. And Hunter was gone from the room.

I was terribly cold. I found I was naked. There was ash on the floor— my clothes had been burnt off of me. The flame had been real; but so was the queen's protection.

Despite the cold, I swam in the pool until my skin tingled.

When I woke again it was mid-morning. Ermine was rattling dishes. My servant never woke me with rattling.

But even Ermine was subdued, for Ermine. "You've done a wonderful thing, Rhymer," she said as she served me breakfast. "We didn't know mortals played that way. The queen and Flame have been at this longer than you've been alive—but she chose well in you, I must say."

Before, when speech had been mine to withhold, I hadn't minded my silence much—but now I felt wretched, unable to ask the only question I would have given much to have answered: what had become of the woman, my servant?

"Don't look so sad," Ermine tried to comfort me, "the queen lost but little in this challenge, really. You'll have your voice back at the end of your time, nice as ever, so you will. It might have been worse—if she had lost the dove, or lost you entire, Flame would be sitting sweetly now, isn't that how you folk say it? And if she showed herself a bit too fond of you, well, you never know, do you, with her? It might have been just for the sake of the game, everyone knew that." Not very comforting.

I found I didn't want to harp. My loss was too raw to turn to other sound as a half measure. I managed to think, Oh, come, Thomas, here you are a hero, sulking like a child; a victor, mourning as if your force had fallen on the field. I thought of the dove, working its magic singing my song in the world of men. I stood in the garden, looking at the fountain where the dove had first wept its tears of blood. Why blood? Why tears of blood? What bargain had the dead knight's spirit struck with the Queen of Elfland—and why had she granted him so much and so little?

Time, I thought wearily; time. Hunter had come to me to finish the story. Someday I must complete the song—it was too good not to keep—for when I returned to my own country. But when would that be? I couldn't count the nights, the meals; even the Dancing Nights were impossible to tell mortal time by, for I had missed some, while I knew that others had been held more than twice each year. How long must I still serve? Why could I not have my voice back as soon as the knight had gone to his rest? And what was "the tongue that cannot lie"?

I should have asked these questions before, while I still could. There was much I should have asked the queen: about time, about Elfland, about my servant, about myself. It hadn't seemed important then, when I lay in her arms in her bower, and made my songs in my fountain court.

I saw Ermine, reflected in the pool, coming up behind me. "You have to change your clothes," she said of my battered brocades; "these are no good anymore."

All the clothes I found now in my wardrobe were true green, elegant and simply cut. I put some on, and felt as if I wore the colors of some great house: the badge of Elfland. I was going to take my harp along with me, but Ermine told me not to, so I knew where we were going.

The queen's bower was empty. The roses and honeysuckle gave off their sweet perfume alone. I went to sit under them—and then I halted, for I had been wrong: there *was* someone there.

A woman slept among the flowers, a woman with long brown hair, dressed simply in green linen. I stood looking at her for a long time. Her mouth hung a little open, her fingers curled under her cheek like a child's. Her lined face was so still; but her chest rose and fell gently.

Did the woman love me? Was Hunter right? I remembered her touch in the hallway, the soothed nightmare—and all the careful, inobtrusive service, that I had accepted blindly because the effort, as well as the servant, were invisible.

I knelt down and kissed her cheek. Her eyelids fluttered open, and she looked at me hazily, as though I were part of a half-remembered dream. Still childlike, she reached up her arms to me, and I took her up and rocked her at my breast.

When I laid her down again among the roses, she looked up at me with her eyes full. "Thomas," she whispered. "I didn't think you'd come."

I looked down at her, saying nothing.

"I loved him," she said dreamily, as if to herself. "He didn't mean to hurt me. That's just the way they are. It's always been like that. When I came here as a child, I was his darling; and later on he did love me, for a while. I can't help what I've become, and he can't help what he is, can he?"

I shook my head.

"Perhaps it's different in the world of men."

Yes, I wanted to tell her, very different—and, no, it is not, not at all. It's just like that, the world of men. I took her hand and kissed it. I felt the touch of her other hand in my hair. "You are like him," she said, "in some ways. . . ."

"No." But no sound issued from my mouth.

"Am I very ugly, Thomas?"

I let my lips form the word, *No.*

"I knew you would not want me, though," she said with gentle dreaminess. "If I had him still, I would not want you. . . ."

Could she be beautiful again? I knew all the stories of magical transformations: the White Bear, the Wedding of Gawaine, Cupid and Psyche. . . . I bent down and kissed her lips, long and warm and soft, without desire.

Her eyes fluttered closed. A small smile played on her lips; she slept, and did not wake. I left her there, a plain woman of middle age, her outspread brown hair streaked with grey, sleeping among the roses.

I served my full seven years in Elfland, harping for the court and sleeping with its queen.

Soon after the challenge she sent for me. She opened the door to me herself, and spoke no word then, nor all that night, denying herself what was denied me. She could be kind when she wanted to be. For the remaining years, I made not a sound.

After the challenge, the Elves accorded me a kind of honor, treating me as kindly as they could, some even with respect. At the same time, they spoke more freely in my presence, as though I were a hound at their feet. Silent, ever silent, I listened to the words of the Elves, their riddles and their poems, quarrels and counsels, games and flirtations. The riddle of the King's Cup I knew now; but I pieced together more from their fragments, I think, than they intended; secrets of that other world, and its workings, knowledge not suited to a man in the world of men. I know who the King is now, and what his last battle; and if I weave that truth into songs, who will believe me?

In the queen's presence I learned patience, and to hold my temper. With even the illusion that words were weapons against her gone from me, I learned what it was to bear another's choices, and have none myself. It was she who chose the topics and let them go; and so I learned that my servant had indeed been a changeling, stolen by Elves and brought up by Hunter, and that since his departure she was "taken care of"; but how, and where, I could not learn, and was too proud to make a dumb show of asking. I learned, too, that the dove had succeeded in his quest, and was now a soul freed to Judgment, and that all with Eleanor had fallen out as Hunter had told me. But who that king had been, and where, I never learned.

The queen's body was a great solace to me; but even the sweetness of her flesh scarcely compensated for the loss of her conversation. It was company I had craved, I knew now, as much as I had craved her bed. Denied true companionship, I took the carnal for what it could offer. In the process I came to know her every mood and need, as a monk knows his letters. With her I could lose myself in a complex tangle of desire and fulfillment, intricate and well shaped as music. And she was gentle with me, loving, almost, for the sacrifice I had chosen, the game I had well played; harsh with me only when it pleased us.

My hair grew long, heavy and dark. The queen liked when it fell around us both like a curtain.

"My raven," she would say, reaching up and rippling it like cloth, "my darkness, my silky child, my night river," naming me with many names, as lovers do.

I touched her face, her hair, her lips, letting my hands speak for me. Touching her, my hands grew another sense, a deeper one beyond the daily touch that tells us if something be hot or cold, smooth or rough. Her body had a thousand textures, and each of them spoke to me.

"Thomas—" She caught my hands and kissed them, fingers and palms and the calluses where I harped. I slipped into her like fish through a stream, and found our way through light and darkness to a kind of resting-place for both of us.

After a while, the queen slid out from under me, leaving my skin chilly where sweat met the air.

"Come," she said, "Thomas, rise."

I dried myself with the silk sheet, and dressed in the green clothes that we had draped on a chair. She took my hand and led me to the door of her chamber; but when the door opened it was on a fair garden, an orchard whose seasons shifted even as I looked. . . .

"Oh," I said. "Oh, no."

"The voyage is done," the queen told me, taking both my hands and looking at me with dark eyes. "The road has come 'round to its beginning."

I fell to my knees in the soft spring grass, and kissed my lady's hands. I could hardly bear to look at her, to see what I was losing. But my time was done, and I must return to the world of men, as I had always meant to. Elfland was not my home, and the queen and her people not my people.

"Lady—" I began, and stopped, realizing that I had my voice again.

"Oh, Thomas," the queen sighed sadly. "You have kept faith with me, and I keep faith with you now. Remember me, when your feet touch Middle-Earth again; remember me, and do not forget me and my realm. I will remember you."

"Lady," I said, "you are my music, always."

But the Elf Queen smiled a rueful smile. "So you say now. But soon your true life will claim you, and these seven years pass as a dream you dreamt on Eildon bank; for you are not one of those who sickens and pines for fair Elfland on their return to the world of men. Before you go, though, I would reward you, Thomas."

I had imagined this moment before, and knew now what my desire was. "Sweet queen," I said, "I want one boon only, and that is that you permit me to take with me out of Elfland the mortal changeling that was my servant."

But the queen shook her head. "Oh, no, Thomas, that never can be."

"Lady, I will make her my charge," I said earnestly. "I will see that she is not alone on Earth, and does not go hungry or lost. . . ."

"Thomas, my Rhymer . . ." she answered me with pity, "the woman cannot leave Faery, though you ask it ever so sweetly. From childhood, she has eaten the food of Elfland. She cannot go back to your country." As I gazed at her in sorrow, she added, "But she has deserved well of me for her service. For these past years she has lain in a sleep of sweet dreams. And when, at last, she wakes, it will be to comfort, and to gentle care, until her days are ended."

"Thank you," I said. "I can ask no more."

"Nevertheless, you shall have my parting gift."

I started as the queen pulled an apple from a tree close by. "It's all right," she said; "you have earned it. From seven years of silence, your tongue has been bred to truth, and great truth. Take the fruit now, and eat it, and know the tongue that cannot lie."

I held the fruit in my hand. Its heady smell of wine and of carnations, with a bit of the green of summer mornings, attacked my senses so that I could barely form words. Nevertheless I joked, " 'The tongue that cannot lie'? Won't that be a bit awkward for anyone trying to do a little buying or selling? I should be hated of princes and merchants everywhere, and women with ugly hats."

The queen tried not to smile. "Refuse it if you will, Thomas. But you'll have wasted seven years of silence: it was for this I laid the ban on you to speak to none but me, that your words might store up power in Elfland. And for the great gift you gave the murdered knight, your gift of true speech is increased tenfold."

Still I held the fruit, and looked at it. You never could have mistaken it for an earthly apple.

"Did you think to return home unchanged? You, who have ridden the steed of Elfame, and waded the mortal river, and sat in the Oldest Orchard at dawn, with the Elf Queen combing your hair? And listened for seven years to the counsels of our court?"

"No," I said. "I am not who I was."

"I am, though." One hand brushed back her hair in an unthinking gesture, as though she hadn't meant to say this to me. "I am always who I was, and always who I will be, now and forever the same. I do not change. But you, you will always change, even when you know the future as I do. It is in your nature, as it is not in mine."

I took a step back from her sad beauty, and said what I never had dared to before: "Is that why you cannot love me? Because that would be change?"

The queen looked at me gravely. "There is no change in that, Thomas; none in the world."

I stared at her, wondering if I dared to understand what I wished to in those words.

"Now, do as I say," she snapped suddenly, "and eat."

I sank my teeth into the crisp white flesh. I don't remember really chewing or swallowing, just being engulfed in the smell and texture of the fruit. But when I was done, I was holding a very small applecore.

"Nothing happened," I said, because I had to say something.

"You may think that," she answered briskly, "until you know better," and walked off through the trees. I followed her, to find her white horse and my Mollie contentedly cropping grass under the branches.

We mounted side by side, and together we rode across the barren plain, and down into the cavern whose warm heart the mortal river runs through. Standing before the river was a man. He was looking into the flow, and didn't turn until we were nearly upon him.

I hadn't recognized him, for the slope of his shoulders was dejected as he gazed on that river. He straightened when he saw us, though, and I knew him then.

"Hail, Queen of Elfland," he said.

"Hail, King That Is to Come."

"Man of Earth," said the King, "I am glad to see you crossing the bourne. Greet them for me, sun and moon and leaf on the tree, when you set foot on Middle-Earth once more. Remember me, Rhymer, for we shall meet again."

"Brother," I said, "I will."

We left him standing by the river he could no longer cross, the mortal river that whispered of warmth and old, old battles. And now I heard the songs of all of them, all the songs that ever were sung by the men and women of my own land; heard and understood and forgot them in that journey of days and years and heartbeats.

As we began to climb out of the cavern, a breath of chilly air drifted down the dark tunnel toward us. I gasped as its unexpected familiarity cut into my senses.

It was the smell of earth.

PART III

MEG

He has gotten a coat of the even cloth,
And a pair of shoes of velvet green,
And till seven years were gane and past
True Thomas on earth was never seen.

—*Trad. (Child ballad no. 37)*

I DON'T LIKE anyone to know that my hearing isn't as good as it used to be, but it's true for all that. There are other ways for a body to keep track of matters, though, and those I know. The start of the old dog by the fire, cautious but not alarmed as he made his way to the door, told me a friend was there, just before the knocking grew loud enough for me to hear it.

Hasty as I could I wiped the baking flour from off my hands and went to unbar the door. There've been rough men about lately, and you can't be too careful these days.

Well, I swung back the bolt, and there was a sight I never believed I'd see: our Tom, Thomas the Rhymer, dressed all like a prince in green velvet, standing there hale and sound. Old fool that I am, my eyes filled with tears.

"Tom," I said, "oh, Tom, we all thought you were dead!"

Without a word, he opened his arms to me. I'd forgotten how tall he was! The velvet against my cheek smelled sweetly of herbs I couldn't name. And he was warm as any living wight, and his heart beat quickly under my cheek.

At last I pulled from his embrace. But he held onto me at arm's length, staring at me. And I gazed back as hard: he looked strangely dazzled; unworldly, even, despite his rich attire. And Thomas, that fountain of misdirection and excuses, had spoken no word since he came in. He only held me, inspecting me as if I were a wee lass being dressed for church, or some fine vessel for a king. I thought of my flour-smudged face, my wispy hair and much-darned smock, and wondered at it.

"Meg," he blurted out at last, "how beautiful you look!"

"Well, there it is! You disappear into the hills without a word for years, and then you think you can win your way back into my graces with a little flattery."

But his look was ever fixed and ever fond, as though he gazed on the world's treasures.

"Oh, aye, a rare beauty," I joked, trying to ease some of the strange hunger from his face; "maybe I should put a little more flour on my nose! Is that the fashion these days?"

But he just looked confused, poor boy. "There," I said more kindly. There was more amiss than his well-fed, well-dressed form made appear. "I'm only teasing—" and imagine the Rhymer without a saucy answer! "The truth is, I'm bread-baking today. It's just oat bread—"

I feared that I would never stop babbling. He was so strangely silent, so dazed and hungry. For the first time I wondered if he might be a spirit indeed, some sending of the Enemy. It would account for much. He'd not said where he'd been—said barely anything. And he looked, I saw it now, not just healthy, but unchanged, as though my memory of young Thomas had walked out of the hills. But the dog at our feet, old Tray, was feebly wagging his tail. Dogs shy from spirits. Besides, we had rowan over the door against that sort of thing. No, Tom was human enough—hadn't I felt his heart beat myself? But he'd seen some strange adventures, and traveled harder than it looked. Well, the story would come out in his own time. So I determined to speak to him as I would anyone. He'd come from whatever, wherever, or castle or hill, to me, and me he should have as ever was.

"We'll eat plain oats, but you can help knead if you'd like, you've come just in time for it. Not in those fine clothes, though—they should be folded and put away."

He looked down, as if he was noticing his splendor for the first time. "Oh," he said. "I suppose so."

He was always a worldly man; he knew what velvet was. (I'd never seen so much of it on one body in my life!) I thought to myself, Go easy, go easy and we'll uncover the trouble. So I chattered on, "I've kept some of your clothes, you see, in the oak chest. Laugh if you like, but I couldn't bear to part with them all at once. . . . Your blue cloak's gone, though; I gave it last Yule to Bran the Beggar, times being so hard as they were. . . ."

"Why should I laugh?" he says. "I didn't say when I'd be back, did I? I suppose . . . I suppose I've been gone a while?"

I felt cold, to hear him speak it so. "It's full seven years, my heart," I answered him, "since you walked out into the Eildon Hills and never returned; seven long years almost to this very day."

"Full seven years," he repeated. "Not seven days? Seven weeks? She said she'd keep faith with me, but she doesn't really understand time . . . I was hoping maybe it had been less."

" 'She said . . .' " I didn't want to ask it, but I must: "Tom, dear one, wherever have you been?"

He stood stroking the green velvet with his thumb, and then looked up at me with a bit of his old hard-edged glint. "Oh, Meg; where do people usually disappear to for seven years?"

That was the Thomas I remembered, too proud to say what needed to be said, hiding it behind a veil of words. It made me wonder if he wasn't acting the whole fey scene, to hide some less enchanting truth.

"Oh, come now!" I exclaimed. And then I wished that I could take the words back; for there was no laughter on his face.

"No," he said. "I'm not joking. Look at me."

I looked at him leaning against my table at the other end of the room. "I see you've gotten a fine growth of hair," I said tartly; for it never did do with the Rhymer to let him get high-handed on you. "Stop messing with that flour, Thomas, and come here where I can see you."

He stood before me, the light from the window full on his face. There was no mistaking what I saw, but I reached up and touched his supple skin with my fingers. "They could be seven days on you."

He stilled my hands with his. "Ah. You see it. Then it's true. I suppose I'm glad. There was no knowing, in that place, what was real and what was not—if anything was." He turned from me, shy of being looked at, began to pace the room, randomly stopping to touch the most common things: a spoon, the table, a wisp of straw. "She said it would all come to seem like a dream, but I thought, how could it, when I lived every moment of it? But coming back here, smelling the old leaves on the hillside, and seeing you with your worn hands and the table with the flour fallen in the cracks . . . it makes the other seem unreal, as though it never happened —no, as though it never *should* have happened."

"Maybe it shouldn't," I said. He'd always been quick and fanciful; whatever had happened, now the Rhymer had the beginnings of a poet's tongue of wisdom in him. "But what's done is done. Come, sit you down. I'm sure you could use to eat something."

I don't know why my saying that should make him laugh. He sat, and then half started up again. "Shouldn't I get out of these ridiculous clothes first?"

"They're very fine clothes," I chided him, "and they suit you wondrous well. Why don't you keep them on just long enough to show Gavin—his old eyes'll pop out of his head!"

"Oh, God," Tom breathed in relief. "Then he isn't dead. I thought— when you didn't say anything—I was afraid, maybe he was . . ."

"The Good Lady didn't give you eyes of wood, did she?" I said, taking out cheese and barley cakes and apples for him the while. "Why, there's his staff, plain to see, and there a bit of basket he's working on, that I haven't the skill for; and there one muddy old boot of his wanting cob-bling. . . ." But even as I spoke, I wondered, How different would it be if he were gone? Wouldn't the old staff still be there? And would I have the heart to move the basket?

I set the dish down hard. Of course I would. Things exist in the world for the use of folk, not to serve as cold memorials. Everything would be different if Gavin were gone. Thomas might even have come back to an empty house. . . .

"Meg," he said, "I'm sorry. Of course they would be."

"Sorry for what?" I snapped unfairly. I'm not as surly an old besom as

Gavin is, but I don't expect my thoughts to be read. "You'll be the sorrier if you don't eat that food, my boy."

Obedient, he began cutting the apple up. But he sliced it into little tiny pieces, as if he wasn't really interested.

He must have heard Gavin coming down the hill before I did. Thomas squared his shoulders, and brushed off his knees and stopped all pretense of eating.

Gavin was whistling "Haste to the Wedding," one of Tom's old tunes. When he opened the door, he must not have seen Thomas, his eyes being unaccustomed to the dim light indoors. "Maggie," my goodman said to me, "I thought you made sure to keep the house barred up when you're here alone."

"I do." I could feel the Rhymer's eyes on the both of us. "Company came."

"Oh?" Gavin turned in the direction I nodded, and stopped frozen. He said softly, like he was approaching some wild creature of the hills, "Thomas, lad, is that you?"

"None other." Thomas sat still, as if he was afraid to move. He always did take Gavin too seriously.

My man drew a little nearer. "My," he said as his eyes adjusted to the light; "where'd you get that fine set of clothes?"

"In Elfland," Tom answered absently—and then stopped, as though he hadn't meant to say it at all.

I saw Gavin draw back, a little hurt. "Now," he said sternly, "you've no cause to be answering me like that." He stood, silent and patient and hurt, in that calm way that I love in him, though some people take it for dullness.

Thomas didn't take it so. "I know I haven't. I'm sorry, Gavin." He didn't try to defend himself. I held my peace; it was best to let the two of them have it out.

"Well," Gavin said bluffly, "the clothes don't matter. For all I know, they *could* come from Elfland, they're that fine on you. But you've been gone a long time—you must have a lot to tell us. You know, we thought—"

"Yes," he said tensely. "I know you did. Meg told me. I'm sorry for that, too. If there'd been any way to tell you, I would have."

"Well, the years haven't treated you badly." Gavin was still a little nettled at the way Thomas was fobbing him off. It's not every day a man comes back from the dead; you'd think he'd have the courtesy to fill you in on a few details. Gavin hung his cloak to air, and sat down by the fire to warm his hands.

"Thank you," said Thomas stiffly. He nibbled at his apple.

"It was a woman, was it?"—Gavin, trying to be casual, gruff disapproval in his voice.

"Yes. It was a woman."

"Beautiful, then?"

"Very beautiful."

"And rich."

"Yes."

"Whyever did you leave her, then?"

"I wanted to come home," Tom said softly.

"Home," says Gavin, lightly scratching his pate. "She was someone else's, then?"

"I won back," Tom said a little desperately. "I had to win my way back to you."

But my Gavin, once he's taken a notion in his head, it's hard to shake it. He'd be on about Tom's women till Doomsday if I didn't stop them now, so, "Gavin," I intruded, "let the boy alone now." And, "Tom, you'll want to be changing your clothes. Out back, go." I pulled some of his old things from the oak chest, and shoved them at him, and shoved him out the door.

Gavin just sat staring after him. "Well!" he said. "Well."

I spoke soft and quick, for the Rhymer not to hear: "I know it rubs against the grain, my heart, but try to give him a little time. You know Thomas as well as I do—words are meat and drink to him. The story'll come out if we wait."

"It's not the story," Gavin said a little sadly, "but where's he been all this while?"

"Gavin," I said, holding onto his hand as though mine could lend him trust, "he says he's been in Elfland."

"To you, too, he said that?" I nodded. "But that's not—"

"But it is. It could be."

"Then the lady . . ." Gavin breathed. Suddenly he started up. There were hoofbeats on the hillside. My heart jumped; it must be raiders. There'd been men without enough land in the region all summer, looking to relieve each other of goods, and not above replenishing their store along the way. Now, I'd let most of the hens run free—it was troublous to collect their eggs, but at least I kept the hens—and we'd sheep to spare, if they weren't too hungry.

We got to the door to see an armed troop of men coming down on the croft. Thomas was already there, still in his green velvet, standing waiting for them without a weapon.

"Thomas," I said, my throat strangely tight, "come inside, and quickly. Those are lawless men—they'll take what they want and go. Get inside!"

"Bar the door," Thomas said, without turning 'round, "and wait for me within."

But we stood where we were, Gavin's hand tight on his heavy staff.

The leader of the force reined up before the Rhymer. He was a great, black-bearded man of middle age, riding at the head of no more than ten horsemen, all well armed.

"What's this?" he cries. "A prince of the hills, or a herald, or a poet?"

"All of those things," said the minstrel pleasantly, "and more besides." He did not move, but suddenly his voice seemed to be coming from a much larger man: "Woe unto you, Blackwell, for your reiving will never thrive, and you'll be dead ere you see Carlisle. And your young son, that sits on his nurse's knee, is the chief of all your kin: for only his sons will bear your name."

The leader's face was the color of cheese. If this was indeed the great Blackwell, a sorry man was he.

"Out upon you, hedge-witch! And turn your curses from me."

Thomas said, "Turn your horse and go your ways. We will not see your face again this side of Tweed Water. So speaks the tongue that cannot lie."

The raider raised his leather-gloved hand, and the whole host wheeled and turned back up the hill. The Rhymer stood there watching until they were gone from view.

"That was easy," he said lightly to us. "That was absurdly easy." But his face was white, his hands unsteady. He brushed aside my offer of an arm to lean on. "It's all right," he said. "If I have to be afraid, better now than before *them.*"

Like anyone who's just had a bad fright, he was become all motion and excitement, passing back and forth across the yard that he had just defended with his words alone.

Gavin, all curiosity now—for how he loves a wonder!—said, "Why didn't you tell us you were become a seer?"

"I didn't know," Tom said, cheerful with relief. "I recognized Blackwell, you see, saw him once when he came to Roxburgh to try and cut a deal. What a bully!"

"But the rest . . . ?"

"Oh, that's all true. He's on his way to Carlisle to meet up with someone; but that horse of his will fall and throw him before he gets there."

"How do you—"

Thomas looked at us like an innocent child. "I just know."

" 'So speaks the tongue that cannot lie.' " I repeated his words. "Well!

You're going to be something to have around. Planning to stay long, are you?"

"I . . . don't know."

"You're welcome," Gavin said. "And not just 'cause you saved me a few sheep."

Tom grinned at him. "Thank you. I would have done that anyway, just to see the look on his face!"

"Come inside," I scolded, "it's colder than you think. And *will* you change those clothes—it makes me sure I'm going to spill something, just looking at them!"

Thomas changed the clothes. His old suit of homespun brown and grey looked hopelessly dingy on him; but he wore it like his own skin: his body relaxed a little, and some of the glamour seemed to go out of him. It was a relief to me. I folded up the velvets, and laid them in the bottom of the oak chest.

Gavin made great to-do over how he must bide indoors to find and mend an old tar-box, while the neighbors' boy, Tod, minded the sheep.

But Thomas was not talkative. He rolled up his sleeves and kneaded bread, and inquired politely about local matters. He was surprised to hear that reivers were abroad—the English treaty had broken down, and the earl's soldiery that would normally protect these hills were off on the king's business, as we understood it. Tom's true ignorance of all this did as much to convince me of where he'd been as any words might: I couldn't imagine the Rhymer living in this world and not following the affairs of the great ones.

Every look, every touch, showed him to be savoring the world around him. It unsettled me a little, thinking of where he must have been to find the familiar so strange. And, oh, the stories he must have of the things he'd seen! I longed to hear of that strangeness, as he seemed to long for the familiar; but at the same time I enjoyed the chance to see my house, my world through his eyes, fresh from a land where they say the sun never rises nor sets. So the old was made new again.

As the two of us worked the bread, he said, "This is good," smelling the warmth already beginning to rise from the dough in his hands. "You don't know how good—to be making something, something real, with a hot fire burning and real people beside me. . . ." He laughed. "I'm not even sure of the last time my hands were dirty!"

From time to time, when he forgot, he would begin a little snatch of a song to himself. Gavin and I would stop, thinking, *The music of Elfland, maybe*— But usually it proved a tune we knew. And our attention would dry up his singing. Even Gavin felt it, and held his peace. One time, though, it was a new song: something about a girl dressing as a serv-ingman, with a strange tune. When Tom stopped, Gavin asked, "What was that one, lad?"

"A song I wrote," Thomas answered shortly.

"It's lovely," I said. "A new song?"

"I don't know. New enough. It was the last one I sang in the—" He broke off the sentence, and started punching dough like a traitor's face.

"In the what?" Gavin asked. Strong feelings always made him jumpy.

"In the hall. Where I was."

It was questions that the Rhymer didn't like. I was beginning to have my thoughts about that, and not pleasant ones, they were.

Gavin tried another track. "You know, your gypsy friend was by. He came a couple of times, asking for you—wouldn't believe we didn't know where you'd gone to. Threatened to bring the law down on us for making off with you, if you can believe that!" Thomas smiled. "And when *that* didn't serve, offered us a silver ring to tell him where you were, or even to get word to you." Gavin turned to me. "We've still got that somewhere, haven't we?"

"Nothing would serve Bevis but that he leave the ring here with us," I explained. "Said he'd be back for word of you, next spring. But that was, what, three years ago? four?"

"Four," Gavin said. "It was the winter Billie Crauder broke his leg."

"And he never did come." I wiped my hands, and went and poked around in our hidey hole in the chimney nook, a small opening built twisty in the stone, until I brought out the little cloth-wrapped packet.

Time had tarnished the silver ring. "Hell's blight." Thomas spoke the moment he took it in his hand. "This was from Lilias Drummond's hand. She gave it unhappy, ill, pregnant with her fourth child, thinking Errol didn't love her, that her family had me killed. . . ." He looked up sud-denly, ashy-faced, his hand clenched around the ring. "She's dead."

I pried the ring out of his fingers, stuffed it quickly in my apron pocket. "Are you sure?" I asked, to get the stricken man to say something.

"Of course I'm sure. In childbirth. A girl. *Damn* Bevis!"

"He didn't know," I said, surprised to find myself defending the gypsy. "He was trying to help her."

"Well, he knows now. No wonder he didn't come back; no need, with Lilias gone. Why didn't he believe it when you told him I was missing?" Thomas demanded suddenly.

"It was the harp," I confessed. "He saw your harp here first time he came. He thought that meant you were nearby. And then the second time, when it was still here and we wouldn't sell it—"

"Not but what *I* told him we'd sold it!" Gavin growled. "But the rogue wouldn't take my word . . ."

"Because you're honest," I had to say, "he saw the lie. But, yes, Tom, it's here. I've kept it wrapped up against cold and damp for you."

I'd thought for so long how Tom would laugh at me: it was a daft thing to do, keeping the harp no one could play, just to have it around the house. But his face was avid with longing.

"I'll get it for you, if you'd like," I said casually, to counterbalance that fierce look of desire. "The bread's to rise, now."

"Would you, Meg?" Thomas asked with careful restraint. "I'd like that, please."

I climbed up to the storage loft, my pocket with Lilias Drummond's ring knocking against my knee. Tom reached up to take the harp from my arms, like it was a small child; only then did he help me down the ladder.

Carefully he unwrapped the harp from its layers of oiled cloth, peeling them back like rose petals. He held it for a moment on his lap, his eyes shut, savoring the familiarity of its weight and shape. Then he raised his hands and began to play.

The sound was horrible: slack and brittle strings harsh with discord. Thomas jumped to his feet, holding the harp white-knuckled out in front of him, as though it had attacked him and might again.

"Out of tune!" he cried furiously. "The damned thing's out of tune!"

"Haven't you got a harp key about you?" Gavin asked sensibly.

The harper's eyes flashed. "Of course not! I haven't needed one for years!"

It cut me to the heart to see him cursing the harp he had loved. I wanted to chastise him, but I held my peace; he'd have to learn.

He raised the instrument over his head, knowing no other target for his anger. I put a hand out to warn back Gavin.

Suddenly Thomas turned his head, looking out past the windows and into the hills. "Not now," he said, "why now?" We sat, frozen. He looked at us. "You like it, do you? Or can't you hear it?" he asked, the edge of anger still in his voice.

"Hear what? No, nothing."

"The horns of Elfland. The riders are coursing something down." He tilted his head, listening. "Some poor soul, maybe." It came to me then, the sound of wind in the heather, I thought it was. "Of course it's not really music. And it's not as good as mine," he added, smugly but absently, still straining to hear.

"Tom, dear," I said, rising to brush the hair back from his wild face, "you're dazzled. Give me the harp, now, and sit."

He shook his head. "There's nothing you can do."

Gavin looked grim. "I'll bar the doors. They'll not have you a second time."

"You don't understand . . . it's with me still. I've left, but the time is so different. . . . Oh, Meg"—he took my face in his hands, but I doubt he saw me—"Meg, I had a fountain, and a courtyard filled with flowers . . . and such clothes and horses and crystal and lights as you never saw. . . ."

"That's done." I gripped his hands. "That's done now. Stay with us."

"Meg," he asked, "Gavin, do you really not mind if I stay here for a while?"

Gavin looked at me. My eyes pricked with tears like a silly girl's. It was so unlike Thomas to ask anything in that diffident tone—it made me realize that I would never have back the Rhymer who'd left the house seven years ago. It was foolish to go on treating him as if he was the same. And his defenselessness touched me. Where once I had to cut, sharp, at his own net of self-protection, now I must be gentle for his lack of it.

"I've always wanted you to stay," I said—and was glad to see that the man who spoke only truth now knew truth when it was offered him.

Thomas sat after supper for an hour and more, doggedly tuning his harp. It was painful to hear; and it never did tune to his satisfaction well enough to play. We were relieved when at last he took blankets and went to sleep in his old place by the fire.

Snuggled tight in our own bed, Gavin whispered to me, "Do you think he's mad?"

I kicked him, it made me so angry. "What good do you suppose it'll do," I hissed, "to think that he is?"

"None, I guess, you harridan."

"None in the world, Gavin Big-Mouth. At least you've got the wit to realize he's not lying to us a-purpose."

"No, he'd never give out such a tale if he were, he's too proud. Is it true, then? Has he been to Elfland?"

"Bless your five wits, I'm sure I don't know! Ask *him!*" Thoroughly worn out with the pair of them, I rolled over and went to sleep. I never did tell Gavin about the changelessness of Thomas's face. I doubt he ever noticed on his own.

Next morning, Thomas looked more human: his hair was tangled, his eyes were crusty, and he needed to shave. He stumbled out to the stream shortly after I got up, and came back in shivering.

"Frost still on the grass," he said, toweling his head dry. "Looks beautiful. Why is it so damned *cold* here?"

"Frost," Gavin said tersely.

"Oh." Thomas blinked. "Right. Listen, I wanted to say to you both how sorry I am that yesterday was so—"

"Yesterday," I said, plunking a bowl of oat porridge in front of him, "you already apologized more than you ever have in your life. If you do it once more, you're going to get a face full of oatmeal."

"I'm sor— All right." He ate his porridge.

"I'm nearly thirty," he said suddenly, towards the bottom of the bowl. "Isn't that strange?"

"Very," I said drily. "What keeps your boyish beauty fresh?"

"It was a spel— Oh. Damn. I wish I'd stop that."

"I'll stop it. No more questions."

"Don't bother," he said glumly. "No need for *you* to change, too." He shivered again; he really was unused to the chill, and it was only autumn yet. I put a little more peat on the fire; we'd have to see about getting him more warm clothes.

He believed he'd been in Elfland, although he'd stopped trying to tell us so. Wherever he'd been, it had changed him. For myself, I inclined to believe him, and only tried not to think on the service he had done there. But Gavin took the changes in Thomas less easily—they were almost harder on my goodman than on the Rhymer himself. After all, Tom'd had seven years to grow into them. But Gavin likes to understand things once, and then keep them that way. So he couldn't help wondering if it was all some story of the Rhymer's, covering some prank, as he'd done of old. And if Tom had returned the glib lad who left us, I own I might have thought the same.

Gavin is a good man, but not always gentle. And so he would pick at Thomas as a child picks at a scab, knowing he shouldn't, knowing there'll be pain, but unable to resist—maybe hoping to find something interesting underneath. Oh, I could have kept it in check with chiding; but I've learned over the years that I can't control everything around me, and, more important, that there are some things that need to work themselves out. It hurt him, you see, to think that Tom might still try to deceive us.

It was a gloomy day, with promise of winter in the air. We'd been all three indoors all morn, Gavin at the loom, Thomas tormenting his poor harp with imperfect sound, until even I wished he'd give it over. Suddenly Gavin knocked the shuttle home and stood up.

"Come, lad. There's still time to make the Silver Cock and back before nightfall. I could use a dram and some society."

Well, two-three times a year the spirit took Gavin to go a-taverning.

Probably as well, now. But, "I'll stay," says Tom softly, so I could barely hear him.

"Never a whit!" booms Gavin with forced cheer. "Don't you want to see what's new in the world?"

"No."

"Whyever not?"

"Because I— Oh, leave it, Gavin! Why can't you leave me alone?"

Gavin flung back the bolt on the door. "Because you're a man," he said, "not some puling changeling. Now act like one."

But with his cloudy eyes and floating hair, the Rhymer looked more Elf than man. He turned his eyes on Gavin, standing stocky by the door. "I'm a seer," he said. "What kind of a man is that?"

"Fine." Gavin was uncompromising. "You're a man with a bit of extra knowledge."

"Oh, is that all?" Thomas asked wildly, like the boy he was when he first came to us. "Ask me something. Anything to come. I'll answer truly."

"I don't want to know about that. I want to know where you've been, and with who, and why."

There it was: the first time since he came we'd really challenged him directly. And we were going to get our answer, I could see by the tensing of his hands.

"I've been with the Queen of Elfland, Gavin. For seven years, on account of one kiss she had of me. I rode with her Under the Hill, and there I served her seven years, at bed and at board. She bound me to service, and to silence, until she set me free at last with the gift of true speech, and so you see me now."

"Fine." Gavin was breathing hard through his nose. "And if I call you liar?"

Thomas flung up one hand, as though he'd been struck. But he forced himself to answer clearly, "Then there's nothing I can do."

"You can tell me the true story, boy."

Thomas drew a deep breath. "Right. Fine. I was with the—with the Queen of—Elfland—I was—" He whirled violently. "I've told you the true story! It's all I can do; I can't lie even when I want to. Don't you think it would be easier for me to make you a tale you'd swallow more easily than truth? Listen to me—look at me—old fool, there's nothing else *in* me but truth!"

Gavin stood where he was, not turning a hair. "Then I'm an old fool, am I?"

"No." Thomas dropped his head. "I'm sorry, Gavin, you're not. Of course you're not."

"But you can only speak the truth?"

"I—*thought* you were an old . . ." Thomas's shoulders started to shake, whether with weeping or laughter I couldn't say, and I'm not even sure he could. "I can still have an opinion, I hope!"

"I just wanted to get a few things straight," my goodman said mildly. He came forward, put one rough hand on the Rhymer's shoulder. "You're a man, all right, Thomas. You're a man who's just lost his temper. Have a drink."

They unsealed the best whiskey, the two of them.

Thomas drank deep. "I don't know if this will help or not." He was still shaky. "Maybe I can lie only in my cups."

"You can lie whenever you want to," I said, scraping flour off the table. "Just put your mind to it."

"We'll see. Maybe I only need to get the hang of it again."

But he didn't get the hang of it that day, nor yet the next. Every question seemed to take him unawares; and if he wasn't careful, he'd answer them all, from "Where did I put my knitting?" to "Will it rain, do you think?" He was right, too.

We kept him there with us for days, learning to know him while he learned again how to know the world. He had forgotten the strangest things: what to wear when it was cold, where I kept the firewood, how to call the dog and pick up a pot hot from the fire without burning his hand. But he had learned how to be a quiet companion, even how to listen, so that I found myself telling him things I would never have dreamed of before; and he could do bird calls perfectly, and tell the weather, and find mushrooms in the woods.

Slowly and patiently, he was relearning the use of his mortal harp. He still cursed softly over it, but with an undertone of affection. He began to play for us, sometimes, when we were working in the house—familiar tunes mixed with very strange ones, so that I wondered if he even knew which were mortal, and which of Faery. Of course, it was all music to him.

He never asked about Elspeth—as though he knew he was not ready to do anything about that sad abandonment, needing still to find himself—and being, as most men are about women they've carelessly hurt, a coward in the matter. I knew that she would come, like bitter winter, like the storm clouds rolling to us dark across the hills.

It was a cloudy autumn day that the Rhymer went out on his own to walk in the hills. Of course he'd been out with me, and helping Gavin with the sheep—but it made me powerfully uneasy to let him go alone, after what had happened years ago in the Eildon Hills. When he wasn't looking,

I stuck a bit of rowan bound with red wool in his pocket; it's as potent a charm as any against Faery. I told myself nothing could harm him now; he knew the earth in a way he never had before, and we had bound him to us as nearly as we dared.

I was counting out warp threads for the big loom when a familiar knock let me know there was company come. Elspeth knew I needed to hear it loud.

Her face was scrubbed red by the wind on the hillside; she'd walked a few good miles to get here, but that was nothing unusual for her. She'd brought a couple of duck eggs for a gift; but I saw she also had her knitting, and was hoping to stay for a morning's gossip such as we often enjoyed.

"Come in out of the cold and sit you down," I said, getting her tea, taking her cloak, all the while looking to see if evidence of Tom was about. I didn't know how soon he'd be back. I couldn't be in too much of a hurry to shoo her away, or she'd know something was amiss.

"I thought I'd help you while I'm here," she said, "but warping that loom's something I never could do—I always get tangled up in the counting!"

"Never you mind," I said. "It can wait, while you let me know how you are."

She plumped herself down on the settle, and took out her knitting decisively. "Awful, thank you. Same as ever. They don't know I'm gone yet—we'll know when they do, you'll be able to hear the howls of rage all the way from the Ridge."

"You'll want to hurry back, then . . ." I said weakly.

"I will *not* want to hurry back. Let them howl. Maybe they'll scare away reivers."

I tried to see her as Thomas would see her, seven years changed. The girlish roundness was gone from her face: she was a handsome woman, but a spare one, with weathered skin taut across her high cheekbones, and a narrow, pointed chin. Her hands always looked chapped, even in summer. Her eyes were still far too expressive for her own good, but her mouth was often a thin, tight line. Elspeth's wild bush of tawny hair was darkening with age; she kept it bound up now.

"What do they want you for?" I asked.

"Stirring the dye pot, today. The smell makes me sick."

"Nobody likes it. . . ."

"But I'm the one who gets to do it! And if I object, they say I'm lucky to be there at all. . . ."

"Elspeth—" I leaned forward and put my hand on her thin wrist, halting her vicious click of the needles. "Why don't you go back to your brother's, where at least you have some respect?"

"I won't be a burden to Iain and his brood. I told you that when I married four years past."

"You were more of a help to Iain than you are to Jack's people on the Ridge."

"They get"—she paused to break a piece of yarn with her teeth—"what they deserve."

Now seemed the time to tell all that I'd long been thinking but never dared say to this proud, lonely woman: "You enjoy making them angry with you—hurting yourself at the same time—it's not right, and you know it. You're throwing your life away for pride—"

"I've nowhere else to throw it," she said pleasantly. "The world is a dull place, and full of toil. Do you think I should run off and follow the soldiers?"

I sat back. "If you want to do it, I'm sure there'll be no stopping you."

"Dear Meg!" She smiled one of her cold, dry smiles at me; a smile of the mouth, not of the eyes. "I know what that sniff means. It's feared the country 'round. I'm sure I deserve it"—at last the smile reached her eyes —"but please don't scold. Tell me how Gavin is; tell me a story; tell me anything!"

"Anything but advice. Very well. I should tell you we're thinking it's time we sold Thomas's harp."

She stiffened. "No. You can't do that."

"Why not?" The Devil's own grim mischief rose in me. "He's seven years gone; he must be dead, or never coming back."

"But if he did— If he did come, he'd surely want it."

"If by some chance he does come, it's not the harp that'll bring him."

"But it isn't yours to sell!"

"Well, whose, then?" I sighed. "And don't you think it should be played? It isn't right it should sit idle, not when the beauty of it has warmed so many cold nights. . . ."

For a moment she looked as though she might break. I wished that she would, that I might hold her in my arms and let her weep her fill. I saw the memory of those nights fill her face, and fade, like a fire, underfed, dying out. "I know." She sat looking at her idle hands. "I do know. It makes no sense to keep it. Of course you must do as you like."

Almost I told her then, to feed the flame alive—but the truth is, I was afraid to. He'd not yet said a word about her, see—and neither of them was the same as the young pair who'd loved in their singular way, years back. There was no telling what either of them would do now.

I promised myself I'd tell him she'd been by, though. It was time he faced up to that.

"I had a dream," she said, not looking at me, "five nights past. I saw him walking down the hill to you, dressed in green, without a harp or any thing. I only saw his back, but it was him."

"You shouldn't think of it," I said, feeling suddenly old, and useless. "Dear child," I spoke out from the heart, "I want you to be happy."

She looked at me bleakly. "I have been happy."

The door to the house slammed open with a cold gust of wind. We both started, for I'd swear I had latched it tight shut behind her.

"Meg!" came a voice from outside. "Meg, look what I've found!"

Thomas edged in through the doorway, balancing in his two hands a perfect bird's nest. In it were two blue eggs, a strange sight for autumn.

He carefully put the nest down when he saw Elspeth.

She was sitting very still, her hands clenched on her knitting. "You're back," she said.

"Yes."

"No one told me."

Despite her words, she never looked at me. It was as if I was become a wraith in the room: the world seemed to exist only because they were in it, staring at each other, like that night seven years back, when they had looked and loved; but overcharged now with seven bitter years.

"No one knew. I've not been back long."

"Are you planning a long stay?"

"I don't know yet."

"You look well," she said. "Clearly travel agrees with you."

He smiled warmly, to let her in on the joke. "If you knew how far—"

"It's no affair of mine."

He stopped then, and looked at her long and searching. But I don't know that his seer's eye held true, for in a lover's heart a past and a future that never were are sometimes clearer than the present that is. "Elspeth," he said to her, "I have something to tell you."

She waited, as I did.

"You were right." He laughed again, a little shamefacedly. "There are marvels. I only thought there should be, but you *knew* there were, so you were right. In Elfland—" His voice took on a poet's dreamy tones: "In Elfland there is a well, an old well-spring in the middle of a green forest. By that well there sits a cup. No birds sing in that wood, only—"

"Stop that," she said, not moving. "I want none of your rhyming now."

"All right," he said with unwonted humility. "Another time. But I've so much to tell you—"

"What," she said, picking up her knitting, "makes you think I want to hear it? I'm a married woman, Thomas, I've no time for your nonsense now."

He looked at her, his face white as death. Truth-bound himself, he seemed to have forgotten that others could bend truth around him. "When? Why?"

"Years ago. A woman must marry, Thomas. Jack wanted me, and his motherless bairns wanted looking after."

"I understand," he said, understanding nothing. His sense must have told him something was at variance, but he'd lost the ability to reconcile seeming and knowledge. "But let me tell you where I've been these seven years; I owe you that, at least."

"I know where you've been. It's written on your young man's face, and on your soft hands that haven't known work a day of the seven."

"You sound," he said wryly, "as if you've been talking to Gavin. It's not like that, I promise you. Elspeth, I've been in Elfland."

"Eating white bread and honey. And sleeping on feather beds."

"Elspeth, aren't you listening to me? I was there—enchanted."

"Oh, that's new," she sneers; "for you, at any rate."

It was strange to hear him eager to tell her of Elfland, when it had come so hard with me and Gavin. "Please listen. I've waited so long—I thought, of all people, you would believe me. I thought you'd understand."

"I understand," she says, "that you left without a word to us, and that now you think a few fine phrases will make it all right. You act as though you think no time has passed, and nothing has changed. Did you never think we might tire of your lies?"

He gave a choking laugh. "Lies? I can't lie to you now. Another gift of Elfland."

"To me, or to you? It's not much of a gift, is it? You'd have done better with a chest of gold, or a pair of seven-league boots. You've been away so long, you think we simple folk don't know now things really are. But it's all right, Thomas, I can follow a more intricate tale, if you must unburden yourself."

"What do you want to hear? That I went to Jerusalem and shared Suleiman's harem? That I went walking by the Eildons, and a rich woman on a white horse with silver bells promised me the riches of the earth if I'd come away with her at once, forgetting everyone I cared for? I went off without my clothes, without my harp, without a girl I said I loved, on some kind of mad poet's whim? If that's the man whose memory you've carried in your heart these years, no wonder you speak to me this way now."

Her face was chalky, with two spots of color high on her cheeks.

"Oh, no," he says, looking at her. "Of course. You thought I was dead. And here I am, hale and whole, and it's a disappointment to you, isn't it?"

She stood like stone, as though, if she moved, she would crumble to dust, or crush him with her rage. "I would like," she said, "just for once, to hear truth from your lips."

He bowed low and gracefully to her. "If you wish. You won't like it, but you will have it."

His body seemed to relax into words it was no effort for him to say. "It was seven years ago, that I lay on the green hillside, and a lady rode up to me on a white horse with silver bells. The ringing of those bells was enchantment, but her kiss it was that sealed it. I must have had a choice: she dared me to kiss her, and if I had refused . . . but the man I was then did not refuse. And so I kissed her lips, all underneath the Eildon Tree, and more besides.

"She was the Queen of Elfland. She took me up upon her horse's back, and we went swifter than the wind, until all living land was left behind. And so we waded through the river of the Earth's blood, and passed through a land where nothing grows, and down along the white road to Elfland. As in a dream, I remembered you, and Gavin, and Meg, and even the king his court—but you were real, and I was bound to the dream, to serve her seven years. For seven years I harped in the halls of Elfame, and wore their clothes, and bore them company. For seven years I spoke no word to any save the queen, and I ate none of their food. And at the end of that time, my service done, I returned to Earth. Not seven days past I came to this door; for where should I come but here?"

Tears were rolling down her face, but she didn't heed them, although she sniffed and gulped as she spoke: "You're such a stinking liar, Thomas. Isn't that the story we all want to tell? That someday someone will come riding up on a white horse, decked with ribbons and bells, and carry us off to a golden palace to be their lover? We *all* dream that, Thomas—but *you*, of course they come for you! For you, the harper, the rhymer, the bonny boy with the handsome face and charming tongue, for you we must believe it happened!"

He'd been looking out at that distant point that storytellers choose. Now he saw her, and fell silent.

"I can't—" he began haltingly. "There isn't—there's nothing else in me. I know no other tale." For the first time, he turned to me, frantic and young. "I know no other tale, Meg! There's nothing else in me. Meg, where have I been, if not there? What's happened to me?"

I shook my head.

"Elspeth"—he turned to her—"I have such tales—you will like them, I was sure you would. Let me tell you of the glade where true songs walk; the hall of blue lights, like a world under the sea; the bower of living flowers; and the knight's ghost that was a dove—"

"No stories, Thomas." Her face was red and puffy, but her mouth fixed firm. "Not this time. I know how good you are. But this time you went too far, and stayed away too long. I've no stomach for them now. I've stories of my own: of winters on the Ridge, children screaming without peace, dirty pots without end, splinters from rough wood; and a man's weight every night binding you to the mattress because you made your vow and you've taken his food for your belly and his clothing for your back and his roof for your shelter—"

"I see," Thomas said grimly. "But that's been dealt with before. Leave him."

Her hand flew to her throat; she threw back her head and laughed mirthlessly. "For what? For *you?* What, will you challenge him with your bright blade? Or shall I poison him with marrow bones?"

"Never mind. Leave him. You've been a good wife, now you can be a bad one. I'm sure you'll enjoy the change."

"Jack's dead. He died last winter. But his kin have offered me a home; it's generous of them, you must allow. What shall I leave for?"

"For me," he said. "For sport, for revenge, for a jest, for a whim. For stories you don't believe, for songs you've forgotten, for adventure you never had."

"For lies."

"What do you care?" He seized her hands, although she tried to keep them from him; seized them and held them. "Call them lies if you want, if it makes you feel better. I never lied to you but once, when I said I was not made for loving one woman. We were both foolish enough then to believe that one. I know better now."

"You know you want to salve your conscience. I know you pity me, because I can tell a sad tale, too—"

"I know I need you," he said. "I need you to take the taste of Elfland from my mouth."

And so saying, he kissed her with a ferocity it embarrassed me to look upon.

When he released her she stood there trembling, the color rising and falling in her face. "A rough wooing," she said, "to win any girl's heart. You were once more subtle, my fine and lovely Thomas. If those are the manners you learned in Elfland, I think you had better go back there and leave the rest of us alone. Good bye, Meg, thank you for the tea."

"Elspeth, wait—"

She was right. He would have done better seven years past; would have begged her pardon, asked her what she wanted; flattered, teased or cajoled her into doing his will. Who would have thought she'd be sorry for the truth now?

"Please, Elspeth—" He tried to bar her way at the door.

But she turned her terrible eyes on him, and he let her pass.

It was Gavin came in past Thomas at the door, as the harper stood there with his face turned to the wind. And, "The Devil take it," bustled Gavin, "are you daft to be letting the cold in? What do you think you're about? That was Elspeth, wasn't it, I saw going down the hill?"

Thomas stood still gripping the doorway as though he might fall. "Stop asking me questions."

"Did you speak to her, Tom, lad?"

"Stop asking me questions!"

I went to Gavin, and hugged him, pressing my face into the nubby wool cloak he had woven, that smelt of sheep and cold and heather and him.

Tom looked at us, but would not speak. I laid food out on the table, but he never touched it. He only stared out the window, gripping the frame tightly; and once more he had that wild and listening look, as though he heard horns where there was only wind in the grass.

If ever man needed to be alone, that man was the Rhymer. So we didn't try to stop him when he took his cloak and his misery with him out of the house. But when night fell dark without a sign of him, we began to worry, and determined to go looking for him if he wasn't back by morning.

So it was that we took cloak and staff and food, and set out towards the Eildon Hills just as dawn began to break. The sky was dense with clouds the color of tin. The dew-damp sedge and little hidden brooks wet the hem of my skirts. But the hills were lovely to see. We walked slow and steady, and Gavin helped me over the rough patches; we saw no one, mortal or fay, only the early-grazing rabbit and the red roe deer.

At last we came to the grassy bank, under the Eildon Tree. Someone had been there before: the ground bore the imprint of a body, frozen into the frost in the cold shadows; but he was not there now.

"I know another place," I said, and so we made our way onward through the hills until we came to the Bourach Mound. There was no knowing he'd be there, or anywhere else on Earth. But not everyone who finds their way out of Faery can find their way back in again.

We found Thomas pressed against the west side of the mound. He was all hunched up, and wet, and filthy, and he shivered even as he slept. He

cried out when we woke him, and spoke to us at first as though we were
not who we were.

Gavin changed Tom's wet cloak for his dry one, and I gave him some
drink. "It's no good," he protested through chattering teeth. "I can't come
back. I don't belong here anymore."

"If not here, then where?" I snapped, for the cold was getting into my
bones, and I can't abide self-pity.

"I c-can't find the way back in—and no wo-woman of Earth will have
me as I am now. . . ."

"Certainly not, all muddy and wet—you look like a scarecrow someone
left out in the rain. And it's high time you learnt to get along on your own
without a woman for more than a week, anyway!"

"Come, lad," Gavin said. "You can't think with a cold head and an
empty belly."

And so the three of us straggled on home.

Although he got warm and dry, by evening Thomas's mood was still
grim, and there was no shaking him loose from it. "I'm useless," he said
flatly. "I can't earn a living. I'm too old to learn a trade. I barely know one
end of a hoe from another—"

"The best harper in the land doesn't need to know one end of a hoe from
another!"

"The best harper in the land is a madman!" he flared. "How can I speak
to anyone now? How can I appear before the king or the Earl of Dunbar,
absent seven years, and tell them where I've been? They'll ask me questions, and I'll sound like a fool. I can't bear to be laughed at," he said
wretchedly.

"Laughed at?! When you can tell them where the next raid is coming
from, and when?"

"Oh, yes; I can start predicting everyone's death. That'll make me very
popular, too."

It went on and on. You know how it is when someone wants to complain; all the good counsel in the world is nothing to one drop of their
precious misery, and everything you suggest is somehow impossible.

Finally I brushed my hands together. "Well, Thomas. I suppose you
must be right. You had better go back to Elfland, where you can be
happy."

"I can't," he sulked. "I tried—"

I said, "You might begin by taking the rowan out of your pocket."

He fished my poor charm out. The dried twigs and berries were all bent and crumpled, and the red wool frayed. Thomas looked at me with annoy-ance and amusement mixed.

"I doubt," he half frowned, "that this would hold much weight with the Queen of Elfland." He tossed it on the fire, and watched it turn to a flame of itself and vanish.

"I think," I told him, "that you should go away for a while. Return to the world, and see if it's as bad as you fear. It's true prophets can have a hard time of it, but you're a man has weathered more courts than one. And your harping and singing haven't suffered any, while you were gone. Write some new songs, and be respectful; what more can they want?"

Tom smiled. "We'll see. At least I wouldn't have to learn to hoe."

"Try it," I said. "You can always come back. It'll give Elspeth time to think things through."

"Aye," Gavin chimed in, "and yourself time to earn a bit of silver: no one wants to marry with a beggar."

"She won't have me," he began to moan.

"Oh, don't be a fool, Thomas," I snapped. "No one would have you now: you're like a half-drowned kitten looking for its mother. Elspeth's got troubles of her own. I think it would be very nice if you rescued her from the Ridge. Do you think you could get a white horse anywhere?"

He laughed shamefaced that I remembered their conversation. "Maybe I can," he said. "It's something worth working for, anyway."

"That's right," Gavin said. "It always is."

"Just like one of your own tales," I said dreamily, looking into the glowing fire: "The Princess on the Glass Hill, or the Black Horse and the King's Son of Ireland. . . . I'll tell Elspeth you've gone off to seek your fortune."

"Only if she asks," Tom said shyly.

Gavin said, "She's a fine girl, that one, for all her ways. It's time she settled down, and you, too, lad."

Like so many of us, Thomas the Rhymer knew the truth about every-thing but himself. In the world, his music was still loved. Those he told he'd been in Elfland could believe him or not, as they chose. After a few fistfights, Thomas learned to settle back and smile when the question came up. No one thinks of rhymers and great music-makers as quite like them-selves, anyway—such a man was as like to have been in Elfland as any-where else.

We knew he was all right when rumors of a new seer in the kingdom began to reach us, even in the hills. They said he predicted the flooding of

Wark, and the fate of young Traquair. The news came on just a little bit ahead of him that summer; before the harvest Thomas was back, wearing the gold of kings and princes. He took in vassalage the old tower of Leirmont, just outside the town of Ercildoun, on the Earl of March and Dunbar's demesne. Like his father before him, the young earl was a good friend to the Rhymer; his castle was to the other end of Ercildoun from the Rhymer's Tower, and Thomas was to harp there when it pleased the earl to be in residence.

All this we learned when Tom came to see us, bearing gifts in his hands and a new assurance on his face. He also showed us several lengths of green silk, an ivory comb and a ring of braided white and pink and yellow gold.

"No white horse," he said. "Do you think this will do?"

"You're wooing the girl, not buying her!" Gavin admonished.

"Oh, I know . . . but no one wants to marry with a beggar!"

Well, the first day she slapped his face, but he left the comb. The second day, she threw the comb at him, but then he made her laugh. And on the third day, Elspeth came down from the Ridge with the ring on her hand, and the cloth in her arms to make her a wedding dress.

"It's a magic ring," she explained to us. "The day Thomas is unfaithful to me, the stone in it will turn black and crack."

"But there isn't any stone," Gavin observed.

Elspeth smiled.

And Thomas leaned over the back of her chair and sang,

> *The lily it shall be thy smock*
> *The jonquil shoe thy feet*
> *Thy gown shall be of the celandine*
> *Thy gloves the violet sweet.*
>
> *The waking all the winter night*
> *And the tippling of the wine*
> *And the courting of a bonny lass*
> *Will break this heart of mine.*
>
> *Brave sailing here, my dear,*
> *And better sailing there,*
> *Brave sailing in my love's arms*
> *Oh, would that I were there!*

And,

Oh, she wouldn't say yes,
Wouldn't say no,
All she'd do was
Sit and sew.

Before the year was out, she was sewing again; and he was singing cradle songs.

That is how it is, now: the tower at Leirmont is never empty, what with the children and their nurses and the folk that come from as far away as Skye to consult with the Rhymer. Gavin and I don't much care for the hustle-bustle; we're happier when the children come up here to play. Thomas says it's good for his bairns to learn a useful trade; and, in fact, among them all the dear mites can bake and weave and guide the sheep well enough to do any croft proud.

But if the winters keep getting much colder here in the hills, we may yet come and live in that tower room that Tom and Elspeth say is waiting there for us, with the fire all lit and the feather bed softly made.

PART IV

ELSPETH

The lif so short, the craft so long to lerne,
Th'assay so sharp, so hard the conqueringe,
The dredful joye alway that slit so yerne,
Al this mene I by Love. . . .

—Geoffrey Chaucer,
"The Parliament of Fowls"

"ERSYLTON. Omnibus has literas visuris vel audituris Thomas de
Ercildoun filius et heres Thomae Rymour de Ercildoun salutem in
Domino. . . ."

—Charter granted by the son
and heir of Thomas of Erceldoun
to the Trinity House of Soltra

LITTLE THESE DAYS can make Thomas laugh. But there's an odd bit of news come up from the village, and I want him to hear it.

Young Tam has gone out, to visit with the monks at Melrose, where he got his education. That's a boy who can both read and write, but where he gets his notions of propriety I do not know: there's no law of courtesy *I* can think of that says that, just because he's heir to Leirmont, he has to stay here every hour of the day to watch his father die.

I know it won't be very much longer, now. I suppose I'm selfish of my time alone with Thomas. I've never minded anyone's dying so much, not even my babies'. I have to watch my husband grow weaker every day, losing the essence of all that makes him mine, as the sickness turns him in upon himself, all his strength going to keep him human.

His face died first: the quick-changing expressions froze to a look of steady endurance, eyes a little clouded looking off to an unimaginable distance where pain does not exist.

The younger boys are a great comfort to me, for all that Evin's and Kay's "help" consists mostly of spilling trays and letting possets boil over —their minds are on other things, you see: the nature of life, and what their friends will say, and a scraped knee, and a girl who smiled yesterday, and might smile back tomorrow. I'd rather that than your true adult misery.

I expect that when this is over, I'll sleep, and grieve, and do all the things that other people do. I am trying to be myself, my *good* self, for as long as I can, just as Thomas is—how can I offer less to him than he is to me? There is still pleasure just being in his company, even if only watching him sleep, or talking and knowing he is listening.

I had rather an hour in Tom Rhymer's company than a year of any other man's. The Duke of Cauldshield said that once. I would give my hope of Heaven for that hour.

I wish I could shake the one false note that rings in my head like a nasty, jangling dance tune that won't quit: Thomas is leaving again. Leaving me, and not coming back this time. He doesn't want to go, God knows. There is no pleasure in this journey, and what awaits him at the end, even True Thomas cannot say.

It has always been a comfort to us that his sight did not extend to the death of any of us. Even Meg and Gavin went on their own; he knew enough to be with each of them at the end, but that was all. But then, one night just a year ago, he turned to me in the comfort of our bed and said, "You'll see me gone, Elspeth. I'm sorry, but I'm glad of it."

And for the first time in twenty years, I called him a liar.

Oh, I used to tease him awfully, always wanting to know. I thought, you see, that there was nothing I could not bear; that if he had knowledge, I could share it. . . . I wanted to share everything with him, his burdens and his joys alike, for love and also to show that I was as strong as he, though not blessed by the Elf Queen—that I'd strengths and hard learning of my own.

And I promised myself that I'd never berate him for speaking truth, for I knew that other women would, and I wanted to show myself what I'd always been, what he even called me: a woman unlike any other.

But it was like the story of the seal-woman's husband, where he promises never to strike her, but of course, he does—well, not *just* like, for Thomas never turned into a seal and vanished; but the same because it is impossible to adhere to grandiose vows under mundane circumstances. And so over the years I came to do those very things I'd pledged not to, not once, but many times . . . but that, I think, is the difference between tales and real life: in tales there's nothing unexpected—and in real life, not so many dire results of rash action, though just as many tears.

We were not two years wed, when Tom was summoned to the King at Roxburgh, and this time I went with him. Much as I hated to leave my little Tam alone with his nurse, I was desirous of travel, for I'd recently miscarried of a bairn, and the winter had been long. Still, I fretted at leaving the child until Thomas said, "Oh, leave off, Elspeth, he'll be perfectly all right! No harm will come to Tam while we're away."

Almost I rounded on him with a retort on his unfeelingness, until I reflected that Thomas did not speak idly—or, rather, that though he did, his words about the future carried weight. So I set to packing with a merry heart, certain that my gowns would be laughed at by the court, and almost managing to care not a whit: they were good cloth, and pretty colors . . . and my husband was Thomas the Rhymer. Let them laugh, if they'd nothing better to do.

It was only a day's ride to Roxburgh, over greening countryside. Rooks and gulls followed the ploughman's red turned-up earth, and we whistled as we rode. Oh, I loved riding a-horseback! It was only an old charger lent us by the earl, broad as a kitchen table, but it was so comfortable with my arms around Thomas, and the world going by around us. At last we saw the high walls of the king's town rising grey before us through the grey-green woods, and Thomas kicked the horse into an unenthusiastic shamble.

There were painted cloths everywhere on the walls, and some woven ones from France. The very stone was painted. Oh, we'd canvas hung to keep out drafts in our tower, and the earl's castle walls had painted cloths with patterns, but these were beyond anything I'd ever seen: scenes, all of them, of forests and fountains, ladies and saints and prophets and monsters. . . . It was like walking past stories. I gripped his arm as we were led to our room, whispered, "Tom! How much would these cost?"

"Lots," he said, as we passed a tapestry outside a doorway.

"Look!" I said. "You can see the boy's face looking into the fountain water, all woven in!"

Tom covered my hand on his arm, dragging me along past the picture. "The boy," he said, "is meditating on vanity, and so should you."

To my enchantment, our room was not without its painted cloth: a unicorn unempoisoning a stream with its horn, while all sorts of strange beasts looked on, gryphons and lyons a-battling and all . . . and our bed-curtains patterned with doves and ivy woven in! Our clothes had been brought up. I laid them in the chest prepared, which had been agreeably scented with lemon balm for spring, though the winter moth-smell of tansy still lingered in the corners.

Then I took a run at the bed, and cast myself onto the cloud of feathers. "Cream!" I cried, rolling in it; "clouds!"

"Are you trying to make me lose all self-control?" Tom demanded with a rattle of curtain-rings.

"How can you lose," I asked, "what you never had to begin with?" And, "Tom," with my face all-but-buried in his armpit, looking past it to the woven bower of doves and ivy, "when the king asks you what payment you want for your services, couldn't you ask him for the bed-curtains this time?"

"Not doves," Tom said, "they make me nervous."

"Close your eyes. Or put them somewhere less . . . dovey. . . ."

"That's dovey."

"Not very. What about a tapestry?"

"You're like the Fisherman's Wife . . . why not ask for the whole castle while you're at it?"

"Just a nice hanging . . . he's got so many. . . ."

"I'd like to ask him for land."

"Land! What would you do with it—farm it?" I mocked.

"Silly fox cub! Someone else will farm it for me. I'll collect rents. And pass it on to Tam, or portion it off to our daughters. . . . We can't live in a tower off nobles' gifts forever—or we'll end up eating nothing but venison and tapestries!"

"I could."

"You've let some of those feathers into your brain. But I won't ask for land now; the time is not yet. The nobles aren't sure of me; they don't know yet what a harmless soul I am. I don't want to cause trouble."

"Never. Do they really think you're a threat to them?"

"I am a threat to them. I could have a lot more power than I want. How do they know I don't want it? I'll harp for them tonight—that always makes me look humble—unless they remember Tristram harping before King Mark."

"Or David before Saul. Will you play them the new song?"

" 'The Lady of the Lake'? Not yet—they'll think I'm boasting about Elfland."

"What for? It's nothing to do with Elfland!"

"Water sprites with swords?"

"But that's unfair! Any rhymer could—"

Thomas chuckled. "Welcome to court."

I did rather well on the curtsey, I think; anyway, nobody laughed. I tried not to stare—or, rather, I did stare, but tried not to look like I was. The king's hall was crowded as Michaelmas Fair, with all manner of people, eating and serving and entertaining at once. In one corner musicians were playing on vielles, but you could barely hear them for the racket of dogs and platters and conversation. I thought of Thomas ten years ago, working to come to the attention of the king, and shuddered for him; it had been a direr task than he'd told us.

Now the king spoke his words of welcome to us; I tried to smile and look properly respectful at once. I turned my eyes to his lady, the French queen, at his side. The queen was no longer young, of course; but she'd a splendid coif, and elegant carriage. It was true my gown was not cut like the ladies' who surrounded her, but my copper-colored brocade did not look shabby, and I did not shame to stand there before them all.

I knew the queen had been kind to Thomas; he'd had her favor, harped for her and her ladies in her bower. Now I saw that she had her pick of musicians, and perhaps his comeliness had helped him win his place there.

"Come here, my dear," she said. She spoke the words so strangely accented I scarce understood their meaning; and then I thought she meant Thomas, until he pushed me forward. I curtseyed again, to be sure.

"Did you have a pleasant journey? The roads not too muddy? And the room you are given is to your liking?"

"Yes, majesty, your ladyship." Oh, dear! I didn't know what you call a queen to her face! She wasn't offended, though, so one of them must be right—or not too wrong.

"And are you a singer, too, and a harper, like Thomas?"

"No, my lady. I'm a—well—a farmer's daughter." Where I come from, that's superior to a wandering singer, but for the first time I felt it might not be. "I married Thomas two harvests ago."

"You have little ones?"

"One, my lady." (What *did* Tom call her in his stories?) "We've a little son, madam," *(ah!)* "and with God's grace, more will follow."

She crossed herself. Her fingers were thick, made no lighter by many rings. "God send him well to fare. You are fortunate in your man. It was arranged by your father?"

"No, madam."

For the first time, the queen seemed to be looking at me as though I was someone new, not just another face she'd had the same conversation with many times before. I did not entirely like it: there was a piercing avidness to her gaze; it made me feel studied, pricked by a fine needle. "The women in these parts are famous for their weaving," she said.

"Some are." I'm not. The lady standing behind her bent to her ear and said something low, and the queen smiled.

"You are fortunate in your man," she said again. "Many will envy you. Few there are who could ever say him nay."

I kept the same idiot smile on my face, for want of anything to replace it with. I felt sick, as though she'd just hit me in the gut—and I couldn't hit back. She thought I'd run off with him, or been seduced, and he'd had to marry me; that I had no portion and no skills. How could I tell her of the ivory comb, and the ring of braided gold? I couldn't think of a thing to say or do but smile, so I did. I didn't even think she meant to be unkind—if she did, I'd never given her cause!

Then I felt Thomas at my elbow, and I understood how Tam felt when he fell down, and then I picked him up: everything all right after all, and safe, no matter what happened. I took his arm, and whatever airy words might be said or darting looks exchanged, he was warm and solid beside me.

"Thomas," the queen said, "welcome to our court once more."

He bowed and thanked her. "I am glad to see your majesty again."

Her eyebrows were raised, waiting for him to say more before she answered. But he'd nothing more to say. She blew out a little puff of held breath. "We hear great things of you, Thomas. You are become gifted even beyond those gifts you had, of music and rhyming. We even hear that you have harped in Elfland."

"Some do say that," he sidestepped neatly.

"And I congratulate you on your bride."

"I thank your majesty. I have known Elspeth since she was scarcely more than a girl. We have always been great friends."

I felt a knot I hadn't even known I had untie itself and slip away. And the queen smiled on me more warmly. "You were away too long, Thomas."

"Madam, I would have come if I could. I do not forget the love song rebutting Sir Lionel's scurrilous claims about women's faithlessness, which I promised to have ready by Christmas . . . I hope you never said *which* Christmas, or I am forsworn, and all honor lost!"

"Alas!" the queen said happily. "Sir Lionel is gone into the North with an heiress and settled down; his views on love are no longer relevant."

"Small loss," Thomas remarked. "But when I have satisfied the king your husband as to his business, perhaps you will grant me leave to sing your majesty the new songs I do have."

Her smile seemed to come from someone else, so clear and uncomplicated with pleasure it was. "Yes. I want you to."

I was famished, and wished the interview were over, so we could sit down and join the others eating. Among the smells of people and dogs I could catch tantalizing whiffs of meats and spices. From the corner of my eye I kept seeing vessels and dishes being carried past, laden with all sorts of colorful things.

"Dear friends," the French queen said to us, as though catching up with my thoughts, "you must be tired, and hungry as well. It is no courtesy for me to keep you talking, although I rejoice to see an old friend."

"Madam"—Thomas made a bow—"it rejoices me to hear it."

Again she seemed to be waiting for more. This time she said, "Ah, Rhymer, the years seem to have blunted your tongue—or is it your life among the settled folk, the . . . farmers and villagers, that has changed you?"

"Neither, madam," he had to answer. And suddenly everything was not all right anymore, and my hand on his arm became an eagle's claw as fierce protectiveness welled in me.

Our inquisitive queen went on, half mocking, "I cannot think the court of Elfland so barbarous a place that you learned these manners there. Were you used to answer the elf lords thus?"

I really think she meant no harm: a light-spirited woman who was used to being indulged and deferred to. But I could feel all of Thomas's body clenching against the truth waiting to come out of him. It would take him some time to relearn the knack of turning direct questions aside with light answers; they could still catch him unaware, and freeze him between speech and silence.

And so I answered for him: "Madam, my husband is not entirely well. He was fevered ere we left, and I fear the journey has taxed his strength." So was the queen all contrition. We bowed again, and someone led us to seats at a table down the hall from the royal dais. "Queen or not," I muttered to him, "she is a silly woman." He held tight to me, not speaking. But he smiled at me with wicked delight: It was a good lie, worthy of the court, it seemed.

We sat between a nobleman's secretary who wanted to talk about wolf-hunting, and a thin little man who wanted to do nothing but eat—he kept stealing glances at me, as though afraid I would catch him at it. But I was enjoying the food too much myself. We didn't get all the dishes the royal table did, but there was still more saffron and meat than I was used to seeing in one place, even at weddings or at the earl's.

I heard Thomas telling the eager young secretary, "No wolves in the Lammermuirs coming this fall; you'll have to go norther for your sport."

"Never a whit," the young man said; "last fall they were out in droves."

"This year's different."

"You're awfully sure of yourself. What did you say you were, a harper? Would you care to place a wager on the matter?"

"I'm not sure," Thomas said, glancing at me, "that my wife would approve of such a wager."

"Nonsense." I pried myself away from the cinnamon-apple pie. "Your wife thinks it's a fine idea; I have such faith in you, my love. And you, young sir, shall come to Leirmont Tower at Ercildoun and bring us a wolf pelt, and we will feast you in return—or not."

(Later, in our room, Thomas commented, "You're right rapacious when we turn you loose."

("The nobles pay you to prophesy; why not their lackeys? Besides, I liked him. I'd be glad to host him."

("Just because his kind are new to you. I assure you, there are dozens like him here."

(But in this Thomas underestimated us both, for Duncan has become a good friend to us; the children like him, and he managed to convince Iain that learning to read would not instantly turn him into a monk. And now that his lord and patron has risen to high influence, he comes to us for more than wolf-hunts.)

By now, the platters were coming less often; the meal seemed to be drawing to a close, and in the center of the hall tumblers had begun their antics—not what I would have chosen to look at after just eating myself, but no doubt the court has developed stronger stomachs.

Thomas waited until another singer had come and been replaced by

some dancers, a trained dog, and bell-ringers, before he offered to play—
that was courtesy, for him not to try to show the singer up directly. His
harp was sent for, and then he sat alone in the center of the hall, facing the
king and his queen. I'd seen him sing at home, of course, and in the earl's
hall, but never before so many. I don't know if he felt nervous, but I did.

He began by harping, and soon the hall was quieter for him than it had
been all evening. Torches were lit as dusk fell. When the tune ended there
was a buzz of comment: people who remembered him; those who'd seen
him lately on his travels; people who had only heard the stories. I thought
he looked a prince of Elfland, sitting at the center of the torchlight, with
his long hands on the harp, his hair long and his eyes distant . . . but,
then, I've never seen a real one.

He sang a simple tune next, one from the countryside, about lovers
meeting. I understand some minstrels won't sing those songs in noble
courts, but Thomas always had. Then, to show off, he gave them part of
his Tristram verses. By now I was just enjoying the music, and so was
everyone else, so I wasn't at all nervous. The little man next to me had
even stopped rolling bits of his manchet into bread balls on the table, and
listened fixedly. The queen was watching Thomas with pleasure.

He'd changed his mind about "Lady of the Lake":

> *Your words are hard and harsh, lady,*
> *Your heart is made of stone,*
> *For to swim this water with a naked sword*
> *It never can be done.*

> *She's struck the water with her hand*
> *And it swirled stark and white:*
> *Oh, will you be a false villain*
> *Or be my own true knight?*

> *You've taken from my hand, she said,*
> *The belt and aye the blade,*
> *Now will you be a coward knight*
> *And let your courage fade?*

> *You've taken from my hand, she said,*
> *The better and the best,*
> *Now will you be a coward knight*
> *And fail like all the rest?*

It was a long song; a story people knew, but he'd changed some of it: now the young king's faery paramour was become at the same time the mother of his chiefest knight, and she foretells their doom to each, how the young king's wife in turn will be the knight's leman, and bring them all to woe. But the two men will never heed the warning, as we know, though Tom's song stops before then. He ends it suddenly, with the lady telling the king,

> *Your blade will turn all in your hand*
> *As light as leaf on tree—*
> *But ere you draw your last world's breath*
> *You'll come again to me.*

Even the young secretary sat gape-mouthed, still enchanted with the song. When Tom finished playing, the king's own page brought him wine from the royal table. But the small man to my other side seemed agitated. "Was that wise?" he said, to the table or to me, I couldn't tell. "Was that wise, to tell them that?"

"Did you like the music?" I asked him experimentally.

"Yes, of course," he snapped nervously. "But your husband knows more than he says."

I was intrigued, but half my eye was still on Thomas. "Doesn't everyone?"

"He's not too proud to use what he knows, and that's pride enough. It's only music, they will say—well, let us hope so."

"What's the danger in making a song of an old romance?"

"Why, none in the world—in *this* world. But hark you, lady"—suddenly his sharp little face was thrust under mine—he reminded me of a water rat—"there are some Hills not to be mined."

"I think," I said coldly, for truth to tell he was beginning to frighten me, "you overreach yourself." For was not Thomas safe from harm? Far from requiring that he keep silent, the Elf Queen had gifted him with true speech.

"Maybe," the man answered, almost a whisper. "But I have seen them, too, and they are not kind."

I never told Thomas about him; I meant to, but somehow the words never got said. When Tom returned to sit by my side, the small man disappeared again into his preoccupation with bread-rolling. He was like a withered leaf, and Thomas was hale and strong, bright with the king's praise-and favor, the glory of the music from his heart and hands.

The king sent for him the next day, to ask the fate of his foe, the young

English king. I was half afraid the queen would send for me in equal courtesy—from Tom's stories, I pictured her sewing all day long, and I had enough of that at home—but I was left to my own. I wandered the halls, looking at the pictures; making up the stories when I didn't know what they depicted. Only once was there any mishap: a well-dressed woman stopped me, clutching my wrist, and pulled me into a window corner.

"Make me a charm!" she begged, without so much as a good day.

"What kind of charm?"

"You know. Make him to love me again as he did."

I had to bite my lip to keep back my laughter. "You must be thinking I'm someone else."

"I know you; you're the Rhymer's wife."

"I'm the Rhymer's wife, I'm not a hedge-witch!" I answered her frostily. "And if you trouble Thomas with any such thing, he'll . . . well, he'll probably laugh at you," I finished honestly. "Go your ways," I said more kindly to her fallen face; "try wearing a new scent, or taking a new lover."

Thomas did laugh when I told him. "We'll make you a wise woman yet! You gave her better advice than I gave the king. He kept saying, 'What should I do?' and I answered, 'I don't know.' So I shall not be court prophet after all, and a good thing, too." He looked out the thick-walled window, towards the hills and the west. "I'd like to go home soon."

I took his hands in mine. "All the gold and the king's praise don't please you?"

"No," he said; "this is no court for me."

So we returned to our good strong tower, and let the seekers come to us; and when the Earl of March and Dunbar was in residence, we went to his castle across the town and made music and talked. I mean the young earl, not his father who gave Thomas his first rewards for his singing there. Young March is a cheerful, busy man, who doesn't mind that I tease him for not having tapestries.

These are bright memories, things we speak on when we speak at all. Other matters I don't bring up, and here is one of them: another time I felt I'd lost him. The memory of that time is sweet compared to this, a bright bauble of misunderstanding, a toy for memory to play with. I keep it to myself, and I think Thomas has made his own peace with what happened. He knows me better than any ever will again, but there are things I've thought and seen that even True Thomas has no business with.

It was in a snowy Martinmas time, when Tam was still small, that a troop of armed men came clattering into our yard. With the country so unsettled, we'd grown used to travelers going heavily guarded. I was sewing in my bower; as lady of the house, it was in my charge to teach my maids their household skills, though most of them plied the needle quicker than I! We sang as we worked. Bets had just finished another shirt, and wanted to take mine from me to do; we were tussling over it when the hoofbeats sounded below, a clutterish mush in the snow.

I didn't look up; it was as like to be the Earl of Dunbar as not, for I'd heard he was returned from attending the king at Jedburgh (and he liked nothing better than to sit at our hearth, to get away from the hustle-bustle attending his return at the castle). But Bets jumped up to peek out the window, and, "Madam, the bonnie colors!" she cried, leaving me in charge of the shirt; a useless victory, for when I went to look for myself, the sewing was forgotten.

Surely I'd seen them before, the green and yellow livery on coat and banner and bridle; maybe at the great feast at Roxburgh, where we'd gone to attend the duke and the singing. I know the colors of our friends, who come to us often; but at Roxburgh there had been so many liveries it looked like a dyers' festival, with so many names that I was hard put to keep them straight.

"Off you go to the kitchen," I told Bets, "and tell them to start heating some drink for the guests, and you, Nan, bid Willie build up the fire in the hall and see to the horses as best he can. I'll be down in a moment to welcome them, as soon as I've put on a fresh coif."

I found Thomas in our own chamber, playing with young Tam, his son and heir, as comely and froward a lad of six years old as any that ever wheedled cakes from his mother's store . . . though even then he was something grave of manner. They were making a country out of our feather bed.

"Build it up," says Thomas, "so . . . now there's a nice mountain, we can run the river valley here."

"A river with real water, Da?"

"What, will you make water in the bed?"

I could have told him the child would collapse in giggles, and he get no sense from him after that. But I was busy fussing with my cap.

"It's crooked," Thomas said without turning 'round.

"Fix it." Seeing him sprawled on the bed, all disheveled and at his ease, I wished there were no visitors, no need to pin the coif in place. But his obliging fingers did the deed for me.

"Tom," I asked, "what's green and yellow?"

"Poison," he answered, "and snakes. Hold still."

'No, it's not a riddle. There's men in the yard. Ouch!"

"You'll wet the bed!" shrieks wriggling Tam.

"It's Errol," says Thomas.

I glared at my husband for setting the boy off, but Tom's face was not on his son, nor on me. It was his Seeing look, gaze turned inward; but now his face was taut, strained, as though the news were ill. When he Saw, his face was always clear as glass. I touched his cheek, and it was cold.

"Tom," I said, "I must go down to welcome them."

He suddenly turned and pounced on young Tam. "Help! A giant is destroying our land!" Together they rolled the feathers flat.

"Tom!" I called for his attention, and though he made not to hear me, I knew he did. "I'll down to Errol now, and you may come or bide as you like, for I'm sure it's you he wants to see, and not me."

He reached up an arm, as if to draw me into the fracas. "Bide you. Let the Earl of Errol send to find you, and announce himself as a great lord should."

"Tom," I protested over Tam's giggles, "I can't. That's not courtesy, not in these parts. Tom, even the duke's lady of Roxburgh came to meet us in her hall. Would you have me puffed up greater than she?" I wasn't sure, you see, not really, of what was right. Seven years wed was not long to learn to be the Rhymer's lady, mistress of a prophet's house.

It was not like Thomas to turn cold at a visit from any man. If Tom hadn't been carrying on so foolishly, I might have been alarmed. There was something he feared or misliked in Errol's coming. Since his return from that Other place, and even since our wedding, he'd still gone off sometimes traveling to court and hall. And if there were some ladies and princes his truthful tongue offended, why there were many more saw the use of it, for couldn't he tell them what they wanted to know, as well as what they did not?

And so they began coming to our tower at Ercildoun, to consult with the Rhymer, as far as his truth would take them. Some went away glad, some sorry, and some merely confused at his riddling answers. For, said Thomas, he'd answer any question truthfully, if he'd a mind to answer at all—but he'd not always tell all he knew. Only once did a man refuse to leave at all. It was a fearsome time, with us besieged within our own house by Sir John Adorn, that wanted to take Tom away with him to be his only prophet. But Tom foretold such doom on him that at first he would have killed us out of hand, but at last his spirit broke and Sir John fled, cursing the very stones around us. And the Earl of March and Dunbar hunted him down on the hills, leaving him enough men to tell the tale of what befell those who forced the Rhymer against his will.

Had Errol's coming been such a danger, Tom would have foreseen it, and told me now. Whatever my husband feared, it was not harm to any of us. Still I took his hand to draw him up from the bed. "Tom. Come down with me."

Young Tam tried to cling to us both, as we were bed and coverlet between us, but I bade him off to his nurse, and went downstairs with his father's hand firmly in mine.

Of course I might have asked Thomas straight out what the matter was (or he might have told me on his own!). A few years ago, I'd not have thought twice about demanding an answer. But I had been learning to respect the Rhymer's silences; it is no small thing to ask a question of a man who is bound to tell only truth.

Our small hall was nothing like the king's or the earl's. Now it seemed to be entirely filled with men, still muddy with riding, warming themselves with the fire and the drink our people had provided. Their green and yellow livery looked strangely springlike in the deep of winter, as though a Maying party had strayed from its own time.

The men turned to look at us, courtesy and curiosity mingled. I thought of what they must be seeing: a tall, sleek, dark-haired man, his youthful face at odds with the heavy knowledge of his eyes; at his side a ginger-haired, sharp-faced woman, her coif impeccably straight—I fought the urge to tug at it to make sure. Thomas suddenly looked at me and smiled, as sure as if to say that it was. I wonder if all husbands can do that trick. Maybe they can; for I myself know often enough without asking what's on his mind, and I've no special sight.

"Be welcome under our roof," I said to them, "all you who come in peace."

Like wheat stirred in the wind, the men turned to show one who stood closest to our hearth fire. I expected to see the fearsome Lord Errol, but there was only a boy, dark-haired, fine-boned and young.

"Mistress," he said, "I thank you for your courtesy." He held himself proudly, and his mantle was trimmed with fur. "I bring greetings to Thomas Rhymer, Seer of Ercildoun, and to his lady, from the Earl of Errol." When he spoke, I thought him older: fourteen or fifteen, maybe, just old enough to be a noble's emissary.

I felt Thomas at my side standing still as stone. I snuck a glance at him without drawing attention to it, and my heart turned like cold stone itself, for he was looking at the boy with a kind of horror. No one noticed it but I, for no one knows the particular set of his face and body as I do, that cried aloud to me, where anyone else would simply see a man being formal.

So I thanked the boy myself, letting Tom keep a dignified silence. I didn't know whether to be angry at Tom, or truly frightened, so I just tried to do all the things a hostess does. I found out that Errol's messenger had brought fresh-killed game to feed his people with, and I arranged a room for him to sleep in here. He agreed to send his men to lodge in the village, rather than let them sleep in our hall.

"Fine," I concluded the business. "Then if you'll be content to wait here, young . . . sir," I finished lamely. An inexperienced messenger, he'd forgotten to give his own name.

He noticed my stumbling, and was quick enough to see the reason. The boy lifted his head a little, letting haughtiness mask embarrassment. "I am Hugh Drummond Carnegie, Errol's son of Errol. The earl my father has sent gifts, and desired me to take counsel of the Rhymer."

"You are welcome," I said again. I was suddenly stricken with the certainty that I'd seen him before. But I couldn't have done: the person I was half remembering, without knowing who it was, I saw no younger than Errol's son, maybe older. It pricked me like an itch you can't quite reach. Not this boy, but a kinsman? We didn't know any other Errols, or Drummonds or Carnegies, for that matter.

I couldn't ask Thomas about it then and there. I took my farewell of young Errol, and took Thomas's arm firmly in mine and out the door. "There!" I hissed in the hallway. "It's Errol's own son, come under the protection of our roof in good faith! You've naught to fear, whatever dark secrets you're harboring. So stop looking like a cornered stoat, and try and be *civil* tonight!"

Thomas lifted his head, looking down his nose at me. "Did I say I was worried? If there were any danger, my dear, I'd tell you."

I glared at him. Did he think, because I was no prophet, that I couldn't see what was before me? But I held my tongue, and went off to the kitchens to oversee the preparing of that night's meal, which had suddenly gone from pies for the household to a wild game feast for a full company.

Young Errol did not want for entertainment, it seemed. At evening, when the board was laid, our Tam appeared in the hall with Errol in tow, chattering at the gallop. It was more of the Toby story: a mythic pony Tam had stabled for years in his fancy, and ridden somewhat far afield. Errol was taking it in good part: "Horses *are* bigger than ponies," I heard him agree, "but of course that doesn't mean their hearts are greater."

"Toby will jump whatever I tell him," Tam said. "I always give him apples. Does your horse get apples? Mine always does."

Errol's son smiled a private smile, and again false memory stung me like a gnat. I knew that look of self-contained amusement . . . but who could an earl's son so remind me of? And would it reflect badly on the Rhymer that *his* son's fancy outpaced his father's truth? Apples, indeed!

Tam brought Hugh of Errol to the table where I sat, and properly seated him at my right hand, with such a grave and courteous air that I was hard put not to smile at the sudden change in his demeanor. Our son served at table with the other boys, as doubtless young Errol had served in his father's hall—how strange, that the son of a minstrel and of farmers should be so gently bred! And he so apt to it, too. Tam waited until his father was seated before he took himself off to fetch the wine.

I looked anxiously at Thomas. But his haggard mood seemed to have passed; he was pleasant and affable as any good host. And the meat Errol's men had brought was excellent; I thought I would save some to send to Meg and Gavin, who seldom tasted such.

When Errol turned his head away from me, I saw he'd braided blue ribbon into a lock of his dark hair. Although I wasn't sure I should, I could not help admiring it. The boy blushed.

"Yes," he said, his voice squeaking as it broke. "It's from my . . . cousin. Lady Elizabeth Drummond. She gave it me for the journey."

A love knot! I thought. I'd heard about them in songs, but never actually seen anyone wearing one. Errol did seem young to be up to such flirtations.

"A young knight," Thomas said smoothly, "bearing a lady's favor on his quest."

Because he'd said it, it must be true—and, indeed, the boy beamed brightly at the notion. Perhaps his head was full of courtly exploits, and not romance at all.

Elizabeth Drummond . . . I thought, and blurted, "I've met her!" Really, I was getting as bad as Thomas, so to speak my thoughts. But I had met her. At the Abbey at Melrose, when we'd gone for Holy Week, she'd been there, soberly dressed, on some sort of pilgrimage. A girl of spirit, quiet and firm, with large grey eyes and heavy dark brows. Hardly a girl, though. "She's so much—" I began, and bit my tongue. So much older than this young lord. Surely not a figure of romance.

"She's a beauty," he said, pitching his voice as deep as possible. Thomas smiled at me, a smile I read as priests can read a book: *See how hard it is to bite back the truth when you see it?* Since I couldn't stick out my tongue, I contented myself with narrowing my eyes at him. He affected not to notice, and aloud he said smoothly, "Master Hugh is betrothed to Lady Elizabeth."

Our guest looked at him a little startled, and I saw plain on his face how he realized for the first time that Thomas really was someone who knows things. "She's fallen heir to lands joining those of my mother's portion," Hugh explained. "It's that I've come to ask you—"

"I know," Thomas interrupted brusquely. "But not now."

Well, he had become like the weather over the Scar! All sun one moment, and black clouds the next. Our guest didn't know but that this was the way of seers; I knew well enough that it was not, and set about to mend the conversation, let Tom and his rudeness shift how they might.

Thus employed, I learned that Hugh had five sisters living, one by his own mother and four by his father's second wife. No wonder Errol wanted him spliced with Elizabeth Drummond: her portion aside, it was time he secured an heir for his son, or else one of the daughter's husband's heirs might walk off with the Errol lands.

What would Tam inherit? I looked across the room at our son, healthy and clever, thank God. I'd lost two babies since, and our daughter Megan was even now being spoiled in the nursery. Or so I hoped. I looked at Errol's only son, and a sudden chill ran through me. He was such a small boy, and delicately made, with the spirit burning bright in him.

"Thomas," I said suddenly, "I must go see if Megan's all right. I'll only be a moment."

He laid his hand across mine. "She's asleep," he said.

Does he know the fate of our children? Perhaps he's never asked himself the question. I've had to bite it back myself; will I ask it before he dies? Will he tell me?

"Tom," I fussed, "what's young Tam doing with that dog?"

He opened his mouth to answer, and shut it again, and said, "You can see for yourself he's feeding it scraps. I think it's his favorite . . . Cavil?"

"Caval," I corrected automatically. "I know. It wasn't a real question. I'm sorry."

"Don't apologize," he said softly, "for my bad temper."

"Tam!" I relieved my feelings shouting. He scrambled up, came to me. "You've no business with dogs when our guests want wine." And I pressed a sweet cake into his small, warm hand.

As supper ended, Errol's men-at-arms begged leave to entertain the company. We'd had a fiddler up from the village to play while we ate; but we're always eager for music from other parts, so we listened with pleasure to a song one of them sang, about the Man-in-the-Moon falling in love and out of the sky. His friends had all heard it before, but they were glad to see how much our people liked it. Only young Tam fell asleep with his head on the dog's gently breathing belly. Another man begged the fiddle, and played a mournful air. Stealing a glance at my husband, I saw he wore his "minstrel" look, immersed but keen-eyed—trying to learn the tune, I think. Then another visitor got up and did a very showy leaping jig he'd learned in the North. I clapped with pleasure; he bowed to me and did it again!

I did wonder that they had strength to sport after their day's journey. But they kept at it, to the delight of maid and man alike. Perhaps they were hoping Tom would offer to play? I could have told them he was not in the harping mood. Indeed, I was ready to rise and signal the feasting's end when one man, enlivened by our wine, called up to his young lord, "Come, Errol! What about your harp, then?"

Tom turned sharply to the boy, who looked desperately uncomfortable, as well he might. But Errol drew himself together to answer his man, "My harp's where I left it, at home. Didn't we bring enough baggage, Davey, for you to look after?"

The men laughed; it was clear the boy was popular with them, and quick enough with his tongue, when he wasn't talking about women. And that would have been the end of it, if my Thomas had not spoken: "I have a harp for you to play."

Even the boy could hear the challenge in it. I pressed my lips together; I would speak to Tom later! Whatever bad blood there was between him and the Errols, he had no business taking it out on this boy, who'd done him no wrong.

Hugh of Errol drew breath to retort, halted in thought, and then said carefully, "How should I presume to harp in your hall, sir?"

"Yes," Thomas agreed silkily. "how should you?"

Errol lifted his head a fraction. Small as he was, he had a trick of holding his chin a little too high, so that he seemed to be looking down his nose at people, when in fact he was looking up. "But if you ask it," he said, "I will."

"Good," said Thomas; and then, loud enough for the room to hear, "You shall have your choice of harps to play, for each harp fits a different hand."

Our people were sent to fetch the harps; Errol's men looked pleased, and I thought, He must be good, he must be! I was beyond saying anything; it was as if my hall was become a tourney ground . . . I scarcely felt that it was mine, scarcely knew what Thomas was about. I was not frightened or angry; I felt I was watching a tale told out. I comforted myself with the thought that, whatever happened, this incident would be over, Errol gone, before too long. Embarrassing someone was not a crime—although it came close to breaking guest law. But Thomas had not been raised to observe it as we had—in him I saw, suddenly, the outlander, the traveler who had known too many different halls.

The harps were brought; he'd sent for only two, though he owned more now. One was a new harp, larger, in the new style . . . and one was his old traveling harp. I remembered it: the one he'd had when I first met him, the first he played on his return from Elfland.

Without even looking at the other, Errol picked the old harp up and began to tune. He did know how, unlike so many knights who can only pluck out a song or two to please a lady. When it was in perfect tune, though, and the hall began to quiet to hear him play, he held it up to Thomas, saying, "Will you not play now, sir?"

You had to admire his nerve. It's the better harper always plays second. Thomas reached out to the harp, only to steady it; for a moment both men held it, neither taking the harp nor letting go. Goading now, the boy said, "When I was young, I often heard my mother speak of your fine harping, of when you played at court."

Thomas lifted his chin, looking down on the boy; and the boy raised his head a fraction more, and I saw in that instant what I could not remember: the two hands on the harp, the raised chins, long noses and imperious eyes, the same.

I made the smallest of sounds, and then I was still.

"You play," Thomas said.

No one else knew but the three of us that any challenge was being issued. Errol's men were pleased to see their lord so courted and honored. Errol sat, cradled the harp—it seemed larger in his small frame than it had when Tom held it—and struck a few notes.

I would not have thought I'd notice, but it did sound different under his hand. He struck some more notes, slowly, as though he were dreaming them. But a pattern began to emerge—a tune I knew, but not as I'd ever heard it, like the same scene witnessed by two different men: Drowned Ys. Errol played slow and patient, testing the ringing of the walls and roof for sound, teasing the listeners with the space between notes. Then the waves began to build, the city bells to ring, and he broke into a youthfully passionate striking of the strings, bringing the final gulls' cries shrill almost to dissonance, sounding the final crashing waves like tolling bells.

At the silence that greeted the end he paused, shook a lock of dark hair from his face as though that were all he'd had on his mind. No one was moving. He looked up at Thomas.

"Can you sing?" Tom demanded.

"Sometimes," the boy said. His voice cracked lightly on the word.

Nonetheless he broke into a new harp tune, a light rolling accompaniment to which he sang, low but true:

> *Young Janet sits in her bower high,*
> *The gold comb in her hair.*
> *The leaves grow green in Carterhaugh—*
> *Oh, would that I were there!*
>
> *She has not pulled the double rose,*
> *Twisted the stem full sore,*
> *When up there starts him young Tam Lin,*
> *Says, Lady, pull no more.*

Now there was an uncomfortable rustling amongst the listeners. "And that's an ill song to sing in the Rhymer's hall," I heard someone say. For we all know the song of Tam Lin, the young knight rescued by young Janet of Carterhaugh, who bore his child within her—rescued by Janet from the Queen of Elfland, who held Tam Lin in thrall.

> *Oh, pleasant is that other land*
> *But an eerie place to dwell,*
> *For at the end of seven years*
> *They pay a tithe to hell.*

Seven years, I thought—and suddenly I was not watching the tale, I was in it. For it was full seven years that we'd been wed. *And at the end of seven years . . .* I felt cold, and more than cold. Who was this boy? He was called Errol's son, but who was his mother? A lady of what court?

The eyes of people not on the singer were on Thomas, wondering what he would do. The Rhymer sat calmly listening, as if it were any minstrel, any song.

> *First let pass the black, lady*
> *And then let pass the brown,*
> *For I will ride on the white steed*
> *The nearest to the town;*
> *Because I was an earthly knight,*
> *They give me that renown.*

It was when I found myself caught in the song, thinking of Janet and Tam Lin and seeing the faery procession, bridle bells ringing at midnight, instead of the hall at hand, that I knew the boy had inherited all his father's gifts.

She's first let pass the coal black steed
And then let pass the brown;
She's quickly run to the white steed
And pulled the rider down.

The harping grew richer, the notes deeper and more harmonious. Thomas had begun to harp.

They played together; the boy sang, and Thomas played along with him, bass runs and treble harmonies from the larger harp blending and coursing with the smaller. I'd never heard anything like it, and never will again.

And then Thomas was singing, too.

At last they turned him in her arms
Into a naked man
She's wrapped him in her green mantle
And young Tam Lin she's won.

Up there spoke the Elfin Queen
An angry queen was she:

O, ye have robbed the fairest knight
In all my company!
And had I known, Tam Lin, she said
What this night I have known
I'd have plucked out your earthly heart,
Changed it for one of stone.

The song ended, but the harping went on. They played that tune, bending 'round its notes and harmonies until it was almost unrecognizable, but always there in essence. Neither looked at the other; neither needed to. At length, like the dizzying flight of an eagle, that winds its way into the air, and finally rides the currents slowly down again, they wound back to the original notes, plain and unadorned. The two harps finished together.

In ones and twos, people were rising from the tables, quietly bidding one another good night in the hush that followed the music, moving towards bed and sleep as though their dreams had already started. Now Errol turned and looked at Thomas. Thomas, still seated at the table, his chair pushed back from it, the tall harp on his lap, his eyes still cast downward. The boy looked long and hard, unsure of what had just happened, unsure of what to say, his lordly speeches useless and deserted. At last he came up to where we were, and simply held out the harp.

"No." Thomas looked at him, from somewhere far away. "Keep it."

"But I—"

"Keep it."

Thomas set his own harp down, careless on the floor, for someone else to look after. He staggered up from the table like one drunk or exhausted. But he found our Tam nestled against the hound asleep, and carefully picked the child up. He stood cradling him tightly in his arms, then carried him off to bed.

It was left to me to say good night to Errol. Almost he asked me about Thomas, I could see it in his face; but I'm glad he did not, for what could I have said? But at least the magic was gone out of him, the magic that attends true minstrelsy: with his delicate awkwardness, his air of being enchanted himself by Tom's weirding, I saw him as any woman's son, any human lady's.

I pretended to be asleep when Tom came in. He knew I was not, but there are some pretenses even True Thomas must honor. I was not angry; maybe he knew that, as well. I was thinking. I counted it forward, I counted it back. Seven years before, he'd returned from Elfland. Seven more years there, and then two before that I'd met him. Sixteen. Could the boy be sixteen? Had it happened before or after the visit where Tom and I first met on the hillside?

Small wonder he'd feared Errol's coming: Errol's heir was not Errol's son. Thomas had deceived him with Errol's wife. Even if Tom hadn't known about the boy, he had known that. What lady was she? Was she small and dark, or the earl dark? Tom was breathing quietly now, asleep. I ached with restlessness, but wouldn't stretch or turn over, for fear of waking him.

He had not been true to me. All those seasons when I'd waited for him at Meg's, a ribbon in my hair in case he should arrive one day unexpected, he'd been off with other women. And then he was away to Elfland, seven years' service doing I well knew what.

I tossed about, to toss off the thought. Thomas didn't stir. Of course I'd known about the others. I'd always known. It was part of his attraction: that fine ladies had him, but he came into the Eildons to walk with me. To walk, but not to stay. And the queen, Tam Lin's queen, was Thomas's queen as well. But I was no Fair Janet, I knew. He had wed me out of shame, out of pity. . . .

In the sleepless dark, all things are possible, the worst most likely, all darkness visible. There he lay, as near as comfort, as far as the other side of death, silent and far away in sleep. I could shake him awake, or murmur the questions: *What happened? Who is he?* And, sleep-dazed, Thomas would open his lips and tell me the truth.

Silently, I reached my arms to him, running hands and arms over the spiritless body until the spirit woke and his will followed after, wordless.

We all three looked tired at breakfast, Thomas, Hugh, and I. Only Tam was frolicsome, who'd slept through last night, and most of the evening at supper. We let him do much of the talking, and he took full advantage.

"My Da knows everything—"

"Tam, hush!"

"Well, he does, it's true! So you must only ask him what you really want to know. And never ask him a question if you don't want an answer. Do you have a Da, too, or is he dead yet?"

Hugh of Errol crossed himself against misfortune. "I have one, too. I'm not sure he knows everything; he seems to, sometimes." He valiantly changed the subject. "Are you riding your pony today?"

"I rode Toby last night. We went to Arabia, and caught a monkey, but he got away again." Oh, no, I thought, not the monkey. I can't take the monkey today. Sure enough, "Mama, can't I have a monkey? The countess had one from—"

"You're not the Countess of Mar," I told him firmly. It never worked for long.

"Tam," his father growled, "if you continue to plague your mother about the monkey, you'll have to leave the room. Do you understand?"

"Yes, sir."

"Go and play with your little sister. You can tell her anything you like."

"She can't talk."

"That makes it easier, doesn't it?"

I scowled at Thomas. He was in a rare mood. I'd told him again and again not to mock the children.

Tom turned suddenly to our guest. "Lord Errol has arrived at Roxburgh."

Taken aback, young Errol blinked. "I was on my way to meet with him there."

"Yes. He's arrived beforetimes. His messenger will be here this afternoon, telling you to make haste to join him. So if we are to discuss your future plans, we'd best do it now."

"Tam—" I took his hand. "Let's go teach Megan to talk."

Shyly, Hugh of Errol sought entry to my bower. He'd some gifts to give me before he left, and according to Thomas's foresight, the messenger was expected shortly. I was sitting up there alone, looking out across the snowy fields, my hands idle. Errol presented me with linen for a gown, some gloves, sewing needles, a pearl-handled knife. His face blazed with a private triumph. The Rhymer's prophecies for his future had been favorable, it seemed. He was so like, yet unlike, his father: the similarity swam in and out of focus; I had never seen Thomas so amiably full of clumsy courtesy. Errol said to me, "The next time you see Elizabeth Drummond, mistress, she will be my wife. She will bear me a son, it's certain. You will come to the christening!"

"No." It was Thomas coming into the room. "We will not go there. So I've brought your christening gift now." He held out a plain silver ring, small enough for a woman's hand. I had never seen it before.

I began, "Where did you—" but stopped myself of habit from completing the question.

"Rhymer," Errol protested, "you've given me so much already, it doesn't seem—"

"It's not for you," said Thomas intractably, "it's for the boy." He put the ring in Hugh's hand.

I took a breath, but the world grew no brighter. "Thomas," I said, "where did you get that ring?"

He looked at me heavily. "I got it from Meg's hand," he said, "seven years ago."

And that was as close as my husband had ever come to lying to me, the best he could do. Before our guest, I did not press him further. And then Errol's messenger rode in from Roxburgh.

I gave them a quick meal before Errol and his troop rode out again. They ate it booted and standing, for if they left soon they could be at Roxburgh by sundown. I did not know what I would say to Thomas when we were alone together. What could I do but ask questions? And what could he do but close his lips and not answer? That was what I could not bear. For what did I care, in the light of day, with my husband by me and the four strong walls of the tower around me, whose by-blow young Errol had been? The question that burned in me, that robbed me of my peace, was only, *Why did you not tell me all last night, when you knew?* And why did he try to lie to me today? What did I ever, ever do to him, in the years I'd known him, not to have his trust now, in this?

I looked at him. In an unguarded moment, he was watching the boy. No coldness now, no stern measuring, but longing and sorrow naked on his face. I crumbled my bread to bits.

Errol had Tom's harp in his arms, his ring on his hand. He stood before Thomas at parting, uncertain as ever. To me he gave the proper words of thanks; to Tom he said, "My father sent gifts for the prophet. But I must give my own to the harper." And he unclasped a gold pin from his cloak, with a ruby at its head, and held it out to my husband. "My mother used to say there was enchantment in your music. But I know it for more than that."

Thomas took the brooch. "Thank you. Praise from a true harper is rare and welcome. I will wear this at my heart, and remember the giver always."

I did not stay even to see if he embraced his son in farewell. I left the Rhymer's Tower, and the town of Ercildoun below, to walk the snow-bound hills as I was used to do, when I was a maiden, before I bound myself in marriage to any man. The wind still cut sharp across the huge open sky, the thorn still twisted on the slanting ground. Far away I saw the line of Errol's men, riding bright and pale as distant spring, away on the road towards Roxburgh. And deeper still I went, where there was no sign of humankind. I started a roe deer, and crossed my tracks with the weasel, the rabbit and the fox.

I was cold and wet when I came home. I had seen ice like crystal encasing the briar, and the black stream water coursing below the silver rime of ice. My hands were mottled blue and red, my petticoats caked with ice.

Thomas came to me where I was drying my feet at the fire laid in my bower. Wordlessly, he bent to the task. I could feel his hands strong and warm through the linen towel.

The fire crackled in the grate. His hair brushed my knee. I said, "Why didn't you tell me?"

Maybe he chose to misunderstand me. "I didn't know I had another son. I only knew when I saw him. And you knew at dinner."

"But you were afraid, even after you saw him. And at the harping, you tried to humiliate him—"

"No," he said swiftly. "No, not that. I only wanted to see if he was . . . how much he was truly mine."

"Well, you were answered. Are you pleased, Thomas?" And when he didn't answer, "Did you truly think me so mean, to grudge that boy your love?"

His hand clenched on my leg and was still, a bangle tight around my ankle. "Please don't." His voice was low, but I heard him well enough.

"Why not? What are you keeping from me?" I was afraid, and it made me angry. "What are you hiding? Who are you protecting?" I seized hold of his hair. "Whose little wedding-breeched bastard is he? Whose bed did you get him in?"

"What does it matter?" he pleaded. "She's dead."

"It matters because I ask it," I said fiercely. "Have I ever asked you before? Have I ever reproached you with any of it? Day and night, do I ask you anything? Thomas, I bite my tongue a hundred times to keep from hounding you with idle questions—and now, when it matters, you're silent as a stone, you're mute as wood to me."

"Is this a trade?" he demanded. "For every hundred unasked questions, you get a free one of your choosing? By whose rules are we playing this game?"

"It's not a game!" I cried. "Is everything a game to you? Is that the way you see us all, a game to be played?"

"No," he said, the edges of his nostrils white with fury. "But I'd like to have some privacy, when I choose."

"Have it," I said. "Have all you like. Sleep alone, and dine alone. I'm sick of the sight of you."

He rose, and left my bower. We did not speak for two more days, nor did my temper cool. Indeed, the list of my wrongs grew ever longer: every little slight, every petty annoyance I'd ever felt became part of the grand scheme of ill that my silence was avenging. At first I'd wished he would go away; his trips were not so unusual, and never had there been a better time for one; but then I became glad that he was there for me to ignore, to pass in the hall, to not ask for the salt.

But at night I missed him. I didn't like being alone in the dark. I thought of things, then, and they were ill things. I began to wonder what he wasn't telling me. On the second night, when even I realized that the truth could be no worse than my imaginings, and that the monster I managed to make of him by day could not possibly be the same man who held me at night, I rose from my bed to seek him out.

He sat alone in my empty bower, harping. He was singing "Fair Annie":

> And would that my sons were seven young hares,
> And I a greyhound to worry them all;
> Would my sons were seven young rats,
> And I a cat amongst them all. . . .

I pulled my quilted robe close around me, and pushed open the door. Thomas looked at me across his harp.

"Just like the ballad," he said. "Were you hoping to come on me singing my confession?"

"No," I said; "I couldn't sleep."

"I'll leave your bower to you, if you want it."

"No, I don't want it."

The harp sighed as he put it down. "Are you still angry about Hugh?"

"I was never angry about Hugh," I said wretchedly. "You're stupid if you think it."

"Do you know what I like?" Thomas spoke softly, almost to himself. "You never expect me to know what you're thinking— To use my gift to know."

"I don't want you to know what I'm thinking," I said. "Not like that."

"Good," he said. "Because I don't. I don't try. So be generous, all right? and don't try to use magic to find out what I'm thinking either."

"I wasn't! I just want to be able to ask— You don't understand."

"I don't understand you, not always. But I understand myself. And that's how questioning feels to me."

"Like people working spells on you?"

"Something like."

I sat by his side. We were both shivering; his fire had died down. He put his arm around me, inside my robe.

"She was a court lady," he said, looking into the embers. "I never knew she'd quickened of me, and she was betrothed to Errol just after we'd . . . been together, that spring. She was not stupid at all; it would be like her to have let him come to her before the wedding, as soon as she realized what had happened, so the child could pass for his."

"Did she love you?"

He shrugged against me. "I don't think so. She wanted me. And I wanted her too. It was exciting. Though not so pleasant when I had to flee the court. People were beginning to notice us."

He'd fled, of course, to Meg and Gavin's. I did not ask him which of those visits it had been. I didn't really want to know, now.

"I think she tried to tell me about Hugh, before she died, while I was in Elfland. She sent that ring by Nora's Bevis. I thought it best for Hugh to have it."

I nodded. "He's a fine lad, Thomas. I'm glad we know who he is, even if he doesn't. He'll do you proud."

Tom said coldly, "That's enough."

I didn't pull back, although I wanted to. "It's all right," I said. "I don't mind it, truly."

"I don't want to hear about it."

"Thomas, you are a fool!" I smiled in the dark, and rubbed his arm, though he sat stiff. "Sixteen years ago, you did what young men do. No one was disgraced, and you got you a bonnie young son. You can't be angry that your lady preferred raising an earl's son to a minstrel's bastard! Not but he's a fine minstrel, anyway. . . ."

"I wish I'd never met him," Tom said. "I wish I'd never known."

"In God's name, Tom, why?"

"Because he'll be dead before the year's out."

The blood turned cold in my marrow. "Oh, Tom, no."

"No," he rasped. "No. As though I caused it. As though I could unsay it." He gulped, and sniffed. "He'll sicken, and he'll die, whether I say it or no."

"I'm sorry," I whispered, like a child that's kicked over the milking.

"He came to ask me if Elizabeth was fecund, if she would bear him a living heir, so he could marry her." Tears were streaming down his face. "I told him yes. But he'll never see his son. I didn't tell him that."

I had asked my question, and been given my answer—but neither question nor answer was what I'd thought it was. Still, it freed him to seek comfort in my arms. He'd been trying to master his sorrow for another woman's child alone; that burden, at least, I could ease.

Thomas does not often weep; over the years, he has come to see things at a remove, as I think he must. This business of Hugh, and my anger at him, had caught him where he least expected. I held him tightly, and at last he was quiet.

There was one more question I needs must ask, for if it was a hard answer, now was the time to bear it. I knew we'd probably not speak of it again; and I knew the wound must heal clean for both of us. I said softly, "Who was she, this lady, when you knew her, before she was Errol's wife?"

Thomas sat at my feet, his head resting on my knee. He looked up at me, his face pale in the darkness. "Not one you ever knew. She died while I was in Elfland."

He'd grieved for the son; now, I thought, he must grieve for the mother. "But do you tell me."

Again he looked into the dying fire. "Lilias," he said. "Her name was Lilias Drummond."

Lilias. I'd been a girl then, teasing the dark gallant by Meg's hearth. *All but one, and Lilias was her name.* The one out of all the queen's sewing ladies who had managed to stay awake for love of the bonnie harper none could deny. Of course I remembered Lilias.

"It's all right," I heard him saying. "You know I've never loved mortal woman but you, my honey, my dove, my heart. . . ."

But the girl who'd been left behind for seven years, to cold and darkness and work and silence, was not so easy comforted. She raised her head within me, and I put my arms around her as she grieved, remembering how as year followed year I'd tormented myself with the thought: that if I had been a lady like Lilias, a woman like any of the others he knew, ready from the start to take him where a man would be, he would never have gone off. For seven years I'd cursed my own virginity, my own spirit, and my girl's pleasure in his wit and company. I should have been Lilias to him; instead I'd been myself, and it had won me loneliness, abandonment, and Jack on the Ridge.

I don't know if I was speaking aloud, or if he let himself enter my thoughts; but he was holding me against his wet face, saying, "Yes, many, many, but you the only one of all, sweet, the only one. . . ."

And I heard myself wail, in someone else's voice, "And your Elfin lady?"

He rocked me, rocked us. "Oh, God, Elspeth, you know what you are to me. She never wept, she cannot give birth . . . like Tam's silly horse, that he can ride forever, but takes him nowhere. I was so lonely there; as lonely as you were here."

"I was so wretched," I sobbed. "Only Meg, and even she not . . ."

"It's over, love, it's over. I'm here. Elspeth, I'm back."

He said it again and again, until I heard and believed him.

I took him with me, to my bed; and though we were storm-wracked, weary from the tempests we'd ridden, we came together in final exultation, triumphing over grief and separation.

The twins were born of that night. And as for Errol's heir, his poor son's son, like our own Kay and Iain he grows daily to a comely youth. We chanced to see him a few years ago, at the Melrose Fair, shooting at the targets: a tall boy, just breaking out of childhood, with heavy dark brows and a sober mien, and a lift to the chin as though he were looking down his nose at everyone, but a bright smile to break a woman's heart.

I don't ask Tom about his fate, or the fate of any of the children. Even now, when there's so little time left to ask anything; the last thing I want to do is plague him with questions. If there's something he wants me to know, he'll tell me; otherwise, I think he can trust my judgment, just as he always has.

Our Megan is off crying her eyes out; she can't help it, she's at the age for waterworks. She came, yesterday, very humble, to ask whether she might order the counting and mending of the blankets before winter, and the chimneys to be swept out and the tapestries put up. Of course I'm happy to have her running the house. She'll be mistress of her own, in not too many years; and a fine one, too, I hope, for she's well dowered. I trust Iain and Kay are minding her, for once; if they're not, no one's come crying to me. Oh, I know I should be there with them; that I'm an idle huswife and an indifferent mother these days—but all that will still be there when Thomas is gone: the herbs and the bedding and the blankets and the sad children. I'll be there for them then, and always.

So now I let the servants and the children run the house, while I hold his thin hand and talk of this and that, letting him answer when he can.

"Do you remember," I say, although I know he never forgets anything, "do you remember that cloak Gavin wove for young Tam when he was small, and how Meg told him it was a Cloak of Invisibility, woven at midnight from the wool of unbaptized lambs?"

"Disgusting," Tom murmurs. "It's a good thing he went to the Abbey for his learning."

"Did you ever know the poor little one lay wrapped in it all afternoon on the hillside, then, waiting for the red deer to come walking up to him?"

The smile was in the softness between his brows, never reaching as far as his lips. "Was that it? And I made it worse, by coming into the hall that night, where Tam sat so quiet, and saying, 'Invisible, are you?' "

"I wondered why he got so angry when you said that."

"So did I. It just popped into my head; I never knew about the deer."

I pressed Tom's hand. "At least he got angry about it. He was always good that way—Iain and Kay just expect you to know everything, they don't even notice."

"Megan argues."

"If we get into Heaven on faith alone, she'll be shoveling coals for eternity."

"Alongside her mother."

"Oh? What are my sins, pray?"

"You argue."

"No, I don't—" Now I laughed, and he lay back, satisfied. "At least we're not afraid of you. That time at Yule, you told poor Ned his sweetheart was come, and in walked his brother's wife! You'll note he did not stay to supper."

"I can't help it. It's getting harder and harder not to know."

"It doesn't matter," I said helplessly. I didn't want to know more myself. "The national sport this season seems to be getting you to eat," I offered by way of distraction. "It's replaced hunting and bear-baiting. We have jam from the Countess of Mar, and game for soup with Dunbar's compliments; and Duncan from the village has sent up a cask of his beer, and some of his own sheep's foot sludge."

"Drink the beer," Tom said, "and give the sludge to the next wandering tinker you don't like the look of. Better yet, save it—heat it—pour it on reivers—"

I held him, hard, by the wrist only, feeling his pulse flashing quick against my fingers.

"Thank them from me," he said when he could speak again. "At this rate, it's going to be quite a funeral feast."

"I don't like it." I blurted the words out. It's bad enough that it's happening; he doesn't have to make jokes about it.

"I don't either," he said softly.

"Tom," I began, "don't you think . . . we might ask for help?"

"I've had the king's own physician."

"No, not that help. We've done all we can with mortal help. But there's others—Tom, Elfland loved you once! There are tales of their healing—"

He stilled me with a touch of his fingers. "No. It's an ill bargain to make."

"Oh, yes!" I said sourly. "And it would upset the priest. But if it would help—"

"No. It won't help."

All the fun goes out of arguing with him like this. And so I never found out whether he spoke from truth seen, or from fear of looking to see.

I took a breath, began again. "Along with the jam," I said, "along with the jam, another request from the countess to take Iain into her service. But I still think he's too young, don't you? And I'm not to be bribed with preserved fruit."

"Maybe send him at Christmas. Just for those few weeks. Extra musicians are helpful, then; he can try it out, and you can have him back after."

"Maybe. Maybe it would be good for him to go off on his own. Kay seems to be getting older faster. Poor Iain, he doesn't understand why girls are suddenly so important."

"He will. . . ."

I told Thomas about the gifts, but not about the people who keep coming with their urgent questions for their future and the country's, or about the scribes who want to crowd the Rhymer's deathbed to take down final prophetic dictation. . . . The earl has actually offered me some of his guard to keep them away, if need be. He says, in his bluff, soldier's way, that "if there's anything the Rhymer wants us to know, he'll tell us." Then he takes out his handkerchief and blows his nose, hard, and damns the weather.

But now two villagers have come to report to me the strange advent of two white deer, clearly hoping the seer will be able to throw some light on it, but too polite to ask outright. I assured them I would tell my husband, and so I will. For it's too good a picture to waste: a normal morning in the village, and suddenly two pure white deer, hind and hart, come striding between the houses, parading fearlessly down the middle of the main street, while everyone hangs back, staring, until they vanish into the forest.

It sounds like a drunkard's fancy, and it made me laugh (when they were gone), as so little does these days. They think it is a portent of some kind. To folk like that, everything is a portent, from a flock of crows to their own sneezes. I suppose it's being wed to a seer out of Elfland makes me a bit prosaic about portents. I hope Thomas will laugh.

I took the tray of broth I'd just heated, and carried it and the story upstairs to the sickroom.

The door was ajar, and I was surprised to hear voices. No one is supposed to go in there without telling me. This was not just Thomas, rambling the way he sometimes does in sickness, but a woman's voice as well.

I set the tray down on the windowsill of the stairwell, preparing the dignified annoyance I have perfected in twenty-one years as the Rhymer's wife—but a strange aroma stopped me. At first I didn't recognize it, and then I didn't believe it: the sweet breeze of springtide—moist earth and swift-flowing water, and the perfume of orchard blossoms.

I stood, frozen, outside the door. The spring smell was coming from Thomas's room, where the voices were.

I recognized his, thin, but stronger than it has been in a long time: "If I were dead, I would probably feel much better than I do. If I'm only dreaming, you are about to turn into a rose, or a chair. So I will enjoy you while I can. I'd forgotten how beautiful you are."

"There." Her voice was the sweet warmth of spring. "Can you feel that, Thomas? I am not a dream."

"No. You're not. You realize that I am a married man?"

"I know your vows you made between you before the congregation. But death is about to part you."

"Why have you come?" His voice was harsh. "I have no more—no more songs—"

"Ah, True Thomas, have you forgotten my promise? I have come to help you."

He made one of those awful pain noises.

"It's all right," she said, her voice so full of solace it almost soothed even me. "It will not be long now. Only a little more, my dear love. . . ."

"Help me—"

"Yes, soon. . . ."

They were sounds he never let himself make when I was with him. I pressed my knuckles in my mouth.

"It will be soon," she murmured, "soon, and then your time is done.

The waiting and the sorrow will be over, and you will be off and away on that bonny road you chose for yourself. Now, hush, my Rhymer; for as I have said, so must it be."

"I can't—"

"It's all right, I have you. Hold onto me—there—so— Just a little more—"

I couldn't bear it anymore. I flung back the door to the room.

A beautiful woman held Thomas in her arms. His face was drawn in pain, his thin hands convulsed. He looked dark and shriveled, shrouded with her long golden hair, his harrowed face pressed to her green mantle.

The woman looked up at me, and smiled. Then she laid him down, gently, on the bed.

Or so it seemed. I saw the crook of her other arm, and the folds of her green mantle encompassing a man's form. Then they were gone. For a moment, the smell of apple blossoms hung in the air.

And the figure of my husband lay, cold and lifeless, on the bed.

I stared at him, perfect in every detail, his face waxy and composed in death.

They had to leave something, didn't they?

I am glad I know. I will not grieve any the less, but I am glad. I am glad she came to help, as I would have if I could; come to love him again as any would who had ever loved him before.

He has my love until I end my days. And, maybe, we will meet again in some land beyond the mortal river. And, maybe, I have only had the loan of him for thrice seven years. I do not know.

I think that he is walking under the blossoms of a very old orchard. I think that he is harping before the Elvin host.

I think that he is singing.

Harpours in Britain after than
Herde how this merveile bigan
And made a lay of good liking,
And nempned it after the King.
That lay is "Orfeo" yhote:
Good is the lay, sweete is the note.
Thus cam Sir Orfeo out of his care:
God grante us alle wel to fare.

—*Anonymous, ca. 1300*

THANKS TO:

Mary R. Hopkins, who first introduced me to the Rhymer.

Professor Robert Butman of Haverford College, in whose class I wrote a one-act play called *The Homecoming of Thomas the Rhymer*. He was good enough to explain it to me.

Mrs. Inez Blair Polson of Earlston, Berwickshire, who showed me the Rhymer's Tower in Earlston, and Jane Yolen of Hatfield, Massachusetts (sometime of Edinburgh), who was brave enough to drive me there.

Martin Carthy, the singer whose version of "Famous Flower of Servingmen" (Child no. 106), more complete than any in Child, I've based mine on—with his kind permission.

Delia Sherman, who not only didn't mind, but actually helped me to rearrange the furniture in a house she'd been living in.

B. J. (Joy) Chute, who taught me, and whose voice will always be in my head asking whether I need that comma to be there, and defending the author's right to have her work published as she wrote it. She was going to read this book, and I think she would have liked it.

All the other friends and relations whose advice I did and did not take, but whose support I always devoured.

In the end, *Thomas the Rhymer* would never have been written without Terri Windling: friend, editor and extraordinary creative mind. For *Thomas* she provided inspiration, and infinitudes of space, music and faith.

Ellen Kushner
Boston—New York—Boston
October, 1986–July, 1989